Soledad Santiago is the ... to the New York State ... General. She has also headed the press office of the New York State Comptroller. She has written for many local and national publications, including *N.Y. Newsday*, *Penthouse*, *The Village Voice*, *GQ* and the *New York Daily News*. She divides her time between New York City and Connecticut.

Her previous novels are ROOM 9 and UNDERCOVER.

'Soledad Santiago is carving out a niche for herself in the thriller genre' – *Associated Press*

'An urban tale that dances across the page so quickly and incisively even the familiar can leave you breathless' – *The Village Voice*

Also by Soledad Santiago

Room 9
Undercover

Nightside

Soledad Santiago

Copyright © 1994 Soledad Santiago

The right of Soledad Santiago to be identified as the Author of
the Work has been asserted by her in accordance with the
Copyright, Designs and Patents Act 1988.

First published in Great Britain in 1994
by HEADLINE BOOK PUBLISHING

First published in paperback in 1995
by HEADLINE BOOK PUBLISHING

A HEADLINE FEATURE paperback

10 9 8 7 6 5 4 3 2 1

All rights reserved. No part of this publication may be
reproduced, stored in a retrieval system, or transmitted,
in any form or by any means without the prior written
permission of the publisher, nor be otherwise circulated
in any form of binding or cover other than that in which
it is published and without a similar condition being
imposed on the subsequent purchaser.

All characters in this publication are fictitious
and any resemblance to real persons, living or dead,
is purely coincidental.

ISBN 0 7472 4716 1

Typeset by Keyboard Services, Luton, Beds

Printed and bound in Great Britain by
Cox & Wyman Ltd, Reading, Berks

HEADLINE BOOK PUBLISHING
A division of Hodder Headline PLC
338 Euston Road
London NW1 3BH

For Johanna Shepard

Special thanks to:

Francesca Dominguez for the purest *alma*
Virginia Giordano for steadfast friendship
Joan Cannon for proofreading and support in trying times
Joan Westmeyer for always asking the right questions
Detective Sergeant William Cavanaugh for technical assistance
Trudee Able-Peterson for her work with the kids of Times Square
Professor Talat Halman for poetic inspiration from my roots
Julie Butler for showing me it's possible to rise above
Cathy Jazzo for phone calls when I needed them
My mentor, Dr Eric Simon, for sanctuary and music

*Better than one hundred pilgrimages
is a single visit to the heart.*

*Yunus Emre
Turkish poet ca. 1241*

1

Lady Liberty, the Colossus of the New World, lights the New York City harbor as she has for more than a hundred years. This Friday, however, she is closed to the public. The federal fiscal year has run out. Capitol Hill and the White House have been unable to agree on a budget. Nonessential services have been cut. Lady Liberty is one of them. Glittering windows of the high-rise city obscure the stars above. The island of Manhattan lies in the middle of the Atlantic freeway, and migration routes span its skies. Buildings as high as the walls of canyons, Central Park, the Hudson and the East rivers conspire to make the endangered peregrine falcon believe that Manhattan is its natural habitat. The falcon is a hunter with deadly talons and a razor-sharp beak. Food is ample here – pigeons, sparrows, starlings, rats, and mice. The falcon swoops down at two hundred miles an hour and flies off clutching his prey in his talons. The average New Yorker is unaware of his presence.

The window became a mirror. My reflection moved toward me. Only my desk lamp was lit. A pool of light splashed my silhouette on the night outside the window. Two teenage girls clad mainly in stiletto heels and garter belts strutted through dense traffic. As they giggled like children their firm young breasts glistened in the spill of headlights. They climbed into the back of a white limo as if en route to a party. I tried not to imagine the details of that festivity. It was my seventh year in the neighborhood New Yorkers call Hell's Kitchen. I was still not used to the heat.

Hell's Kitchen runs from Eighth Avenue to the Hudson River, from Thirty-fourth to Fifty-ninth Street. It is one of the city's oldest residential neighborhoods and a teeming immigrant community. In this contradictory pot Times Square melts with the infamous Minnesota Strip and the Garment District with the grand theaters of Broadway. When America watches the golden ball drop at midnight on New Year's Eve, they're tuned in to Hell's Kitchen. It was here that Damon Runyon strolled for inspiration, Margaret Mead taught Sunday school, Lee Strasberg pioneered 'the Method' at the Actors Studio, and Sylvester Stallone wrote the very first *Rocky*. On hot summer nights the horns of the big cruise ships harbored in the Hudson echo down the streets. In my window two familiar eyes appeared. A knuckle tapped on the pane. I walked to the door next to the window and opened it.

She was unique. She had soft round African features, but her skin was white and her dreadlocks golden. Her eyes, like her clothes, were black. She wore an imitation snakeskin jacket and Spandex pants. Like all the other street kids that year, the symbol of her status, her beeper, was tucked conspicuously onto her waist. Not the cheap model, it could hold a dozen numbers in its memory.

From her ears dangled single-edged razor-blade earrings. A snake ring that swallowed its tail hung from a chain around her neck. She hunched forward into the windowpane with the intensity of a four-year-old, but her body looked eighteen. Back then I believed that she was fifteen.

'Porsche. Come in.'

Across the street a limousine pulled up to Samsara Video. The store offered highbrow European films, a collection of porn, and twenty-four-hour film development. All the way up Tenth Avenue green lights turned red. A siren wailed as an ambulance fought its futile battle to return to St Clare's Hospital before its cargo expired. Traffic didn't budge.

'Walk with me?' Porsche asked.

I took the keys from my belt. As I locked the door we were bathed in pools of pink and green neon. EDEN HOUSE – 24-HOUR HOTLINE – 555 – HELP. The hotline was for the desperate, parents and children alike. The sign itself was designed to attract children like Porsche, children who roamed the night. Runaways who sold their bodies for food, for drugs, for a place to sleep and the short-lived illusion of love that sex can sometimes be. Porsche had come by the halfway house a dozen times in the last three months. She had never stayed.

We crossed the street and headed for the river. As we passed the video-rental store, she peeked sideways at me as if there were something she wanted to say. Instead she returned her eyes to the sparkling slivers of glass trapped in the cement at our feet and was silent. We followed our long shadows until they slipped under us and became short.

'It's like Indian summer,' she said at last. 'When I used to live in the country, Indian summer was the best.'

Traffic kept its steady, empty rhythm. I had never heard her mention home before.

On Forty-seventh Street and Eleventh Avenue, we entered the open-air bazaar of human flesh. We walked through catcalls from the cars and sneers from the pros. The half-naked girls strutted back and forth among cruising cars, basking in the attention of possible purchasers – as if being bought were proof of value. Males of all ages in every make of car imaginable leaned out of car windows like buyers at a fashion show. None of the girls had reached the age of twenty. A wave of angry rap music rolled from a Mustang 5.0. The six males squeezed inside were no older than the girls they were looking to purchase. They were laughing and drinking beer and singing 'Happy Birthday.'

As we crossed the street a cream-colored BMW followed. It was Dr Love, one of the neighborhood's oldest and meanest pimps. He was almost forty: for a pimp that was ancient. His twenty-five-year-old son, Blue Fly, had been pimping for years.

'Keep walking,' I told Porsche.

When we reached the other side of the intersection, Dr Love got out of the BMW to block my way. His purple-black face was framed by the yellow brim of a large hat. In his gaze was a calm, even hate. I stood there staring up at the twenty pounds of golden ropes and chains – the whole continent of Africa and a large golden fist – that he wore on his chest. He said, 'Howya doin', mama?'

I said, 'I'm not your mama, and if you really believed in your roots, you wouldn't do the shit you do. Slavery's dead – or haven't you heard?'

He pushed his hat back. 'The little white woman's getting tough. Learning the language, too.'

His laughter roared over me. If he hadn't been so evil, he

would have been handsome. I knew he was just as hard on the black girls as he was on the white. Harder sometimes.

'You like to think you're down, but you're just a white girl from out of town,' Dr Love said.

'If you say so,' I answered.

Neither of us budged.

'I been looking for you.'

'Looks like you found me.'

'You're bad for business. We want you outta this neighborhood.'

'I have no plans for relocating.'

He tried to push past me, to get closer to Porsche. I stepped between them. He glared at her over my shoulder. 'Get inna car. Blue Fly wants to see you.'

'I'm through with him,' Porsche said defiantly. In her voice I heard a tremble.

'That's not what he say.'

I recognized the battered old Chevy when it came around the corner. O'Shaugnessy, the precinct's community-affairs officer. His first name was Jesus, but everybody in the precinct called him 'Hey-Zeus.' Jesus O'Shaugnessy was the first Irish-Puerto Rican I had ever met. Lately he had developed a knack for being around when I needed him. Now his car pulled up alongside us. Porsche had disappeared into the shadows of the sidewalk ahead. O'Shaugnessy leaned out of the open window. His green eyes flashed wickedly. 'How's business?' he asked Dr Love.

'Not as busy as you.' The pimp sneered. 'Find your killer yet?'

'Wanna confess?'

Dr Love turned and walked to his newly waxed car. As he

got in he tipped his hat to me. 'Hey, mama – don't forget what I said.'

'I asked you a question,' O'Shaugnessy called after him.

'I don't know nothing,' Dr Love yelled back.

'What else is new?' O'Shaugnessy called cheerfully.

The old pimp sped off into the night. O'Shaugnessy sucked on a tooth and said, 'He's not going far.'

Then he stared at me until I offered, 'I owe you one.'

'Can't you find some other line of work, Annie?'

'Why does everybody ask me that?'

'Cuz you're a pain in the ass?' he suggested.

I rested my arms on the roof of his old car and leaned down toward him. 'What about those murdered girls? Any leads?'

'You know I can't discuss an investigation in progress.'

My fingers tapped a beat on his corroding vehicle. 'Right.'

As he drove off I turned to follow Porsche. When I caught up with her, she was walking fast, biting her lower lip viciously. 'Shit,' she threw over her shoulder without looking at me. 'Shit, why did we have to run into that prick?'

'He seemed to be looking for you.'

'Cuz I'm making it without Blue Fly, and I told his other girls they could, too.'

I said, 'I can't decide who should get the Asshole of the Year Award, Dr Love or Blue Fly.'

'Blue Fly – cuz he learned from his father and improved on it. Like father like son.'

'Is that how it works? Our parents make us who we are?'

Dr Love's BMW cruised by in the intersection ahead. O'Shaugnessy's Chevy pulled up and squeezed the BMW to the curb. They got out of their cars, grandstanding, pointing fingers in each other's faces and yelling things we couldn't hear.

'Damn,' Porsche said. 'That cop musta doubled the speed limit.'

We slapped each other five. Her laughter was infectious. When we stopped laughing, I said, 'Why don't you leave the life for real? I'll help you. I promise.'

'I don't know. Maybe it's too late for me. Every time I try to go straight, I get so nervous I think I'll explode ... so then ...' She spread her hands. I knew the blank was filled with drugs, which meant money, which meant sex with perverted adults. 'I got no skills,' she said, 'and I gotta eat.'

'There's too many crazies out here now. Three murders in as many months. The streets aren't safe.'

She smiled sadly. 'Were they ever?'

We crossed Twelfth Avenue. Behind us the pulse of the city quickened. Ahead loomed the aircraft carrier *Intrepid*, now a museum, its cold gray steel welding earth and sky. Traffic was heavy. The weekend exodus had begun.

'That girl that was killed last week – I knew her,' Porsche said.

'You knew her?'

'We did a trick together once.'

'You have any idea who killed her?'

Porsche shrugged. 'The life, the life killed her.'

'You think a john killed her?'

'I dunno ... is it *true* her tits were cut off?'

'No, it was her hands.'

We walked onto an empty pier. Its rotting wood creaked beneath our feet. We sat down and dangled our legs over the edge. Beneath us, the river's many tongues lapped idly at the decaying pillars. On the other shore, the rest of America began with New Jersey. I waited for her to speak.

'What about you?' she asked. 'Grapevine has it you used to be a nun.'

I had gotten used to the question. A lot of the kids were fascinated by my leaving the Church. It was as if they sensed some kind of parallel with their leaving home.

'That's what you came to talk to me about?'

'Not all of it . . . So you don't really know nothing about sex.'

'You changed your look,' I said, changing the subject.

She nodded and rubbed her eye socket with her fist like a tired child.

'Yeah. To tell you the truth, I'm changing everything. It's like you said, Annie. I wanna be independent. Anyway, I gotta leave the neighborhood for a few days.'

A passing headlight transformed her golden-red hair into a wild halo. Within it, her face shone white as bone.

'What for?'

'Just till Blue Fly forgets me.'

She reached inside her pocket. I saw the fuzzy, pitiful thing in her hand. A kitten.

'Will you take care of her for me till I get back?' The request was a challenge.

'Why not just come into the program now?'

'I want to, Annie, but I wanna go away first. A couple of the girls are going to Great Adventure. You know – the park? They got a car and I'm invited.'

'I run a shelter for kids, not animals.'

'Just say yes or no.' Porsche got up. She paced around the pier. The odor of decomposing fish wrapped in gasoline rose from the darkness of the river. She came back and sat down.

'I'm sorry,' she said. 'I'm rotten, I know it.'

'Not rotten,' I told her, 'just confused.'

Porsche raised the kitten to her cheek. 'I found her crying in an abandoned building. I guess somebody just threw her out.' She reached into her pocket and produced a half-empty jar of baby food. 'She's gonna be able to eat real cat food soon,' she said wistfully.

'What's her name?'

'Beelzebub'

'You named her after the devil?'

'Well, she *is* a little devil, she shits on my coat and stuff. But if she had a litter box, I bet you could box-train her fast. Cats are real clean animals. I had a cat in . . .'

Our eyes touched. It was the second hint she had given me that she remembered something like a family.

'Home,' I said. 'You had a cat at home.'

She smiled a smile that made her seem at once fourteen and forty.

I asked, 'Could you go back?'

'I don't think so. It was a long time ago.'

'You're fifteen. How long could it be?'

She got up, cradling the kitten to her breast. A chorus of sirens consumed the silence between us, then faded like a train whistle moving down the track.

'Why'd you leave the Church?' she demanded, crouching down beside me again.

'There was nothing for me there . . . The Church was empty.'

In the night shadows the kitten looked like a fetus. I took it into my hands. Its fur was bare in places; I wondered if it was sick. Porsche said, 'If you buy her a litter box, I'll pay you back.'

'What about it, Porsche? What about getting out?'

'I told you, I'm working on it. I'm working on leaving the life.'

I didn't say I didn't believe her. I didn't say she had lied to me before. I especially didn't say that if something didn't happen soon, I might not have a program. We watched the city's distorted reflection in the murky river. My beeper went off. I took it from my belt to see who was calling. It was Manhattan South. The old wood beneath our feet protested as we got up.

'I have to head over to the precinct.'

She nodded. Another kid in trouble. Nothing new to either one of us.

Traffic on Twelfth Avenue was still steady. To avoid the market of human flesh, we entered a deserted block. Somewhere in the darkness ahead, a howl rose and fell. We both saw her at the same time. She stood in the middle of the street, a small mongrel with mangy hair being mounted from the rear by a German shepherd. Three smaller dogs sniffed at her belly and waited their turn. Above, the waning crescent moon sailed the night as steady as the ship that carries souls to purgatory.

I said, 'I'll take the kitten, but you have to promise to show up at the storefront in a couple of days.'

'I promise.'

2

'This isn't the Garden of Eden. It's just an ordinary jungle,' Officer O'Shaugnessy was saying as he fingered the stubble on his chin. This was a guy whose beard grew so quickly, he always looked unshaven. He was holding court for three mesmerized rookies.

'Poetry or philosophy?' I inquired impatiently.

Into his mouth he shoved a remnant of pizza so old it gleamed like plastic. Smelling trouble, the rookies cleared out.

O'Shaugnessy leaned back in his dilapidated swivel chair and thumped his feet on his desk. Take-out food containers, Styrofoam cups, and soda cans scattered. Old coffee stained a week's accumulation of newspapers. Grains of rice formed a pattern intricate enough to be a genetic code. O'Shaugnessy shoved some rubble aside with his beefy hand and indicated a chair. I didn't sit. 'Look,' he said, 'don't tell the boys I beeped you. You're gonna make me look soft and ruin my reputation around here.'

'Who's the kid?'

'Some runaway preppy they picked up while I was making my rounds.'

'A rich kid. Why can't his folks help him?'

'You prejudiced against rich kids?'

'No, just overcrowded. I don't have room for kids who can go to thirty-thousand-dollar treatment programs.'

There was a hole in the sole of his left shoe. His socks didn't match. I wondered if he would care if he knew. He rested his hands on his stomach and tapped his thumbs together in a kind of salsa beat. 'Didn't expect to be seeing you so soon,' O'Shaugnessy said, not without pleasure. 'You look like it's been a long day.'

'I spent most of it at City Hall.'

'Any luck?'

'*Nada*, not one dime.'

'They're full of shit downtown,' he said. These days, fighting City Hall was the biggest thing we had in common. The mayor was slicing the budget for cops as if they were a social program.

'What about this kid?' I asked.

'He's eighteen. I called his folks. Technically I gotta let him walk. You want him or not?'

'What's his name?'

'Colin Winklesworth the Third.'

'You're kidding!'

Over the tips of his shoes, he said, 'Do I look like I'm kidding?'

'What's he into?'

'The usual.'

I followed O'Shaugnessy down the stairs to the metal door that led to the cages. The room on the other side was painted light green. Abandon-all-hope green. An empty desk and two adjoining cells lined the far wall. It was early and one cell was still empty. Colin Winklesworth III pressed his young Kennedy face against the bars of the other. He was dressed like a sixties version of a Native American. A red bandanna held his shoulder-length sandy hair in place. A turquoise-orange tie-dyed T-shirt hung over stonewashed jeans, the pants legs slashed from top to bottom. The denim had been combed out so that strands of fabric covered his legs like soft white fur.

On the cement floor behind the boy a head peered out from under an old army jacket and mumbled obscenities. A mat of hair hid one eye, the other was missing. Something oozed from the socket. The smell of unwashed human flesh filled the basement room.

'What's *he* doing here?' I asked O'Shaugnessy, because the old man was obviously deranged and probably homeless.

He shrugged and stepped up to the bars. 'Colin, this is Anna Eltern. She has a program for kids like you. That is, if you wanna get out of here.'

If Colin didn't know O'Shaugnessy was bluffing, he hadn't been in the streets for long.

'Not funny, O'Shaugnessy,' I said.

'Whattaya say, kid?' he pressed.

My temper flared. I grabbed O'Shaugnessy's arm, walked him to the corner of the room, and hissed, 'See here, O'Shaugnessy, if I'm gonna catch this kid, it'll be my way!'

He raised his meaty hands in a gesture of surrender and smiled wickedly. 'Hey, just trying to help. If you can turn a kid like that around, his family'd probably throw Eden House some serious *dinero*.'

'You're disgusting.'

We both turned back to the cage. I took the bars between my fingers. The metal was cold, the smell of the old man unmitigated by any ventilation. 'If you want,' I told the boy, 'you can spend the night at my center.'

Colin didn't answer. He didn't move away either.

'Tomorrow, if you don't want to stay, you don't have to.'

Colin studied the tongue hanging from his unlaced hightop sneakers. O'Shaugnessy nudged my arm with his elbow, but I backed him off with a hard stare. Something peeked its scrawny head out of my pocket and mewed.

'What the hell is that?' O'Shaugnessy asked.

Colin reached through the bars. 'Whose is it?'

'One of the kids I work with.'

I placed the kitten in the palm of Colin's outstretched hand. He stroked it with a finger. Then, without looking up, he asked, 'Did you mean what you said before? About leaving if I want to?'

I nodded. O'Shaugnessy played noisily with the keys on his belt. The old man stirred, moaned, and mumbled. Colin sighed. 'Okay then, I'd like to try it.'

O'Shaugnessy unlocked the lock.

'I can't leave without my guitar,' Colin said.

'No problem, kid. Nobody here knows how to play it anyway.'

'What about me?' the army jacket whined without raising his head. 'Just because I'm old, I gotta die here?'

At the front desk Captain Mulholland, bouncing a wad of keys in his big Irish palm, chatted with the boys. Mulholland adjusted the golden-apple lapel pin that betrayed his recent return from a City Hall powwow and said, 'The mayor's office is looking for miracles just because some jive-ass hearings about runaways are coming to the city. There's gonna be a lot of attention on midtown.'

'This is Hell's Kitchen and it's always gonna be Hell's Kitchen. You stamp out the vermin, new vermin rises up. Don't they get that?' the desk sergeant pronounced from his lofty perch.

O'Shaugnessy vaulted the three steps that led behind the sergeant's desk. When he'd gone, the captain looked right through Colin and me. In his hand the keys jingled like a wind chime. 'This bastard perp left no clues. Only the broom. Not one fingerprint. Nobody seen him come, nobody seen him go.'

'He don't come, do he?' Now the desk sergeant did look at me.

The captain laughed. 'I guess he can't cuz our vic was definitely raped, but there was no sperm. So we got no sperm sample.'

'Jesus, can't none of these perverts get it right anymore? A broom handle, for God's sake!' The desk sergeant polished his badge with a sleeve.

'From now on we tell the press squat, and we crack at least one of these cases *before* the damn hearings get here. That's all there is to it. We gotta keep the press from crawling up our asses and bust this thing,' Mulholland told his men as he headed for the exit.

There were many sex killings in the neighborhood. Most went unreported. Last July when a girl's throat had been slit in a peep show, that was kinky enough to hit the papers. So a month later, when a girl was raped and murdered in a hot-sheet hotel, reporters were still watching the Midtown South police blotter. The papers had offered their readers the young girl's death in gruesome detail. After that, the local community board had started agitating the mayor's office for the promised neighborhood revitalization that had never arrived. It had been a long hot summer. From July to September three young girls had been murdered in the Times Square area. The latest just last week.

O'Shaugnessy came back. He barked at Colin, 'Now get your ass outta here,' and handed him his guitar case. To me he didn't even say good-bye. Jekyll and Hyde. Whenever other cops were around, O'Shaugnessy turned mean. I walked by him feeling his eyes on my body.

On the precinct-house steps, Detective Green, a black homicide detective with a chip on his polyester shoulder, kicked a few shards of broken glass with his foot. Like all the detectives, he wore the flag on his lapel.

'What is this shit? Clean this up,' he yelled up at the lone rookie in the doorway. 'Where's Dowd, goddammit?'

'I dunno, sir.'

'Well, how about finding him, shithead!'

'Yes, sir, will do, sir.'

Unlike the older precinct houses, this one had no green-orbed bulbs flanking the entrance. It looked more like a warehouse than the home of the guardians of the peace. The renovation at Midtown South's true headquarters on West Thirty-fifth Street was almost complete. Everything here was just temporary. On our way down, Colin and I passed Detective Green at the foot of the steps.

'Fucking Dowd,' Detective Green grumbled. 'Why doesn't the captain can him?'

In the five years he had been working the precinct, Green had yet to acknowledge my existence.

For a moment the warmth of the evening deceived me, and I felt that it was spring, with summer just around the corner. I searched Colin's pupils for a sign of who he really was. I saw only a tiny reflection of myself. He turned to walk away from me. 'Where do you think you're going?'

'You said I didn't have to stay if I didn't want to.'

I was tired, very tired, of being tested, but I said, 'If you cut out before you've given it a try, I'm gonna hafta go back in there and tell Officer O'Shaugnessy.'

Colin's face soured, but he fell in step beside me, the thump of his guitar case against his long, lean thigh punctuating the silence between us. His eyes wandered toward the Port Authority Bus Terminal, which, from where we stood, had no lights and no windows. The terminal was New York's gateway to America. Inside the building the night was just starting. Boys who wanted to sell themselves for a fix of forgetfulness could do it easily at a place called 'the Wall.' On the second level and made of gray-tinted Plexiglas, the Wall surrounded the up escalator and the stairs that went down. It was the purchase point for young male flesh.

'What are you on?' I asked.

He shrugged. 'I'm a garbage head.'

That meant he swallowed, smoked, or injected whatever happened to be handy.

I touched his arm. He glanced furtively at my fingers. I removed them. 'Colin, don't go back out there tonight.'

We turned up Tenth Avenue toward Forty-third Street and the center. Once inside the front door, you had to pass Rich Cannon, the security guard, to really get in. Rich was a six-foot body-building black man, and he was armed. His presence was designed to frighten off predatory pimps. The kids loved him and he loved them.

'Hey,' he said as I stepped in.

'Rich, this is Colin.'

'Howya doin', Colin?'

Colin nodded vaguely.

'Who's on duty?' I asked Rich.

'Father Toomey. Want me to call him, Annie?'

'No, thanks. Just buzz us in.'

Rich pushed a button under his desk. The door opened, and the dayroom stretched ahead of us with its friendly red and purple lounge chairs arranged around low tables on which were scattered an assortment of magazines, books, and games. The television was on. Residents were allowed to watch the news and, if all their work was done, one additional hour of television. A dozen kids were riveted to the screen, following troop movements in the Saudi Arabian desert like any other action-adventure series. A couple looked up as we passed.

'Hey, Annie, we miss seeing you around.'

'I'm gonna be around more soon,' I promised.

'Annie's got another stray. Welcome, dude.'

The kids reached out and slapped me a gentle five as I passed. Colin didn't react. I didn't introduce him, because his face said he wasn't ready. In the back, behind a Plexiglas wall, Father Toomey, my assistant director, worked at his desk.

'Hang here for a minute,' I said to Colin. 'I'll be right back.'

The father sat holding his mechanical pencil, his eyes bleary. At sixty he was still handsome. A thick head of silver-gray hair topped his ruddy complexion. The broken capillaries on his nose and cheeks were a road map to his past. Toomey was a recovered alcoholic. Under his black shirt and black pants were the lean muscles of a man who was now a religious jogger. Except for the lock of hair that always threatened to fall forward over his eyes, everything about Father Toomey was orderly.

'I need to admit somebody,' I said from the open doorway. He didn't answer. 'I need to process somebody,' I repeated.

He looked up at me over his reading glasses. 'Is City Hall going to give us that emergency grant?'

'I'm afraid not.'

He put his pencil down. 'That's bad news. It means Open Intake is suspended.'

I stepped into the room and closed the door so that Colin wouldn't hear me. 'Open Intake is my first and most basic policy. You know that. It's my promise to the kids.'

'I do know that, Anna, and *you* know that at the last meeting the board voted to suspend Open Intake if no emergency funds came in.'

'I've got to take this boy in. The precinct gave him to me.'

'We're full, completely full.'

'What about the storefront?'

'The board has warned us about that. We have no permit to use the storefront as a residential facility.'

'This is an emergency. There must be something we can do.'

I tried to put some authority into my tone. After all, I was the founder and director. But the Father reminded me that I was no longer running my own show. The moment I had incorporated in order to accept donations, I had lost that power. Now I had to answer to a board of directors. The same board that had approved my hiring him to assist me. Toomey reminded me of all that by raising one eyebrow. After a while I said, 'We need more space. Do you think you might deign to do a little fund-raising?'

'That's your turf.'

'You were in the diocese finance office. You were a Wall Street liaison. You must have lots of contacts.'

Toomey rubbed his neck beneath his stiff white collar. 'I came to this program to leave all that behind. The finance office practically destroyed me. It made me into a drunk.'

'Still,' I said more gently, 'we need more space.'

'We can't pay our bills as it is. We're a month behind on the mortgage . . . you know that.'

Two months earlier City Hall had frozen our budget, along with those of thousands of other social-service programs. We had been treading water ever since. In a cruel twist of fate, word of mouth had spread, and just as our budget was shrinking, the number of kids coming to us grew daily. 'Under the circumstances, don't you think we could improvise a little?' I asked.

He ran his finger down the ledger. 'Maybe you'd like to look at these numbers.'

'I know what they add up to.'

'They add up to our shutting down this facility at the end of the month,' he said.

On the other side of the Plexiglas wall, a card game and a dance contest had started. Colin sat hunched into himself and stroked the kitten. Toomey's office was so soundproof, I heard no music, no laughter, no conversation. 'What about these kids? Where do they go?'

'I pray for their souls and you should, too, Anna. But I must caution you again not to jeopardize the program by breaking the rules set by your board of directors. You can't always operate from the heart – sometimes you have to use your head. You haven't got the money. You haven't got the room . . .'

He was still talking when I left his office and stepped back into the dayroom. As I passed the clusters of chairs teenagers reached out to touch my hand, my skirt, my hair, like much smaller children would do. Colin hadn't moved. I called to him from across the room.

'Annie. Hey, Annie, how's it goin? Y'all never have time for us anymore.' Seventeen-year-old Melanie's accent betrayed the southern roots she usually denied. She had come into the program with a newborn baby. Mother and child seemed to be thriving.

I stroked the auburn hair from her eyes. 'I'm sorry I'm away so much, but you have to keep doing your part. No slacking off just because I'm not around.'

'I'm not slacking off,' she protested. 'I get my ninety-day pin this week.'

'Ninety days drug- and lice-free.' Hot Sauce winked out of his wise-ass sixteen-year-old face. He had earned his nickname hustling in the streets. I was waiting for the day he'd be ready for a new name, or maybe even his birth name. But it wasn't time yet.

Melanie slapped him playfully. 'And no sex either,' she said.

'Yeah, Annie, we all practically saints,' another kid offered.

'But I got some issues, Annie, issues I gotta talk to you about.' Hot Sauce nodded his head to emphasize the seriousness of his words. The kids had learned to spout the jargon of self-improvement. But that was okay; we needed a common language.

After I made an appointment to talk to Hot Sauce, I said my good-byes. Colin glumly followed me into the night outside. Over us rose the towers of Manhattan Plaza.

'We're going around the corner to the storefront,' I told him. 'The main facility is full tonight.'

3

I opened the door and felt at home. The storefront was shaped like a railroad car, but it had once been a barbershop. Mirrors were built into its oak-paneled walls. It was divided into three areas – my office by the window, the hotline phones in the middle, and a makeshift emergency shelter behind a curtain in the back. It had three bunk beds, a bathroom and shower, as well as a minikitchen. Winding suspended stairs led to my apartment on the floor above. Behind the curtain there was young laughter and the pungent smell of chili.

'Annie!' Millie's face brightened. 'Any luck?'

I shook my head. Millie sighed. Millie lived in the apartment above mine. She was the mother I would have wished for myself. She was sixty, recently widowed, and she had adopted all of us. Her chubby frame was hunched over the stove. Five kids, ages twelve to sixteen, sat on the floor picking Lotto numbers.

'I want four.'

'It's been proved white guys don't win the Lotto.'

'He's not white, he's Irish.'

'This is a group ticket, everybody picks a number.'

I maneuvered Colin in front of me. 'Everybody, this is Colin. He's thinking about joining the program.'

'Yo, dude.'

'Hey, homeboy.'

I introduced the kids to Colin. Lucky was a freckle-faced sixteen-year-old Irish kid from the neighborhood. Since his heroin-addicted parents had abandoned him, he lived with his grandmother. His battle with crack addiction was driving the old lady into an early grave. They both came to us for counseling. Occasionally we let him stay to give the old lady a night off.

Red was a light-skinned black kid whose parents were cocaine addicts. His father was sometimes violent. Those were the nights Red spent with us. He was fourteen.

'What's happening?' Eclipse said. She was a chocolate-brown sixteen-year-old. Her mother was a prostitute, and Eclipse had been stopping by at the storefront ever since her mother got lazy and started bringing her johns home. Eclipse was a shy, quiet girl whose wide-set eyes often said more than most people's words. That night she was unusually talkative. The fourth kid in the storefront was Elvira, a thirteen-year-old Polish kid whose parents kept throwing him out because he was gay. His real name was Elton.

Then there was Domingo, the youngest. He was only twelve, and he had been living on the street on and off for two years already. Domingo considered himself an urban guerrilla. That meant he thought stealing and prostitution were more noble than being on welfare like his mother. He dropped in for a break now and then. He had never stolen from us.

NIGHTSIDE

After the introductions everybody's attention turned to the kitten.

'Who does it belong to?'

'All of us for now,' I said, and explained that Porsche would come by to pick her up in a few days. Porsche had been in and out so often that the kids knew her.

'The kitten needs a litter box and some baby food.' I pulled a few dollars from my pocket. 'Anybody want to chip in?'

A lot of small change materialized on the floor. Millie's eyes dampened. I knew what she was feeling. Our kids – we thought of them as ours – were starved for love. Not just to get but to give. They cared more for a stray cat than any adult had ever cared for them.

'Who's going?' I asked.

'I'll go,' Colin volunteered.

He was the one person I didn't want to go. The regulars knew that. They had all been new once.

'We'll all go,' Domingo decided. 'You can leave that here.' He tried to take the guitar.

Colin jerked back. 'Don't touch my guitar, man.'

'C'mon, Colin,' Eclipse said soothingly.

Domingo put his hands on his hips and looked up at me. 'Why is he so touchy?'

'I'll take care of your guitar, Colin.' I reached toward him. He let me take the guitar.

'Stopping off anywhere?' I asked Domingo.

'Just the candy store for today's Lotto ticket. And when we win, our troubles will be up in smoke. Cuz we do have troubles, don't we, Annie?' Domingo, the littlest warrior, looked up at me defiantly.

25

'It didn't work out at City Hall,' I admitted.

'It's like I told you,' he said. 'You can't depend on no handouts.'

'Don't forget dinner's in fifteen minutes,' I told him.

The kids rolled out the door in a happy, chattering platoon. I unfolded the legs of the card table we would eat on. In the kitchen Millie was unusually quiet. Finally she said, 'Father Toomey had a meeting with the volunteers today.'

I took a stack of plates from the cupboard. 'And . . .'

'And he said Open Intake is about to be suspended. How are you going to deal with that?'

'I just can't picture myself sending kids back out to the street. It's a betrayal of everything I ever told them.'

'If you ask me, Toomey's ruining the program.'

'It's not Toomey. It's the budget cuts and the board.'

'Why do you need that stupid board? This is *your* program. You started it. You built it.'

'You can't legally run a not-for-profit program without a board of directors, Millie. I need them.'

We both remembered that night seven years ago when six teenagers knocked on my door asking for refuge from their pimp. I had taken them in, and somehow six kids became thirty. From the beginning I had promised myself never to turn any child away. That's what Open Intake meant. When I formed the corporation and things became official, my policy hadn't wavered. And now the budget crisis and the board were about to change everything I stood for.

'You're spending too much time away from the program, Annie.'

'I don't like it either, but I have to try to raise some funds. I need another plate for Colin.'

Millie handed me a plate. 'Where are you going to put this new boy?' she asked.

'I guess he'll stay with me.'

'Be careful,' Millie warned. 'You know the board wouldn't like that. Plus, Father Toomey is out to get you.'

'You're paranoid, Millie. Toomey's a pain in the ass, but he's very good at what he does.'

She shook her head. 'Too good, if you ask me. He's trying to take over the program.'

'He can't do that, Millie. He's the least of our problems.'

When the kids came back, we sat down to eat. First we joined hands and each of us said a few words of blessing. Everybody but Colin, who stayed silent. After the bowls had been filled with chili and after Millie had been complimented, Eclipse asked, 'What's gonna happen to the program? Are we gonna win?'

'What do you mean?' I asked.

'You know, the funding. I saw it on TV. They're cutting everybody, not just us, even schools and hospitals.'

'America is broke,' Domingo added.

'We'll win this battle,' I told them.

'Battle,' Lucky echoed. 'It's kinda weird, ain't it? Like bein' at war with your own country just cuz you wanna survive.'

I studied the happy pattern of Lucky's orange freckles thinking about the undeclared war he waged on his own grandmother. She, too, was just trying to survive. Colin stirred his chili listlessly and pretended to eat.

'You're gonna like it in the program,' Eclipse told him softly. 'They help you get your act together.'

'I seen you in Port Authority, right?' Lucky asked Colin.

'Could be,' Colin said.

'Have you seen me?' Domingo demanded.

'Could be.' Colin stroked the kitten on his lap. 'But I don't remember. There's a lot of faces out there.'

'What's his name?' Lucky asked, pointing to the kitten.

Colin looked at me. I shrugged because I didn't want to say 'Beelzebub.' That shrug wasn't exactly a lie, but it wasn't the truth either.

'Let's name him.'

'How about calling him Cat?'

'That's weak.'

'Besides, he's a she,' Colin said.

Everybody laughed. 'Big deal, he, she ... who cares?' Elvira said.

'Jezebel. How about Jezebel?'

'I vote for Little Devil,' Colin said. Everyone at the table looked for my reaction. But I didn't react. Just as clearly as if he were sitting there in the room with us, I heard my grandfather's voice: *Driving out Beelzebub with the devil is like fighting fire with gasoline*.

'Little Devil, that's cool,' Lucky said.

Domingo studied my face. 'Okay?'

Odd that Porsche and Colin had given the kitten two versions of the same name. I shrugged.

'She used to be a nun, but she ain't no zero now.' Domingo slapped the table and slipped into a rap he created as he went along.

> *'Nun is a person and zero is a place*
> *Some of us are hungry and some of us got grace*
> *Little devils used to be angels in God's face*
> *You can't walk the streets without no Mace.'*

'C'mon, guys, let's eat,' I said.

Later, as the kids got up to do the dishes, Lucky asked me how to feed the kitten.

'Like this,' Colin answered. He opened the baby food, inserted his pinkie, and then slipped it into the kitten's mouth. The kitten sucked on his finger as if it were a nipple. The kids watched in rapt attention.

'I'm going to turn in,' Millie announced. 'I'll be back in the morning.'

She kissed the kids one by one. Except Colin. When she approached him, he stepped back.

'No hug?' she asked.

He put his hands in his back pockets. Millie said, 'That's okay, I can wait.' She turned to take me in her arms. Into my ear she whispered, 'You need a break, Annie.'

'I'm okay, Millie. Really I am.'

As I locked the door behind Millie the kids started another card game. Colin sat watching, the kitten in his lap.

'Hey, the dishes need to be dried and put away,' I said.

Eclipse jumped up. I said, 'The boys should help, too.'

'Aw, let 'em play.' She winked at me. I knew that meant she wanted to talk.

There was only one dish towel, so Eclipse dried and I put away. She polished each plate as if it were silver. 'Me and Porsche was on Thirty-fourth Street last week, and just for fun we went into Macy's. They have some dishes there,

Annie, you can't believe how beautiful they are.' She ran a finger around the edge of a plate. 'All with flowers and gold. We were gonna buy a set. We thought they cost a hundred dollars. It turned out a hundred dollars is for a big plate, a little plate, and a cup.'

'A setting.'

'Yeah.' She handed me a plate dreamily. 'Someday I wanna have plates like that, but first I have to have a house to put them in.'

'If you go back to school and graduate, you can get all the dishes you want.'

'Those plates probably break real easy, though.'

'Not if you're careful.'

We were almost finished before she asked, 'So how *is* Porsche?'

'The same, I guess.'

Her liquid eyes looked up at me. 'I'm kinda worried about her, cuz she went off on Blue Fly in front of everybody.'

'What did she say?'

'He's got this john he makes her go with for free, and she said she wasn't gonna do it anymore. She said she's going free-lance.'

'Hopefully she'll come into the program for real, and then she won't have to worry about Blue Fly. And what about you? When are you coming in?'

'I can't leave my mom,' Eclipse said. 'She quit the life. So it's gonna be all right at home.'

I kissed her forehead, afraid to say the wrong thing. 'You're always welcome here.'

She lurched into my arms, then pulled back just as

quickly. 'You're good people, Annie. You're white, but you don't act it.'

Eclipse said good-bye to the boys, and I walked her to the storefront door. After locking up, I sorted my telephone messages and answered a few calls. The neon sign on the window pulsed to the rhythm of the wise-ass chatter from the kitchen. I sat down in the window alcove and watched the night outside heat up. The video store had moved across the street just last summer. It had robbed me of the illusion that Eden House was changing the neighborhood. After a while Lucky came and sat across from me, his foot nervously tapping the floor. The flashing neon sign bathed him in red, then green.

'I seen my parents today,' he said.

'How are they?'

'They didn't see me. They was on the subway steps fighting. My mom was hitting my dad with her shoe, screaming something about he took her hit.'

'That must have been hard for you,' I said softly.

His freckles shifted with the effort of his muscles to hide the anger that covered his hurt.

'How's your grandma?' I asked.

'She's goin' nuts cuz I keep smokin' that crack. I say I'm gonna stop and I mean it. Then something happens. It could be good or bad. Next thing I know, I'm in the crack house.'

I wanted to offer to refer him to a rehab program. But waiting lists were now six months long, so I kept my mouth shut. Tomorrow I would have to tell my own volunteers to stop recruiting. Lucky and I sat in silence. I said, 'If you're staying tonight, you should call your grandmother now.'

He didn't smile. I had never seen Lucky smile. But I felt him breathe easier. He had been waiting for this invitation. He made his call. I kicked off my shoes. Then, for a while, we both just sat watching the night outside. I felt good that this was the sanctuary where he didn't have to grandstand. And where I could just be me. Lucky went back to the others. A little later I followed.

'Lights out, guys.'

'The bunks are all full. Where's Colin gonna sleep?' Domingo asked.

'On my couch.'

A low murmur went around the room. I had never before invited anyone to sleep upstairs. Domingo pointed a jealous finger at Colin. 'Hey, ace, *you* got it *good*.'

Colin's face paled with anger.

'C'mon, let's get the kitten set up in the bathroom upstairs,' I told Colin.

As Colin and Domingo stared each other down the other kids noisily divvied up the bunk beds.

'See you all in the A.M.'

'Night, Annie,' the kids chimed.

I headed for the winding stairway. Colin followed with the kitten and the litter box.

The apartment above was shaped like the storefront below. In the back was my room, in the middle the kitchen and bathroom, and in the front the living room. 'You can put that in the bathroom,' I told Colin.

'The cat needs a water dish.'

I handed him an old soup dish. He took it and Beelzebub into the bathroom. I made up the couch in the living room, then sat down, waiting for Colin. But Colin didn't come.

After a while I went to check up on him. The bathroom door was open. He sat at the edge of the tub, balancing the water dish on his knees, holding the kitten by the neck, trying to get it to drink. The kitten mewed miserably.

'I don't think you can force him to drink, Colin. Just leave the dish on the floor and close the door behind you.'

Colin ignored me. I said, 'I made up the couch for you. It's almost time to turn in.'

'How come you're doing all this?' he asked.

I took Beelzebub from him gently. 'It's what I do. It's my job.'

'Having all these people in your house is your job?' He raised a quizzical brow.

'They're not in my house, they're in the storefront. *You're* in my house.'

'Why me? My own mom doesn't want me in her house.'

'Is that a threat or a challenge?'

He actually met my eyes then and grinned. 'I dunno.'

'Well, I'm not your mom, and this is a temporary situation. The deal is I get you into the program and you start fresh.'

'How?'

'We make commitments to each other and we keep them. We write a contract so we know what to expect from each other. Not just you and me but the other people in the program, too.'

He nodded thoughtfully and reached for Beelzebub. I knew better than to push any further. I showed him where he would be sleeping. I had placed a towel and toothbrush on the bed for him. Then I returned to my end of the apartment. When he was finished in the bathroom, I went to shower and then turned in myself.

Under the window by my bed the radiator hissed. I tried to turn the heat down, but the valve was broken. Steam escaped from the burning hot metal. I opened the window and lay down on my bed. My thoughts raced in circles. Downstairs I could hear the kids giggling.

Tired as I was, I couldn't sleep. I thought about Porsche, her ashen face, that sadly adult smile. Where was she now? As I began to doze off I heard the rush of running water. From my bed I could see the bathroom. The door was open, the light on. Colin stood hunched over the sink. I got up. 'What's going on, Colin?'

The hands hanging at his sides clenched to fists. He turned. He had taken his bandanna off, and his long, sandy hair was wild around his face.

'I'm sick,' he said softly. 'I can't sleep.'

'We'll go to the infirmary tomorrow.'

'I'll go crazy if I can't sleep.'

'Tomorrow we'll go to the infirmary,' I repeated.

'Tomorrow will be too late,' he whispered.

'Go back to bed, Colin. Tomorrow we'll deal with it.'

I watched him hobble to the front of the apartment like a broken old man. Then I closed the bathroom door behind me and checked the medicine cabinet. The Tylenol with codeine my dentist had given me was missing. Had I used them up? Or had Colin helped himself? As I swung the medicine cabinet shut I met my face in the mirror. I ran my hand through the dark curls I had cropped that year, grateful that my hair needed so little care. I looked haggard and a bit too thin, my eyes seemed larger and more haunted than usual. Budget cuts, I figured, were beginning to take their toll. I went back to bed, put my head down, and slipped into a dream.

I was at the First Station of the Cross, where Christ had been betrayed. I kissed the ground on which the Father stood, then looked up at the ledger he was holding. With his long, bony finger, he pointed to my cell.

I put the binder around my breasts. I laced the corset. I wrapped myself in fourteen yards of fabric. With fourteen safety pins, the cloth became a habit – no buttons, no zipper. On my shaved head I placed the bonnet. Then I pinned the veil. My peripheral vision gone, I stared at the wall, where no mirror was allowed. A high, thin shriek pierced my chest.

When I woke up, the phone was ringing. I was bathed in sweat and freezing. At the end of the long, narrow corridor of the railroad flat, Colin lay on the couch bare-chested. In his fuzzy jeans he looked like a satyr, half animal, half man. From the street below a passing headlight cast shadow bars over the ceiling. The phone continued to ring. I picked up. On the wall the clock said it would soon be dawn.

4

'It's me – Anna.'

On the other side of the door, I heard the shuffle of Millie's slippers. Fuzzy robe, furry slippers, silver-blue hair in rollers fastened with pink plastic toothpicks, she let me in. 'You're up a mite early,' she said. Her head looked like a receiving station for Radio Free Europe.

'Millie, can you go down to my apartment before the kids wake up?'

'Come in, please, Annie. Where you going so early?'

'My grandfather had a heart attack. I'm going up to Danbury Hospital to see him.'

'Why didn't you say so, honey? Come in. Have a cup of coffee with me before you go.'

Without taking off my coat, I sank down at the kitchen table and let the warmth of her home embrace me. Millie placed a cup of coffee in front of me. Her imitation Tiffany lamp cast a rainbow of colors onto the cabinets around us. She sat down, framed by silk geraniums that lined the sill of the make-believe window to her bedroom. Millie's apartment was shaped just like mine downstairs. But it was homier.

'I haven't been back since last Christmas.'

'But they did call to tell you,' she said.

'My sister called, not my mother. My sister said Grandpa's been asking for me ... What if he dies?'

'Don't think the worst, Annie. Just go and make peace.'

'I had the strangest dream, Millie. I dreamed I was wrapping myself in a habit, the old-fashioned kind. The kind I never wore. They're made of a nasty rough material and held together by safety pins. Once you've pinned yourself in, your freedom of movement is gone. I woke up more tired than I was when I went to sleep.'

'Sounds like a prison.' She tucked a loose strand of hair into place.

'What do you think it meant?' I persisted.

'You did get woken pretty early, and by bad news.'

'The dream, Millie, the dream was *before* I woke up.'

'Well, which of your bad habits feels like a prison?'

'I don't know, Millie. I don't drink, I don't smoke, I don't ... none that I can think of.'

'Maybe that's it. You don't ...' She left the sentence dangling.

'Look who's talking.'

Millie's jaw tightened. 'You're wrong about that, Anna. I had a good life with my husband. After he died, I just never wanted anybody else. But you're young, Annie. It's not natural for you to be so alone. You ever ask yourself why your best friend is a sixty-year-old woman? When are you planning to start your own life?'

I got up. 'You'll take care of the kids?'

At the door Millie hugged me. 'Don't be mad, Anna – you asked, I answered.'

'I never really noticed before, but I'm surrounded by people obsessed by sex. I just don't happen to think it's the most important thing in life. I'm living. My life is full.'

Millie's sigh heaved her large breasts. 'I never said s-e-x, I said life. You know – love, friendship, relationship and all that goes with it. Not just kids.'

'I love those kids and they love me, Millie.'

She changed the subject. 'When will you be back?'

'I'll call you. I have to figure out a way to get Colin into the program officially.'

Millie touched my face tenderly. 'I hope your grandfather's okay.'

'The hotline, Millie. You have to let the volunteers in to staff the hotline.'

'Relax. Have I ever let you down? As soon as I get dressed, I'll go down to your place.'

I entered Edison Park through an opening in the Cyclone fence. Inside, hundreds of cars were lined up as neatly as gravestones. In the tiny illuminated shack at the exit gate, a twenty-four-hour guard kept watch. I unlocked my old clunker, drove to the gate, and inserted my plastic ID into the computer. The gate didn't go up. I tried again. The gate didn't budge. I got out and walked back to the guard shack. I tapped on the window. 'Excuse me. I'm in a hurry, and I can't get my card to work.'

His brown face folded in disdain. 'You pay your bill?'

I rummaged in my purse for my checkbook. On the halogen lamp above the guard shack, a spider tightened her web around a luminous fragment of moth wing. The attendant punched computer keys; I wrote a check I hoped wouldn't bounce and pushed it through the slot under the window. The printer began its rattle. I wondered out loud where the other guard was. The one from Trinidad.

'Him dayside,' the face behind the window said. 'Me nightside.'

That told me where he was learning his English. 'Nightside' was cop slang for the night shift. Reporters used it, too. They weren't much different from cops.

'Where you from?' I asked. His expression shifted ever so slightly. 'Persia,' he said, handing me a receipt. There hadn't been a Persia since 1935.

My muffler spitting and coughing, I sped up the West Side Highway past the George Washington Bridge onto the Saw Mill. Tufts of milky mist danced over the parkway. In them the past welled up like a picture show, my years at home, my years in the Church, and the years since I had left the Church. Doors that closed and doors that opened. It was almost as if I'd had three distinct lives. But the door that intimidated me most was the one that led back to childhood. I had gone home little more than once a year for Christmas since leaving the Church seven years ago.

The car began to sound like an airplane. No matter how fast I drove, the speedometer didn't leave zero. That meant I had to gauge my speed by the cars I passed. And I was passing a lot of cars. The other drivers slowed down just enough to glance my way disdainfully and shake their heads. I began wishing I owned a better car.

As the sun rose through blazing leaves I asked myself why I had buried myself in Manhattan. At the time it had not felt like a choice. After leaving the Church, New York City seemed to be the only place where I could begin again. In New York you could shake the past. I missed the turn onto I-84. By the time I reached Danbury Hospital, the early-morning sky had turned bone-white.

Inside, an antiseptic stink filled the hospital corridor. The silence had texture and depth. I turned when I heard footsteps behind me.

'This is a restricted area. Can I help you?'

'I'm looking for my grandfather. Vincent Bugliosi. He had a heart attack.'

The nurse's hands fluttered to fix her hair. Her eyes became wide with pity. Had I been blind, I might have missed the point. Still, I waited for her to say it.

'He passed,' she said.

'Can I see him?'

'Oh,' she said. 'It's too late for that. He's not in the room anymore.'

Cobwebs of naked forsythia surrounded the clapboard house. Ghosts, scarecrows, and witches clung to windows draped in orange and black bunting. Although there were no children in the house now, the routine had not altered. On October 1 my mother decorated for Halloween. In the center of the yard a plastic picket fence protected the family Union Jack. The flag was at half-staff. Cars and trucks choked the driveway. The garage door was open.

I turned the engine off and sat there studying the contents of the garage, which all through childhood had been the entrance to the house. It was bursting with the debris of our lives, baby carriages, car seats, toys, decaying newspapers, dismantled lawn mowers. A greasy dust clung to starters, battery cables, ladders, hoses, rakes, flat tires, rug remnants, fishing poles, saws, doorknobs, broken handles of garden tools. Nothing had ever been thrown away.

I broke tradition. I used the front door, the door reserved for guests. In the living room every piece of furniture stood where it always had. I headed for the voices deeper inside the house. By the time I reached the kitchen, I was just a confused twelve-year-old.

My mother sat at the head of the kitchen table, her head in her hands, an untouched cup of espresso in front of her. At each elbow sat my two younger brothers, Tony and Vinnie. I was struck by how much they looked alike. Three years apart; they were both state troopers. They acknowledged me with stricken faces. Tony had a pad and pencil in his hand. As I stepped in, my mother looked up. Her glare seemed to say that giving birth to me had been a mistake. Aunt Cirella, my mother's sister, took my hand. I wondered where my sister was.

'He was asking for you,' my mother accused. Behind her head hung a plaster cast of the Last Supper.

Because I didn't know how to touch her, I just sat down across from her. She opened the sugar bowl. The sugar was damp, yellow, old. She raised her spoon; it slipped from her fingers and bounced on the linoleum floor. She leaned to pick it up. When her head was under the table, we could all hear her begin to sob. Tony tried to put his arms around her, but she pulled away.

'Coffee?' Aunt Cirella asked.

'Yes, please.'

My mother shredded a lavender tissue with her fingers. 'You look so much like Grandpa,' she said. 'It's like the genes skipped a generation.'

In the yard outside, a slight breeze moved my childhood swing.

'Grandpa was going to take that rusty old thing down,' she said.

In my head I saw pictures of Grandpa and me: hiking, fishing, gardening, doing homework. There was barely a corner in the house Grandpa's carpenter hands hadn't worked on. If to me he had been a father, in her heart was he a husband?

My sister appeared in the arched doorway. She wore a clinging black knit dress. Her patent-leather spiked heels matched her wide belt. Although she was twenty-eight, her face was still like a child's, sullen and beautiful. She folded her arms and stared at me as if I had taken her spot. 'You want to sit?' I asked.

She hoisted herself up onto the kitchen counter and pulled the last cigarette from a pack.

'Thanks for calling me,' I said.

She crumpled the empty cigarette pack and tossed it into the open garbage.

'A little late, though,' Tony said, 'cuz she was out half the night.'

Angie shot Tony an evil look. My mother's eyes went from Tony to Angie. She seemed confused. 'It was probably a heart attack,' my mother said.

'Grandpa planned for all of us to come together,' Angie persisted. 'Grandpa always was a great planner. He went to Grandma's grave every day. Every day for seven years he groomed her grave. He always decorated it for the holidays. He was putting pine branches on her grave when he laid his head on the headstone and vomited.'

I asked, 'How do you know all that?'

'Because after that he got in his car, drove home, and called Tony.'

'I listened to Grandpa's heart and took him straight to the hospital,' Tony interrupted proudly. Then his face fell again.

'We're making a list for the memorial service.' My mother took the pad from Tony's hand and pushed it across the table to me. 'You do it.'

Angie said, 'Give her the pen, Tony.'

Tony put the pen on the table. My mother pushed it toward me. 'You were always the organized one, Anna.'

For the next thirty minutes, between coffee and small talk, we added to the list. After about three hundred names I asked, 'Did anybody tell Dad?'

Vinnie's face went red. Tony's fist pounded the kitchen table. 'What's that bastard got to do with anything? We don't even know where he is.'

'Yes, we do. We know where he is.' Angie exhaled through her nostrils. 'We *all* know he moved back to New Milford last year.'

Normally this confrontation would have led to a shouting match. But in deference to the occasion Tony and Vinnie glared at Angie until she began picking at her panty hose. The subject was closed. Mom lit a cigarette and said, 'Grandpa's going to have nothing but the best. A beautiful announcement, Father Damian at the service, not that new guy who can hardly speak English, good food at the reception, and a beautiful casket. One of those modern ones.'

'They cost five thousand dollars,' Angie objected.

I downed my coffee in several gulps, vowing not to get involved. My mother said firmly, 'Everybody's got to chip in.'

'No problem, Ma, just tell everybody what their share is.' Tony patted Mom's hand.

'I'm gonna hafta give you mine after Susie has the baby,' Vinnie added. His wife Susie was seven months pregnant.

Angie slid off the counter. 'I ain't got no money and everybody knows it.'

'We'll pick up your share and you'll owe us,' Tony told her. Vinnie nodded.

I put my mug down on the table. It echoed like a gavel pounding. I heard myself say: 'I think a simple coffin would be fine.'

'You see that, you see that, Ma! She don't give a damn about anybody but herself.' Vinnie glared at me. 'You haven't changed.'

'Look who's talking!' Angie yelled.

Aunt Cirella left the room. Tony shook his head in disbelief. He hated family fights. Vinnie pointed a finger at Angie. 'You and that bastard of yours must cost Mom a heap.'

'I hear you got a little expensive action on the side yourself.'

'Look what you started,' my mother said to me.

I said, 'If you're determined to spend the money, there's a lot of living people you could make donations to.'

'Like that scum you work with?' Vinnie sneered.

'If you weren't so damn ignorant, I'd get mad at you, Vinnie.'

'Don't talk to him like that. He works, he supports a family. You don't even know what family is!' my mother yelled.

My finger traced the pattern on the Formica table. Then softly I said, 'I do know this isn't it. This is a pathetic imitation.'

'You never loved Grandpa,' my mother accused. 'You never loved any of us.'

'I loved him with all my heart.'

'Oh yeah, yeah, yeah.' Tony wiped a tear. 'That's why you never came to see him. Not even to have an ice-cream cone with him.'

I remembered how much Grandpa loved his ice cream and having someone to share it with, and a lump grew in my throat. I said, 'I don't expect you to understand.'

Angie grabbed me by the hand and dragged me toward our old room. In the kitchen the shouting continued. 'I got something that's all mine to show you,' she whispered.

The Blessed Virgin stood on the old bureau. Between our beds stood a crib. The crib had been mine, and it had been Angie's, too. Even from the doorway I could see the baby that sucked on its clenched little fist. I felt the quick stab of jealousy. 'How come you never told me?' I asked.

'We haven't exactly been in touch,' Angie said.

The baby began to cry. 'Boy or girl?'

'Boy.'

'What's his name?'

'Raymond Daniel, but I call him Coffee.'

Just like my kids, I thought, with their many names.

'Can I pick him up?'

'Go ahead.' She sat down on the bed, kicked off her high heels, and leaned down to rub her feet. The baby cuddled to my breast. Its skin was a beautiful brown.

'Who's the father?'

'What's that supposed to mean?' she asked, studying her face closely in the mirror. 'Even your thing with Christ didn't last, did it?'

I said, 'I left the Church, I didn't leave God.'

'Well, I left the man, I didn't leave the kid.'

She wiped some lipstick from a tooth and picked up a perfume bottle. 'His father is a big, beautiful black man.'

'Where is he now?'

'Same as Dad,' she said, moving the Virgin closer to the perfume. 'He fell in love with a bottle.'

The baby grabbed for my nose. 'He's gorgeous.'

Sighing, she sat back down on the bed. 'It's all so easy for you, Anna. All you do is leave. I'm stuck here. I can't afford to go nowhere else.'

'They all hate me,' I said.

'No they don't.' My sister leaned back on the bed. 'They just act mad when they're hurt.'

The door opened. Mom stuck her head in. 'Somebody has to go with me to Grandpa's house to get his good clothes,' she said, looking at me. She said it as if Grandpa were going to a party.

'See,' my sister said. 'She loves you.'

In the driveway my mother headed for her Buick.

'Let's take my car,' I said.

'I'd rather take mine.'

'Then you drive.'

But she wasn't up to driving, so she climbed obediently into my clunker.

'You doing that bad?' she said when we were on the road.

'What do you mean?'

'This car, is it safe?'

'I think so, yeah. I don't use a car much in the city.'

'Grandpa always drove a Cadillac. It was an old Cadillac, but it was a Cadillac. He was such a proud man.' Her bottom lip quivered.

'I'm proud, too, Mom. I'm proud of what I do, not what I drive.'

For a while we both listened to the muffler banging. Outside, the autumn colors were breathtaking. 'Is pride the reason you want an expensive coffin?' I asked.

'Respect,' she said firmly. 'To show respect. What will people think if we send him off in some cheap thing?'

'I don't care what people think, Ma. And neither should you.'

'You say that because you're just passing through. I'm the one that has to live here with the looks and stares. Our family already stood out enough over the years.'

Grandpa's house stood on a fork in the road. He had built every room. Like so many other houses in the area, it had once been just a summer cottage. The house had grown with the family. I stepped out of the car and listened for the brook where as children we had swum.

Inside the garage I smelled Grandpa's basil drying on the heating vents above. A row of cactuses older than I was stood next to his workbench. Plants potted and brought in to survive the winter scratched at my ankles. My mother and I waded wordlessly through the wreckage born of a family philosophy that prohibited throwing anything away. Someday two broken things might combine into one thing that worked. I reached into Grandpa's tin of nails to find the hidden key.

The house was damp and moldy; it smelled of illness. On the kitchen table a trail of bread crumbs connected a half-eaten loaf of Italian bread to a half-empty coffee cup. My mother sat down as if to finish them for Grandpa. I climbed the narrow stairway to my grandparents' rose-colored room. Thick velvet curtains kept the large room with twin beds and twin vanities in perpetual twilight.

'You were their favorite,' my mother said, coming into the room.

'I was the first grandchild, that's all.'

She opened a drawer and sorted through Grandpa's shirts. 'I want you to take pictures of Grandpa tomorrow. You were always such a good photographer.'

'Not since high school, Mom.'

'You even had a darkroom in the garage.'

'I didn't bring a camera.'

'I have one,' she said. 'Dad is going to look beautiful.'

I left my mother searching the closet. On the old sun porch, purple and blue forget-me-nots bloomed in their pots. I opened Grandma's box of mementos: black-and-white wedding pictures from the old country, the deed to the land the house stood on, photographs of Grandpa and his brothers building the house, baby and school pictures of Mom and her brothers, Mom's wedding pictures, baby pictures of me and Angie, family picnics, graduations, my confirmation pictures, the boys' confirmation pictures, dozens of old report cards, Vinnie and Susie's wedding photos. My eyes sifted through the photographs like fingers through sand, unable to grasp anything solid. I sifted and screened and strained until I was dizzy with fatigue.

I saw my grandparents sitting next to each other in their favorite chairs, and me near them on the stool by the grotto where a little veiled girl eternally prayed to the Virgin. This had been the favorite spot of my childhood. I remembered my last conversation in this room. It was after Grandma died. Grandpa sat in his chair, watching *Jeopardy* on his black-and-white television.

'I'm leaving the Church, Grandpa.'

He didn't answer.

I tried again. 'I have to leave. The Church failed me.'

'The Church doesn't fail. People fail,' he said without taking his eyes off the game show.

I said, 'Maybe the Church isn't the Church she was.'

'Maybe the people aren't the people they were.'

I played with the wedding ring I would be taking off soon. My wedding ring to Jesus. 'Grandpa, I'm not leaving God. I'm leaving the Church. There's a difference.'

'I'm glad Grandma didn't live to see this.'

I didn't say that if Grandma were still alive, I wouldn't have the courage to leave. Instead I said, 'I'm so sorry, Grandpa. You don't know how sorry I am.'

Grandpa got up and turned the television off. He tapped his bony fingers on my chest. 'It's what's in here that counts, Anna. You made a vow. When you break it, I'll be afraid for you.'

My mother came up behind me. In her arms she carried Grandpa's best suit. In her hands, his shoes.

'Need some help?'

She shook her head and turned to hide her tears. I grabbed the shoes and pretended not to notice. In the car, on the way back, she said, 'After the service you can go back to those kids you love so much.'

'We're having a lot of financial problems in the program now.'

'I've had financial problems all my life.' She looked out the window at the dark shadows of the hills. 'You love them so much and you feel nothing for your own family.'

'That's not true,' I said.

Back at the house I called Millie to tell her my grandfather had died and that I would be gone for a few days.

'You okay? You sound awful.'

'It's just hard. I'll be back right after the service on Monday. Okay?'

'Wanna talk a bit?' she asked.

'No, Millie, I really can't right now.' I was afraid someone would pick up the extension and hear me say the wrong thing. 'We'll talk when I get back.'

'You take care of yourself, Annie.'

After dinner my mother sat at the kitchen table with a cup of coffee. Outside, the temperature had dropped and frost silvered the windows. The hills beyond were silhouetted in moonlight. I sat down across from her.

'Why can't we invite Dad?'

She got up and threw the rest of her coffee down the drain. 'What's he got to do with us? He's been gone for twenty years.'

'You threw him out, didn't you?'

There was a long silence during which she scrubbed the coffee-pot as if she had just baked lasagna in it.

'All those years you lied. You said Dad left because he didn't love us. But really you forced him out.'

She didn't answer. I heard Angie flushing the toilet behind the kitchen, making enough noise to let us know that she was listening. My mother sat down.

'I got tired of that drunk's abuse,' she murmured.

'It was a long time ago. Maybe he's changed. You know he loved Grandpa.'

'What are you talking about? They couldn't stand each other!'

'I'd like to see Dad, that's all.'

'You want to see him, go see him. But don't spoil Grandpa's funeral for me.' She started to cry. I took her into my arms. As I held her I remembered the many tears she had cried in my arms, from the time Dad left us until I entered the convent. She seemed smaller than she used to be. After a while she blew her nose into the handkerchief she kept in her apron.

'You were always the oldest,' she said, sobbing. 'That's the problem.'

'I don't mean to blame you, Mom.'

She folded some wetness into the center of her handkerchief and shoved it down into her pocket. 'I let Grandma railroad you into the Church. You were just a kid. I had a lot of doubts about it back then, but I just let it happen.'

'You really don't know me, do you, Mom?'

'How could I?' she accused. 'You're never around.'

She got up and turned on the garbage disposal in the sink. I listened to the gnashing of its steel teeth. She turned to me. 'What did happen to you in the Church, Anna?'

I looked out the window at the rusty swing set of my childhood. I said, 'I grew up.'

It wasn't the answer she was looking for. She combed her salt-and-pepper hair with her fingers. In her flannel pants, collared T-shirt, fuzzy slippers, and the apron with its food-chain pictures, she looked every bit like a man in drag.

I heard Angie behind me. She touched my shoulder. 'C'mon, let's tuck the baby in.'

In the bedroom we shared, Angie lit a votive candle. 'I took this from church. I didn't have any cash on me, and I figured God wouldn't mind.'

The candle stood in a red plastic container. It cast a pink light toward a lacquer painting of the crucified Christ. A crown of thorns sharper than nails bit into His forehead. His eyes that seemed to follow you wherever you went shed red tears.

'Why is that still here?'

'Remember how scared we used to be of those goofy eyes?'

'Yeah, I remember begging Grandma to take it down.'

'But she didn't, did she?'

I chuckled. 'I think she hung it across from my bed so that I could learn to be good. She said if I was obedient and my heart was pure, I had nothing to be afraid of.'

'She was one mean old bitch.'

'Grandma? She was the sweetest thing. I had my best times up at Lake Candlewood.'

'You must be kidding. I *hated* it up there. Grandma

whipped my ass every chance she got. After she died, Grandpa took up right where she left off. He was a holy terror.'

'Oh, c'mon, Angie, what are you saying? They were more like parents to us than Mom and Dad.'

'Oh, wow. Big deal.'

We were both quiet. Not angry at the past, but at each other. Afraid to keep talking.

'Angie, why do you think we remember it all so differently?'

'Cuz you went into that convent and buried the truth. Except I don't think you can do that. When you bury things that aren't dead, they rise up like zombies.'

'Have you been to see Dad?'

'What for? I hate his guts.' She propped herself up on an elbow. 'So what's it like . . . life in the big city?'

'It's not all it's cut out to be.'

'It must be better than here.'

I remembered changing her diapers and said nothing.

'I have to get out of here,' she said.

'Where would you go?'

'Could I come to you?'

'My situation isn't too great right now.'

Her sheet rustled. I heard the whisper of cellophane. The smell of sulfur pinched my nostrils. The match flame was doubled by the mirror. 'Do you think you should be smoking right next to the baby like that?'

'Because he was born, I'm supposed to stop living?'

'No, just be responsible.'

'You haven't changed one bit, have you?'

I watched the glowing cigarette ember and kept quiet.

When Angie spoke again, it was only three words, measured and cold. 'Have you, Anna?'

My palms were damp. I noticed that the room was overheated and I was suddenly very tired.

'Have you?' she pressed.

'I don't know, Angie. People don't see themselves.'

'Now that I'm grown up, people don't call me Angie,' she said. 'My name is Angela.'

My eyes began to burn. The baby stirred.

'I guess to me you'll always be my kid sister.'

'I got this picture of you in my head, you know, when we were Girl Scouts. We had those sashes that went across our chests. Everybody had a few medals and ribbons. Everybody but you. You had so many, your sash ripped. You didn't just have them across the front like everybody else, you had them across your back, too.'

'What are you trying to say?'

'You always hadda be the best. You always hadda be right. Right up until the time you went into the convent, you strutted around like a little general.'

The baby began to cry. Angie turned on the lamp that stood between us on the night table. She put out her cigarette, picked the baby up and placed him on the bed next to her, and pulled her breast out of her slip. Without opening its eyes, the baby found her nipple and began to suck. She said, 'I bet you still haven't even had a man between your legs.'

I turned off the light.

On Monday Grandpa was buried in his Cadillac of a coffin. He wore his best pinstripe suit, his gold watch, and held his rosary beads in his hands. In his vest pocket Mom had placed a four-pack of Tiparillos. His makeup had smeared onto his stiff white collar. When my turn came, I walked up to him clutching the camera. I knelt. I touched his folded hands. The rosary beads rustled as they shifted. I kissed his cold smile. I focused my mother's camera.

5

I was speeding but I didn't know how much. I was scheduled to speak at the United Nations at three o'clock. Inside my head clumps of dirt and rock were still falling onto Grandpa's coffin, and my mother was still crying.

The Saw Mill River Parkway funneled traffic into New York City. By the time I reached Manhattan, I had a tic in my eye. After the last tollbooth into the city, the skyline came into view. A thick mist distorted the silhouette of the George Washington Bridge. The city ahead seemed a bleak, lifeless canvas. I headed downtown, parked my car in the lot at Forty-second Street, and anxiously waited for the crosstown bus. The air seemed as thick as water.

I sat on the bus watching Forty-second Street as if it were a sideshow. Hustlers, hookers, and transvestites entertained each other with stories of the easiest john and the best high. Behind a yellow-tinted cigar-store window stood a sad-looking Domingo, my youngest charge, hands in pockets, wreathed by pink and brown vibrators, ribbed condoms, strawberry-flavored rolling paper, and switchblades. I wondered what he was doing there. Why wasn't he in school? There weren't too many runaways out yet. They had worked the night and were still sleeping, in hallways, under stairways, in flophouses, or in some john's bed. For many the john was the closest thing they had to a friend. It started to drizzle, and the players headed quickly for shelter in the nearest doorway. 'Players' – that was the name they gave themselves.

After the strip came a kind of demilitarized zone. Here there were no movie houses, no stores, just office buildings. High above, a 'zipper' circled a building to tell the news of the hour to neck-craning headline readers. On the other side of the same building, the world's largest moving billboard routinely caused traffic accidents.

The street below was drab and poorly lit except for the painted facade of a steel hut that, at night, was illuminated like a stage set. This was headquarters for the Times Square Redevelopment Project. For years now City Hall had been talking about changing Times Square. But the only change had been for the worse.

The bus traveled almost to Manhattan's other shore. By the East River I stepped up onto eighteen acres of international territory. Back in the hopeful days after World War II, the Rockefeller family had given this land to the United Nations. The multicolored flags of the member nations fluttered in a gray drizzle. Tourists walked reverently among the three buildings – the meeting hall, the twenty-nine-story secretariat, and the low, rectangular conference building. I felt like a visitor to the pyramids. I looked at my watch and walked faster.

In Conference Room C, attendees sat around a gigantic oval table with a hole in its center. As I searched for my nameplate I studied the names of the other attendees. There were thirty of them. Each nameplate represented an

NGO – Non-Governmental Organization – involved with children's issues and problems all over the world. This was the Committee on Children that had been formed in 1985, during the International Year of the Child. The committee still met monthly. An impeccably dressed black woman leafed through the information packet in front of her. I knew immediately that she was the other speaker. Her square haircut emphasized the round beauty of her head. She opened her briefcase and extricated a folder. The agenda told me she was Dr Anita Green, medical director of a teenage health clinic at Harlem Hospital. Under the table she tapped her foot. I sat down next to her.

A harassed-looking woman appeared behind my chair. 'I'm Janice Walker. I coordinated today's program. Have you two met?'

The doctor and I nodded a polite hello.

'We've been waiting for James Beardsley, the new special counsel to the Senate Committee on Children,' Janice Walker said. 'His office just called to say he'll be arriving momentarily. The shuttle was late getting out of Washington. Do you want to start or keep waiting?'

'I think I'd better start,' Dr Green said crisply.

Although I had never met him, the new counsel to the Senate Select Committee on Children was my reason for accepting this invitation to speak. I had heard that the committee was putting together a funding list for an experimental pilot project. I wanted James Beardsley to hear about Eden House. I knew he would be a powerful voice on the committee.

Miss Walker introduced us to the attendees and asked that questions be held until after both presentations had been made. Dr Green began to describe the difficulties of being an adolescent in a neighborhood that is no longer a community – the anxieties, the flight into drugs and early sex, the many devastating medical consequences. After stopping to pour herself another glass of water, she explained the various medical and psychological problems her clinic dealt with. She was a good speaker, and we all listened attentively. When she got to the topic of AIDS, the room seemed to tense. She said, 'To many of you the AIDS epidemic is old news. For us at Harlem Hospital, the crisis is just beginning. If the current trend continues, within the next few years fifty percent of the children we see will be HIV positive. That's a statistic that will also hold true for Ms Eltern's client population,' she concluded, and turned the program over to me.

The room was full of silence. Even before I began to speak, I saw the index cards tremble in my hand as if I had never done this before. But I had done it a hundred times.

At the other end of the room, the door opened. The faces around the table turned to look. 'I'm sorry,' the latecomer said. 'Bad weather in DC.'

Then he sat down behind the nameplate that read 'James R. Beardsley.' This was the new special counsel. I blinked. The tic under my eye went crazy. My throat itched. I coughed. I took a sip of water. I looked at him again. The face didn't fit the name. Nothing fit. Was I hallucinating?

I launched into my speech.

As I described a national exodus of children to New York's Times Square, my eyes kept going back to Beardsley's side of the table. But Beardsley wasn't Beardsley. It was as if I were inside a giant kaleidoscope being shifted by an unseen hand. Beardsley's expensive pinstripe suit became a soiled collar; his shirt was torn. Around him writhed the jungle. He was David. Father David. The hair was thinner, the beard was missing, and he wore glasses. But it was the same face, the same reddish-blond hair, the same eyes that were neither green nor blue but both.

I talked about what happened to the young runaways from across the country who enter New York City through the Port Authority Bus Terminal on Forty-second Street. How the predator – the pimp – is waiting. Often kids never make it outside the labyrinth of the terminal building before a pimp has recruited them. I explained the vicious consequences of becoming a piece of meat in Hell's Kitchen's flesh market. And then I was done, and the question-and-answer period began.

'Miss Eltern, I see in your bio that you worked with Covenant House in Guatemala? Can you tell us how that work prepared you for what you are doing now?'

The link was obvious. In Guatemala and at home I was working with kids who had been brutalized by adults. I explained that Guatemala had suffered under a brutal military dictatorship for thirty years. In that time so many people had been murdered that the country was full of wandering, homeless children. And now, despite a so-called democracy in Guatemala, the military still ruled the hills. For sport they murdered children. As I spoke, a thousand buried memories collided. I did not look toward Beardsley's side of the table.

I barely made it out of the conference room before my

briefcase opened and spilled its contents onto the floor. In my hurry to leave, I hadn't closed it properly. As I knelt to gather my papers two hands began to help me. I knew those hands. I had loved those hands. They were David's hands.

'Good talk,' James Beardsley said, giving me the papers he had picked up. I shoved them back into my briefcase, thanked him, and tried to disappear into the crowded hallway. He was an optical illusion. I had to get away from him, but he kept pace. 'Have you sent the committee a proposal?' he asked.

'Yes, I have.'

'This is an experimental pilot project. In fact, it's my baby.'

'Sounds promising.'

'I'm personally going to read your submission. I'll let you know what I think.'

Behind us a wall was covered with photographs, larger-than-life mothers and children from all over the world. Around us a class of fourth-graders followed a tour guide in wide-eyed anticipation. I felt the nearness of the children, heard their excited chatter. I heard myself say, 'You look just like someone I once knew.'

Like David's, his eyes changed with the light. They were changing now.

'A priest,' I continued nervously. 'A priest who worked in Guatemala.'

'A friend?' Beardsley asked.

'Yes,' I whispered, 'a good friend.'

I searched his eyes for a memory of what we had been to each other. But there was nothing.

'What happened to your friend?'

'He spoke out against the death squads once too often.'

We reached the Plaza under a sky that seemed about to drizzle again. We passed a fountain sculpture. For a moment I listened to the water fall into itself and looked down at the smooth black stones at the base of the pool. 'Those stones are from the Isle of Rhodes,' Beardsley told me. 'As ancient as civilization itself.'

'Civilization,' I said bitterly, 'is a myth.'

He laughed easily. 'That's quite a statement, Ms Eltern.'

'How can we call ourselves civilized when the world gets more brutal every day?'

'One could debate that,' he said.

I didn't respond. Beardsley said, 'As long as I'm in the city, I'd like to see your program. Could you arrange that?'

'Why?'

At the sharpness of my tone, he cocked his head slightly. 'For my report to the committee,' he said.

'We're battling budget cuts.'

He said, 'These days, that's a given.' We began to descend the stairs.

I felt a kind of paranoia. As if I were being followed. I looked around. A limousine gleamed on the curb at the foot of the platform. The driver watched us intently. Between the limo and the steps, a small barefoot woman panhandled on the wet sidewalk.

She reached her hand toward Beardsley. 'I'm hungry, mister.'

As he gave the woman a dollar I noticed the seal on his expensive leather wallet.

'Am I getting the impression you don't want me to visit

Eden House?' he asked, when the old woman had moved on.

'Not at all.'

'Good,' he said briskly. 'Around ten tonight, then?'

We stopped in front of the limousine.

'That's too late. There won't be anything to see except kids getting ready for bed. I could give you the neighborhood tour, though.'

He ran his hand down his hand-sewn silk tie. I said, 'Maybe your chauffeur could pick up some jeans and a T-shirt for you.'

'You're patronizing me,' he said, 'but I have casual clothes in the trunk.'

My lips twitched into a smile. 'Just so you can blend, you know.'

His chauffeur opened the limo door. 'Ride?' Beardsley offered.

'No, thanks. I have some errands to run.'

He slipped into the backseat. The Lincoln Continental with the tinted windows pulled out into traffic.

I walked back to Eden House. Lunchtime shoppers crowded the sidewalks. Above us towered the luxury of Tudor City and the Grand Hyatt Hotel. At Grand Central Terminal the homeless spread their miserable stench. I thought about Grandpa and David and how I had not said good-bye to them. I remembered David's farewell in a tiny Catholic church in Guatemala. No open casket like at Grandpa's funeral. No casket at all. David's body had never been found.

Mute stone lions in front of the main branch of the public library guarded the line between east and west. Commerce changed. Here the street was the store. Gutters, doorways, awnings, and alleys offered guns, drugs, porn, and children's bodies. Above, movie marquees with burned-out bulbs hung like crossword puzzles with missing letters. A sudden downpour blurred the grimy sex-shop windows.

I took refuge in the newsstand at the corner of Eighth Avenue. This was the gateway to no-man's-land. Because they couldn't decide whose turf it was, neither street nor transit cops policed this subterranean domain. I bought a paper. The falling rain wrapped its clean smell around the odor of damp newspapers and decay. On the ramp below, Domingo came out of the barbershop. I followed him through the smells of urine, feces, and vomit into the mouth of the subway and the video arcade.

There were only a few machines, and it wasn't too loud. Freelance kids waited for low-life johns on the prowl. When I caught up with Domingo, he was concentrating on a video war with the machine.

'What's up?' I asked.

He focused some cross hairs. He blew a bunker off the screen. The machine congratulated him with 'The Star-Spangled Banner,' just a few victory bars.

I touched his arm. 'Hey, what's happening?'

'Nothing much.'

He blew bunkers off the screen until helicopters, tanks, land mines, planes joined the battle against him. Still, he kept racking up bonus points. For two quarters he could play all night.

'Come back to the storefront with me,' I said.

'Toomey threw all of us out.'

'What?'

Domingo glanced at me, his hand on the joystick, wiping out enemy targets.

I said, 'Whatever it is, I'll work it out.'

'I don't think so,' he said. I watched the reflection of his handsome features superimposed on the game screen and remembered a snowy night in Manhattan.

I had just parked the soup van when I saw the boy. He was standing in the doorway of a movie house. Above him the marquee was dark. Between us the snow was falling fast and hard. I stepped through the snow curtain and went to get him. A cigarette hung from his lips. He was wearing a cheap three-piece polyester suit, the vest neatly buttoned. He was shivering.

'Are you hungry?'

The boy let some smoke deftly escape his nostrils, looked me up and down, and said, 'Are you?'

At first I hadn't known what he meant. Then he took the cigarette from his lips, devoured my clothes with his eyes, and slowly, ostentatiously flicked his tongue over his lovely lips. 'I know how to make a woman's body feel good,' he said in a voice that was as deep as he could manage at his tender age.

'I'm old enough to be your mother.'

He smiled wantonly. 'Where do you think I learned?'

That was eight months ago. Winning Domingo's trust had been slow going. But gradually he had begun coming around to the storefront. He had begun to understand that I could love him without it being sexual. But today Domingo's mistrust had returned. He was too angry to speak to me.

I climbed the subway stairs back to the street and ran

through the rain to the center. It was lunchtime and the dayroom was empty. So was Toomey's office. I found the priest in the cafeteria pushing a tray on the food line. I dried my hair with some paper towels and grabbed a tray. The kids let me slip in line behind Toomey.

'Good to have you back,' he said.

'Father, just now I found one of our kids in the street.'

'A lot happened while you were in Connecticut.'

'He says you threw him out.'

'City inspectors were at the storefront. It's a fire hazard. Luckily I was able to avert a scandal.'

'He says you threw everybody out.'

Toomey sighed. 'I've been trying to reach you since Saturday, Anna. The kids wanted to talk to you. I kept trying to explain the situation to them. They got belligerent. I had to padlock the door. Your beeper must have been off.'

'I want that padlock off the door immediately.'

He slid his tray forward to the beverage section.

'Where's the key to the padlock?'

'Coffee or tea?' he asked.

'I'll get it, thanks. Where's the key?'

He took coffee; I took tea. He headed for a table and sat down. I sat down across from him. 'It sends the wrong signal,' I insisted.

He reached into his pocket and slapped a key onto the table. 'I didn't know symbols held any meaning for you.'

What was he insinuating? Was it some kind of jab about leaving the Church? I had grown tired of debating the roots of righteousness with him. We were in a crisis. There was nothing academic about it.

A chill rose from my wet feet. I put the key in my pocket. I dunked my tea bag. All around kids chattered. I wondered where the kids Toomey had thrown out were now. As I got up Toomey offered condolences for the loss of my grandfather. 'My beeper's back on,' I told him.

6

I spent the rest of the day playing catch-up. I had been away so much lately that a lot of residents had little problems and complaints. I spent a few minutes with each kid. I met with a group of volunteers, attended a few workshops, and sat in briefly on some classes. Since I had been busy fund-raising, Eden House had changed from a program with no unnecessary rules into a bureaucracy mired in regulations and the accompanying paperwork. In order to reverse that, I would have to be around more. But if I didn't raise more money, there wouldn't be a program. By the time I left to meet James Beardsley that evening, I was tired and depressed.

Toomey's grenade-sized padlock hung from the storefront gate. I inserted the key he had given me. The rusty lock creaked, but the key wouldn't turn. I rattled the lock. I yanked the key out. I shoved the key back in. It still didn't turn. Too tired to face Toomey again, I went upstairs to my apartment. As I unlocked my own door I heard the kitten inside crying. I hit the light switch. The kitten shivered at my feet. I picked her up. I opened a can of baby food and suckled her with my finger. She ate reluctantly. By the time I finished feeding her, it was ten o'clock. I rushed down to the storefront to be ready for Beardsley's arrival. When I got there, the phone was ringing. It was Millie.

'What happened here, Millie?'

'I'm so sorry, Annie,' she said. 'I warned you about Toomey. It's just lucky he didn't find Colin in your apartment.'

'Where was Colin?'

'Down in the storefront with the others.'

'Toomey threw everybody out?'

'Not exactly. He just started talking about the inspectors who were coming and how you could lose your license.'

'What license?'

'I don't know, building code or something. Toomey said it would destroy the program, so all the kids just kind of disappeared. I waited a long time, but they never came back.'

'Oh, God.'

'He asked the two volunteers who were staffing the hotline to call in next week. He said that since we couldn't service the calls ourselves, the board was rethinking the hotline.'

'The board?'

'That's what he said.'

Across the street in the glare of the video-store window, girls in halter tops and Spandex pants moved like dolls on a stage. In the darkness behind them lurked the pimp's Eldorado. As I said good-bye to Millie the Lincoln Continental with the tinted windows pulled up in front of the storefront. I rushed out the side door to intercept Beardsley before he could realize that the storefront was padlocked.

He got out. He wore a black polo shirt with a white collar and a blue jean jacket. He stared at the locked storefront like a date who hadn't been invited in. 'Locked up already?'

'Yes, sir. Closed early tonight. But your tour guide is ready.' I sounded overenthusiastic and I felt my cheeks color.

He held the car door for me. I dug my hands into my back pockets. 'Let's walk,' I said. 'You'll see more.'

'Sure.' He slammed the door shut.

'Don't you want to tell your driver when you'll be back?'

'He'll be here. That's his job.'

'When we get to the Strip, you'll want to walk slightly ahead of me. If you're already with a woman, most of the girls won't bother with you.'

'Okay.'

'If you decide you want to go inside anywhere, just give me a nod.'

'Okay.'

We crossed Forty-third Street in the shadow of the giant enclave known as Manhattan Plaza. The sweet smell of baking apple pies wafted from the Little Pie Company. An enormous Chinese vase with deep red flowers in a field of blue blossomed in the window of an elegant dry-cleaning shop known as the Dragon Lady. In Curtain Up, the corner restaurant, flickering candles illuminated the roster of actors' names on the walls. The grand old Broadway theaters were just a few blocks away, and a new off-Broadway had cropped up just behind Manhattan Plaza. We stopped for a red light. Then we crossed Ninth Avenue.

A Cyclone fence towered over us, its razor-blade edges

biting into the darkness. Under it two rats fought over a pigeon carcass. Behind it an enormous welfare hotel, with wire-mesh-covered windows and fire escapes, loomed like a prison. Across the street a pocket park long since claimed by drug dealers was sealed for the night. A rusty swing set creaked in a chill gust of wind from the river.

We headed toward the tenements on Eighth Avenue. Herb gardens in flowerpots were wedged onto windowsills, and the sounds of television, music, and children echoed behind cheap lace curtains. At the end of the block a mural of sweating workers covered the windowless Union Hall. A few homeless men had spread their newspaper blankets in the sheltered corners of the entranceway. The corner was dark. It smelled like a toilet. On the steps down to the locked subway, a body stirred.

Traffic was heavy, and we stopped for another red light. Ahead, Eighth Avenue and the Strip were as lively as a bazaar. Next to us, three teenagers negotiated the price of a Saturday Night Special.

'Thirty.'

'This baby ain't got no bodies on it.'

'Fifty . . . that's my last offer.'

We crossed toward an outdoor store wrapped around a corner. The Korean owners sat on stools, impassively guarding an assortment of African tote bags, baseball caps, money belts, and Nelson Mandela T-shirts.

Teenage midnight cowboys with glazed eyes milled in front of pimp bars and peep shows. It was the autumn's first cold night, and the young hustlers shivered in their pale summer clothes. Beardsley stood there as if he had stepped onto the floor of the New York Stock Exchange and didn't know what to bid. A crowd of theater goers washed by us, their faces tense yet fascinated. We started up the street.

'This is it,' I said. 'The nation's biggest round-the-clock sex supermarket, the infamous Minnesota Strip.'

Beardsley hadn't gone more than a few steps when a young boy stepped in front of him. The boy offered his thin hand. 'My name is James,' he said.

I walked on and waited in a doorway. Beardsley took the hand with the easy warmth of a born politician. 'Mine, too,' he said, then tried to withdraw his hand.

'What a fortuitous coincidence.' The young hustler didn't let go. 'I sell what you're looking for.'

'What's that?' Beardsley studied the hand he couldn't seem to get back. His voice stayed calm.

'If you will accompany me to the hotel around the corner, I will make all your dreams come true.'

'Dreams?' Beardsley sounded surprised.

'We have the most beautiful girls, white, black, Oriental, Spanish, too. Twenty-five'll get you in.'

'Twenty-five for what?'

The young James shrugged. 'Whatever.'

'I'm afraid not.' Beardsley jerked his hand back.

His namesake stepped in closer and put a hand on James Beardsley's shoulder. To do it, he had to reach up. 'Tell you what – just because your name is the same as mine, just for that I'll arrange a discount. No S and M, though.'

I stepped out of the doorway. 'Hey, you're late,' I called to Beardsley accusingly. To the runner I gave a dirty stare.

'Oh,' the boy said, 'I see how you're living.' He pivoted to intercept another potential customer. 'Good evening,' we heard him say. 'My name is James.'

Beardsley and I continued up the avenue. The sidewalk at our feet was as littered as a movie theater after the last show. Beardsley was silent as we walked through the spill of garbage and neon.

'That clean-cut-looking kid was a pimp?' he asked at last.

'No, just the legs.'

'Legs?'

'He negotiates time, place, and fee with the john, then brings him to the location. The johns prefer dealing with a kid like that. It's less intimidating than dealing directly with the pimp.'

We passed through the glow of a second-story pool-hall window. It stained Beardsley's handsome face crimson. I pointed. 'There's a nightly auction in the Afterhours up there. They sell everything. A kid goes for about ten grand.'

'You're exaggerating.'

'Ten thousand isn't much when you realize each of these kids earns the pimp about three thousand a month.'

'If you know all that, why don't the cops?'

I shrugged, trying to remember when I had last felt the incredulity he was now expressing. I was as angry as ever. But not much surprised me anymore.

'They get busted. But a few days later they're back in business.'

A teenage panhandler leaned against the doorway of a five-dollar hot-sheet hotel. I recognized him as one of the kids who had come and gone from the Eden House program under Open Intake. He saw me, too. 'Hey, Anna.' He rattled his cup. I went over to him.

Beardsley followed.

'Can I get back in the program?' the kid asked.

'Not tonight, but soon,' I said. 'Right after graduation.'

Beardsley stuffed a bill into the boy's cup.

'Thanks, mister,' he said. 'God bless you.'

'Come next Monday,' I told him.

'What if I don't make it that long?' he called after me.

Because I had no answer for him, I kept walking.

'You okay?' Beardsley asked when he caught up with me.

'I never had to turn kids away before.'

'You can't blame yourself.'

'Who, then?' I asked. 'You?'

He looked up at the sky. 'God?'

I kept my eyes on the craziness of the Strip. 'Tonight is kind of quiet. The cold is coming. Then they'll *really* suffer.'

'Come to Washington and testify.'

'What will that change?'

'If you come next Wednesday, I can still squeeze you into the agenda. And that will make it easier when I lobby the committee to fund your program.'

Another kid tottered past us toward the gutter. His vomit-splattered pants fit him like a tent. They were held up by a rope. His thin body was eaten by hunger and lice. His eyes were too big for his face. I had seen those eyes before, in Guatemala City, where children sleep on newspapers in the street. At least in Guatemala it was never winter.

A storefront peep show beckoned. Pictures of young girls in G-strings plastered the windows. They smiled invitingly. For a quarter they danced and talked dirty behind a screen. If you knew how, you could cut a private deal for more.

'Is this the place where the girl was killed this summer?' Beardsley asked.

'That was down the block.' I pointed to Circus World on the corner.

'Am I right that no one was ever arrested?'

'In this neighborhood, Mr Beardsley, dozens of murders go unsolved. That one made the papers only because it was in a peep show.'

'Isn't there something the government can do?'

'The death of a young girl who's been branded a hooker doesn't provoke much public outrage. The government doesn't care.'

'Can we go inside?'

I said, 'If you want to go inside, you might as well see the most notorious of them all.'

I studied his eyes for a moment. Not that I hadn't been inside these places. I dropped in now and then just to raise holy hell. But I had never gone in too far. I didn't know how I felt about going in with James Beardsley. Still, he probably had the power to get these places shut down. And I would have given anything to see that.

I led him to Circus World. Across the street from the Port Authority Bus Terminal, the ever-moving orange, yellow, red, and purple marquee looked like an invitation to a child's birthday party. Inside, light fixtures shaped like balloon bouquets lit black walls with red-bordered mirror-chip trim. We climbed to the mysteries upstairs. When the clerk at the token booth saw me, his eyes searched quickly for the bouncer. I was half hoping they'd stop me. But he seemed as afraid of me as I was of getting in. We both did a pretty good job of hiding it.

Women alone were not allowed in, but I was with Beardsley, whose money was already in his hand. He bought five dollars' worth of tokens. As we climbed the narrow black stairwell the air became musky and stale. No windows, no light. My heart fluttered in my throat.

At the top of the stairs, near rooms the size of telephone booths, naked girls with dead eyes waited for customers. If you chose one of these girls, you entered the tiny room. Each room offered a stool and one glass wall. Provided you had enough five-dollar tokens, the girl on the other side of the glass would show you anything you wanted to see. As long as you were on the opposite side of the pane, it was legal. Last summer a girl had been dragged into one of these rooms and her throat had been slashed.

We went deeper into the blackness toward the dollar token booths. 'Go ahead,' I said. 'I'll wait.'

'Come with me.' He sounded nervous.

I opened a door and stepped in. There was only one chair in the narrow space, so I had to sit between his legs. I knew instantly it was a mistake. But I was too proud to say I couldn't handle it. 'Put a token in the slot,' I said, forcing nonchalance.

A shade covering the window in front of us went up. A nude girl gyrated on a pole that seemed to be the center of a circle. Balloon lamps, mirror chips, and the painted grimaces of clowns on the wall framed her young, unhappy face. She lowered a hand to the shaved spot between her chubby thighs. The shade came down. In the dark I waited for Beardsley to exhale. He inserted another token. The shade went up.

The girl was masturbating, her expression so cold and sad that I felt drained hollow in an instant. I could barely breathe. I wondered if Beardsley saw it like I did. Or did he think she was sexy? To get farther away from him, I leaned closer to the window. My forehead touched the grimy pane. I saw other heads in other boxes greedily watching the girl. Suddenly I realized I was in a box, too, the only woman in the circle. I don't know why the shock was so profound. Was it that the other faces were so unexpected? Was it the eerie sight of half a dozen disembodied heads? Or was it that I knew they saw me, too? It occurred to me that this was the ultimate definition of 'voyeur'. Watching the watcher. I pulled back into the darkness.

Feeling Beardsley's warm breath on my neck, I leaned forward again. One man was watching me with eyes like chips of flint, as if he had been waiting for me to reappear. Round, bald, overweight, his face twitched as if in agony. A disinfectant spray wafted down over us through the slit at the top of the wall of our booth. Then I realized he was masturbating. He grimaced at me as if he knew me. Where had I seen him before? At the precinct house one night after a john sweep?

'Let's get out of here.'

We descended the steep steps to the street. Beardsley held my elbow. We stood for a moment in the hustle and bustle of the avenue, and I felt the terror of an irreconcilable contradiction. My revulsion had dissolved into the desire to touch him, to hold him close. I pulled away and noted the whisper of his fingers as they tried to cling. Then my emotions settled into place. I resumed the tour by pointing up at the neon sign right next to the Circus World marquee. It read: IDS PURCHASED HERE. Just yards from the bus terminal's exit, any runaway, green from the backwaters of America, could purchase a new identity and get a job. That is, if a pimp hadn't already picked up the kid in the terminal itself.

We walked up to Restaurant Row on Forty-sixth Street, and I showed him where the theater crowd gathered for midnight suppers of French, Italian, Chinese, or Japanese food. The street ahead was patrolled by Guardian Angels in red berets. These self-styled teenage cops were appreciated by the restaurant owners, who couldn't get enough protection for their customers, but they were not much liked by the NYPD. After the block that housed Manhattan Plaza, this was the safest in the neighborhood. On the Great White Way, curtains hadn't yet come down, so Forty-sixth Street was still quiet. I led Beardsley toward Playland on Broadway.

On an island in the center of the street, the Army Recruiting Center was still open. From a giant billboard red neon lips blew a cloud of smoke over an endless stampede of cars and taxis. Above, the 'zipper' announced that in the Midwest a disgruntled employee had shot seven McDonald's patrons. In front of Nathan's, the hot-dog palace, a pudgy black woman in Salvation Army shoes poured her soul into a portable microphone.

After her song she rang a small bell, as if calling God to her table. She wiped her brow with a cloth handkerchief and cleared her throat. 'There won't be no Jews in heaven. No Muslims and no Mormons neither . . . only us . . . us who accept Jesus as our personal savior, only us who welcome Jesus into the pastures of our hearts. We'll be walking those flowery fields in the Promised Land. That's right – no Jews in heaven.'

Beardsley chuckled. 'What does she think Jesus was?'

Sounds of electronic violence spilled from the video arcade onto the sidewalk – machine-gun fire, explosions, crashes, screams, death chortles. Behind grimy window glass, plastic monster masks grimaced under an inch of dust. A sign offered fake photo IDs from Ivy League colleges or authentic dog tags. We stepped inside. It was like diving into an electronic foxhole.

In here kids hustled for themselves, down-and-out kids whom nobody wanted to buy anymore. These children stood mesmerized by the make-believe wars they waged, their fingers wrapped around a joystick. We walked down the aisle between two rows of machines toward a pasty man in a Plexiglas booth. Through a slot he exchanged bills for quarters.

'Get some change,' I yelled. Beardsley shoved a dollar into the slot. A beefy black kid with a Mercedes-Benz insignia on his gold-plated front tooth pushed Beardsley brusquely aside. 'Hey, man, it ain't your turn.'

'How you doin', mama?'

A café au lait Puerto Rican with hazel eyes put an arm around my waist. I studied the flame of red hair trained to rise from his head and said, 'I ain't your mama.'

He rubbed a hand over his crotch. 'But you *could* be my baby.'

As he moved on, his hair seemed to fall into itself like the crest of a wave.

Beardsley walked among the rough trade, the hard-case drifters already so damaged by life that at seventeen and eighteen nobody wanted to buy them anymore. They watched other players, hoping for a stray quarter, a chicken hawk who might offer a meal, a bed for the night. In the meantime they played Forgotten Worlds, Robocop, Shadow Warrior, and Ninja Star. The noise was making me queasy.

Beardsley stood watching a man in a business suit play a game called Crime City with a kid who looked about fourteen. I pulled him along to the next game.

'That guy is your classic pederast,' I said.

Beardsley blanched. 'How do you know?'

'This is a pickup place. The johns play a game with a kid for a while and then proposition him. They do it carefully, because this is also the spot the precinct sends its undercovers to make arrests when they haven't made their quota.'

People were starting to stare at us, so Beardsley inserted two quarters into a game called Deep Freeze. A boy joined him on the machine's second joystick. Figuring he'd best handle this one himself, I stepped outside. After a time Beardsley came to stand beside me. His brow was damp with sweat. I felt an odd satisfaction. His arrogance had finally failed him. He sighed.

'Ready?' I asked him.

He nodded. I led him toward the Forty-Deuce. The tour wasn't over yet. We headed toward the porn shops, the massage parlors, the burlesque joints and topless bars. The summer tourists were gone and the street was quieter than usual. Runaways and teenage players mingled with the old hustlers, the few over forty who weren't dead yet. They gathered under dilapidated movie marquees like figures in the wax museum.

'Crack it up. Smoke, blow, hot pussy. What you looking for, brother?'

An old hustler stepped in stride with Beardsley. I allowed them to pass me.

'I got some nice young girls.'

Beardsley turned to call me. 'Anna.'

The hustler looked disappointed. 'Why didn't you say so, brother? Why didn't you say you had a lady? I got some nice blow keep you up all night, satisfy the lady right.'

'Thanks. We got everything we need,' Beardsley said, pushing into an oncoming crowd. We avoided each other's eyes.

In front of the porn bookshop a group of kids parted as we passed. Eclipse stood in front of the brightly lit window, her blue-black face as regal as Nefertiti's. At first I didn't recognize the girl next to her because of the dark wig. But then I did. It was Porsche. She was smoking a joint, laughing. When she saw me, she laughed so hard, she had to support herself on the shop window. She was wearing a jacket I hadn't seen before. It said 'Born to Lose.'

'What's so funny?'

'You . . . you and that serious face of yours. Don't you ever smile, Annie?'

'I've been expecting you.'

She looked over my shoulder. 'Who's the cutie pie?'

I turned. 'A friend.'

'Don't I know you?' She smirked, her eyes on Beardsley.

'You *don't* know him,' I snapped.

'Oooh, whatsamatta, he your man?' She stepped around me and shoved a finger into Beardsley's chest. 'I *do* know you, mister.'

He smiled nervously. 'If you say so.'

'Yeah.' She ran her finger down toward his belt, slowly. 'I know you, sweet daddy.'

He looked down at her, mesmerized, like a fly in a web. His pupils widened and his skin took on a heated glow. Or was it the pool of light from the store window? I pulled Porsche around to face me. She took a long drag of the reefer in her hand and stared at me. A tuft of sweet-smelling smoke snaked from her perfect nostrils. 'Jealous?' she asked softly.

'That's not funny.'

'C'mon, Anna, I'm just playing.'

'If you don't come by, I'm gonna throw that cat out.'

She passed the joint to one of the other kids. 'Have a heart.'

'Then come and get her.'

She pulled the black wig from her head. 'I'll be by. I'll be by later tonight, okay?'

'Okay,' I said. 'Okay.'

She turned back to Beardsley. 'Round the world half-price for you, baby.'

He ran a nervous hand through his hair. Eclipse and the other girls giggled.

'Okay, enough's enough,' I cut her off.

Porsche winked at me. 'Lighten up, Annie. Lighten up.'

At that moment I could have killed her. Instead I grabbed Beardsley's hand and tugged him across the street. My heart was pounding.

'Had enough?' I asked, letting go of his hand. He seemed unruffled, but his hand had been clammy.

He nodded. We walked back toward the storefront. He said, 'They can be vicious, can't they?'

'They learn from the best.'

'The pimps?'

'Yep. The masters of cruelty.'

I nibbled on my lip, wondering at the storm of emotions raging in me. Was Porsche right? Had I been jealous? As we walked Beardsley turned the conversation to Eden House and our financial problems. When we reached his limo, he stopped. 'I'm sincere about helping you, Anna.'

I nodded, not sure what to believe.

'Take my card and call me. I'll arrange for you to testify.'

He reached into his back pocket. He tried his other pockets. When he had stopped patting himself, he said, 'My wallet's gone.'

I was as embarrassed as he was flustered. 'You sure?'

He went through all his pockets again.

'I'm sorry,' I said. 'I feel responsible.'

He studied the tops of the buildings as if looking for an exit from the pit in which we stood. 'To be expected,' he said with a deep sigh.

'Have you any idea where it happened?'

He shook his head. I hadn't noticed anything either.

'They're like that. I should have warned you.'

His driver had gotten out, but Beardsley seemed to have forgotten the script, lost a page, missed a transition. He stood there, confused and violated.

'Was there much money in it?'

'A couple of hundreds and some smaller bills. But it's not

the money. It's the inconvenience of losing my license and credit cards. Besides, the wallet was a gift for serving on a presidential commission. It's irreplaceable.'

'Do you want to come in and use my phone to cancel the cards?'

'I have a phone in the car,' he snapped. The driver opened the car door. Beardsley got in. For a moment I thought he was going to pull out without saying good-bye. Then he powered the electric window down.

'I'll have my secretary call you to work out the details,' he said as if nothing at all had gone wrong.

7

I sat in the storefront window alcove watching the activity across the street while James Beardsley wandered around in my thoughts. I wondered exactly how his wallet had been lifted. Like a jigsaw puzzle, I took the evening apart and put it back together. I fought with the memory of his breath on my neck. How could I possibly have been aroused in that horrible place? Was Millie right? Was I that lonely? I heard the rattle of the padlocked gate. When I opened the door, Porsche stood there looking over her shoulder. 'Let me in,' she said, and it was a challenge. 'I told you I'd be back.'

'Come around.' I went to the hallway door. She was out of breath and trembling, her lip and eye swollen.

I said, 'Let's go upstairs.'

At the top of the stairs I asked, 'What happened to you? An hour ago you were fine.'

'Blue Fly caught up with me. One of his girls went back to Baltimore, and he blames me.' She sucked the blood from her split lip. 'I'm happy for her. Where's my cat?'

'Why does he blame you?'

She shrugged. 'Cuz he's the asshole he is. Is my cat here?'

'Somewhere here.'

Porsche crouched down to peer under the furniture. 'C'mon, lover, where are you?'

I opened the refrigerator door, studied its contents, and asked the mother's universal question, 'Hungry?'

'Come here, lover. I'm back. I said I'd come back.'

Beelzebub came out from under the table to charge behind the refrigerator. Porsche sat on the floor as if her legs had abruptly given out. 'Nobody loves me.'

'Some people would like to be given the chance to try.' I handed her an ice pack from the freezer. She put it over her eye.

'I guess I could eat something,' she said.

'How about I make us some sandwiches while you go wash off all that makeup.'

'Can I take a bath? I'd love to take a bath.'

'Sure.'

I followed her into the bathroom. In the mirror I saw her fear. She scratched at the glass as if to reach the self trapped behind it, the one without bruises. 'My money-making days are over. I'm a freak.'

'No, you're not, honey. All that will go away.'

'Promise?' she whimpered.

'I promise.'

She knelt in front of the bathtub to turn on the water and to hide her tears. She shrugged off her 'Born to Lose' jacket and put her beeper on top of the laundry hamper. Underneath the jacket her arms were thin and bruised. Her narrow shoulders shook. I stroked her damp hair from her eyes. 'Go ahead now, have your bath. Use my robe when you get out.'

NIGHTSIDE

In the kitchen I washed and sliced tomatoes, buttered four slices of bread on both sides, and set two places at the table. From my room I brought a clean T-shirt, underwear, and a pair of shorts and placed them in front of the bathroom door. Still trying not to think about what had happened to her out there, I turned on the television. Gabe Pressman was telling me that a child had been shot. A nine-year-old boy. His spinal cord had been severed as he slept on his mother's lap in the backseat of the car. The family had been on the way home from a birthday party when a bullet crashed through the car door. In the last few months twenty-four children had been killed in the crack turf wars that teenagers were waging in the boroughs. I dozed off.

When I woke up, Beelzebub had crawled under my armpit. I picked the kitten up, turned the television off, and walked down the hall to tap on the bathroom door. 'Porsche, you okay?'

No answer.

'Porsche.'

I opened the door. The bathroom was dark. Porsche floated with her eyes closed, her pale hair spread in the water like an electric halo. Without the makeup, she was a child again. A sleeping, battered child with large breasts that floated up in the water. Her lips seemed blue.

'Wake up, honey.'

She didn't stir. I knelt by the tub and whispered, 'Porsche, honey...'

She moaned. I put my hand into the cold water and touched her shoulder. 'Look who's here.'

Beelzebub meowed anxiously at the tub's edge. Porsche opened her eyes. 'You found my baby.'

She leaned out of the tub to kiss Beelzebub. I put the kitten next to the clothes I had brought for Porsche. 'Here's some stuff for you to wear.'

As I grilled the sandwiches Porsche stepped into the kitchen, clean and young, Beelzebub clinging to her like a brooch. In her hand she carried my bathroom candle, its flicker highlighting the special beauty of a face where cultures and continents met.

'I'm sorry, I fell asleep on you,' she said, tossing her golden hair back.

'That's okay. I nodded out myself.'

She put the candle down on the table. 'Can we put out the light?'

'The switch is right behind you.'

We sat down across from each other and nibbled at our sandwiches. She raised her eyes to study me. 'You want to talk?' she asked.

To hide my anxiety, I gave a one-word answer. The word I had learned from her and the others like her. 'Whatever,' I heard myself say. 'Whatever.'

She stepped into the vacuum created by my nonchalance. 'I'm ready to go into the program now,' she said.

I chewed for a while. 'You sure about that?'

'Yeah. I'm sure.'

'You can't just come in for a vacation.'

Even by candlelight I saw the anger that suddenly flared in her eyes. 'You always wanna be so tough, Annie.'

'You waited a little too long. There's no room in the program now.'

'Oh,' she said. Just 'oh,' and lowered her eyes. 'I guess I'm dead, then,' she added softly, as if it didn't really matter anyway.

In the sad silence that fell, I made a choice that would change our lives forever. 'You could . . . stay here.' The hell with Toomey and the board.

Porsche looked up again, her hope pitifully disguised and showing.

'It would have to be our secret, though. You'd have to stay in the apartment even when I go to work.'

'How long?'

'Until the graduation on Sunday when some spots open up in the program.'

'That's cool. I'll cook for you. I can iron, too.'

With her split lip she had difficulty chewing the sandwich, but she finished it. As we did the dishes she asked, 'Got any cigarettes?'

'You know I don't smoke.'

'I could really use a smoke.'

'You know how I feel about that.'

She gave me a look that said I should know cigarettes were the least of her problems. 'I'm just a little shook-up right now, Annie.'

Because I didn't want to lose her over something so insignificant, I said, 'All right, just this once. I have to pick up some milk and a few things for the refrigerator anyway.'

'Thanks.' The smile she offered was a twisted little grimace. As I left she sat down on my bed and cuddled her kitten.

Tropical vegetables filled the *bodega* window. Inside, a

couple of neighborhood men nursing beer cans sat on milk crates talking Spanish. Through its glass door I was studying the contents of the refrigerator when I heard a disconcerting sound in the corner. Blue Fly had come in behind me. The pimp sucked on a tooth while he sliced the bottom off a pack of Lucky Strikes. His knife was wickedly thin and looked razor sharp. I opened the refrigerator and felt its icy breath. Blue Fly eased close enough to whisper in my ear, 'You let me at that honey pot, maybe your head would clear.'

I carried my milk to the counter. Behind it Pedro, the owner, sat reading the *New York Post*. The headline said TOP COP RESIGNS. He stood up. 'Good evening, Miss Anna.'

I asked for Marlboro Lights. 'Don't tell me you started smokin'?' he asked, putting the paper down to get the cigarettes. My eyes skimmed the by now familiar story. A scandal had been brewing in the NYPD ever since a reporter had discovered that the bureaucracy buried the files of allegedly dirty cops rather than investigate them. The alleged abuses ranged from sleeping on the job to dope dealing and homicide. Now the top cop was resigning because of his wife's poor health. Or so he said.

'Hey, Miss Goody Two Shoes,' Blue Fly whispered hoarsely. 'No kiddin' now – I want my girl.'

'She's not your girl, and even if I knew where she was, I wouldn't tell you.'

'No trouble in my store.' The chubby *bodegero* glared at Blue Fly. Then he handed me my milk, cigarettes, and change. Blue Fly followed me to the door. 'Tell that little bitch she ain't so slick.'

'I told you, I don't know where she is.'

Because I didn't want him to follow me to my door, I dodged cabs to cross the street. 'That's cool,' the pimp yelled after me. 'But if she doesn't stay away from my girls, she's dead meat!'

I stepped into the video store to give Blue Fly time to leave the block. A bell chimed over the door as I entered the gleaming white room. Wire racks created a labyrinth of aisles. In the back a bullet-proof window, shaped like a television screen, was framed in neon. It had air holes and a slot for passing tapes, money, and credit cards. This make-believe television was the clerk's booth. Next to it there was a door leading into the booth. Inside, the booth had yet another door to another unseen space. The watchful eye of a video camera shifted toward me.

I wandered through an incredible collection of French, German, Portuguese, Italian, Iranian, Russian, and Czech films. Films from all over the globe. I went all the way to the back of the store. There in a secluded corner was the pornography. Pictures of women in leather and lace, women on their knees, women with their legs spread, women tied and gagged, covered the narrow cardboard boxes that advertised the videos available in the booth in the back. Behind me I heard the bell chime and the door open. I hoped I was hidden between the aisles. A moment later Blue Fly was at my elbow.

'You a member?'

I walked to the front of the store.

'This is a members-only club . . . You can't rent if you're not a member.' He blocked the doorway to the street. 'Honey, this is America . . . I'm a member, are you?'

'Get out of my way.'

As I crossed the street back to my own storefront, he called after me: 'This is the free-enterprise system – everybody gets a chance. But don't nobody like to get ripped off. Especially not by a little girl!'

Back home Porsche sat on my bed chewing at her fingernails. I handed her the cigarettes. She ripped the pack open, lit a cigarette with trembling fingers, and puffed furiously. A little cloud of smoke rose between us. 'Thanks,' she said, 'thanks. At least I'm not doing any drugs.'

'Honey, I ran into Blue Fly...'

'Blue Fly'll forget about me in a couple of days.'

'He wants you to stay away from his girls.'

'Cuz they're hicks he brought in from the sticks, and I feel bad for them. I talk to them like you talk to me, you know.'

She pulled nervously on her cigarette. I said, 'All the more reason for you to stay put when I go out.'

'Like Anne Frank,' she said. 'I read her diary.'

'Yes, like Anne Frank.'

Then, to seal the deal, she handed me the cigarettes I had just bought for her. 'Here, you can hold on to these.'

I pulled her shoes off and brought the covers up to her chin.

'This is your bed, isn't it?'

'I'll sleep on the couch.'

She reached for me like a little girl. I hugged her and kissed her good night. Her cheek was warm and smooth.

It was somewhere after midnight when I woke up again. I ran down the corridor toward Porsche's screams. She was sitting up, her eyes blank. 'Don't,' she pleaded. 'Don't!'

'Porsche, honey—'

'Please . . . please,' she whimpered, boxing shadows.

I sat down on the edge of the bed. 'Porsche, sweetheart . . . it's me . . . Anna.'

I took her bruised face into my hands. She pounded at me with her fists. When I offered no defense, her frenzy dissipated and her eyes found me. 'Anna . . . Anna . . . what happened?'

'You had a bad dream.'

She crawled into my arms. 'Anna, can I stay with you?'

'Of course you can.'

'I don't want to be alone.'

'I'm just down the hall, sweetheart.'

'Don't go back there – stay with me?'

I lay down on top of the covers.

She said, 'You'll be cold,' and pulled the sheet and blanket back for me. I climbed in next to her. She laid her head on my chest. I felt the warmth of her small body against mine, and the rhythm of our breaths began to synchronize.

'I can hear your heart beat,' she whispered. 'It's fast like a bongo drum.'

'Porsche – what was that nightmare about?'

'It's stupid,' she said, 'cuz it happened so long ago.'

'It must have been bad if it keeps coming back in your dreams.'

'It's stupid,' she repeated, clinging desperately to her toughness.

'C'mon,' I coaxed.

'T'was in this foster home. It was pretty good, really.'

'Uh-huh.'

'Except Deena, our foster mother, she had this asshole husband who was mean when he drank. I had to take care of the little kids a lot, but I didn't mind.'

She stopped. I felt the memory stiffen her.

'Tell me. It'll help.'

'I had a pet hamster – DC. I brought him from my real home. He was so cute. One night Jerry, her asshole husband, he was watching the tube and drinking and DC got away from me. He ran up on the couch. I tried to get him back, but Jerry was too fast. He hated DC. He always said he was gonna drown him. He took him to the bathroom. He held him under the hot water. I tried to stop him. DC was squealing. He sounded like a bird. Jerry threw him in the toilet. But he was so drunk he didn't flush, and I fished DC out. His paws were all burned up. So he ... he chewed 'em off.'

I pulled her to me and wondered what other memories she wrestled with in the dark. After a while she said, 'It must be so lonely when you die.'

'Not if you believe in God.'

She raised her head to find my eyes. 'Do you?'

'In my own way I do.'

'I keep seeing myself in a coffin,' she whispered.

'You *can* save yourself, but you have to want to. And you've got to get out of the life for real.'

'I touched my mom's hands when she was dead. You know how they fold your hands when you're in the coffin?'

'Yes.'

'Her hands were cold, really cold.'

She lay down again. I thought about Grandpa and never saying good-bye.

'My moms caught an OD, and then I got split up from my brother.'

Softly she started to cry. She cried until she fell asleep. It was a while before her legs stopped their involuntary twitch. Before I slept, I realized she had never mentioned having a father.

8

'Anna,' Rich Cannon said cheerily, 'I hardly know your face. Where've you been hiding out?'

'Around.' I smiled stiffly as he buzzed me in.

The kids sat in a circle in the dayroom. They looked happy and well nourished. I joined the circle. Everybody wanted to know how the struggle was going. I tried to sound confident that all would soon be well.

'Anna ... is the ship sinking?'

'We're plugging the leaks. Have you been walking the walk?'

'Not him. He just talks the talk.'

Father Toomey came in carrying the big clipboard of weekly work assignments, which I used to carry. Work assignments were rotated based on the previous week's successes and failures.

'Anna, I got my GED yesterday.' Lanky, eighteen-year-old Roger beamed.

I gave him a big hug. 'Congratulations.'

Somebody else said, 'I'm accepted at Manhattan Community College.'

Another happy hug.

I told them: 'There's a demonstration today. A lot of

social-service programs from around the city are meeting at the Harlem State Office Building to send City Hall a message. Anybody who wants to go with me, we've been asked to speak. We'll be leaving in about an hour.'

'Do you have to speak to go?'

'No, if you just want to come along, that would also be great.'

I headed for my office. A dozen messages waited on my desk. Most of the calls were from agency heads who were looking to form some kind of coalition to fight the budget cuts. They wanted to hold a press conference on the steps of City Hall. I had been ducking these calls ever since the latest announcement of cuts. I still hadn't decided where I stood. Coalitions were iffy things.

Toomey came in. He looked cheerful and less haggard. 'We're having an emergency board meeting,' he told me.

I said, 'The key you gave me didn't work.' And then his words sank in. 'You scheduled a board meeting without consulting me?'

'Our mortgage payment is coming up, Anna. We don't have the money to cover it, and you haven't been available at all. What did you expect me to do?'

'I saw you yesterday.'

'This just happened.'

'Sit down,' I said softly.

The network of broken capillaries that mapped Toomey's face turned purple. He sat.

'What else have I missed?' I demanded. 'Why don't you fill me in?'

He shrugged. 'Not much. Obviously there haven't been any new intakes, and with only two secretaries left, all our paperwork is slowed down...' He folded his hands on his lap. Ice cubes floated in the watery blue of his eyes.

'What about the suppliers?'

'We've always paid on time, so I'm confident they'll keep supplying even if we fall behind on payments for a few months.'

'Maybe we should see if we can get a second mortgage?'

'That's a possibility, albeit remote.'

I knew he was right. 'How were you planning to structure the meeting?'

'Well, I've prepared an interim financial report. Maybe you want to present it.'

'You present it. It's your report.'

'You'll chair the meeting?'

Instead of answering him, I asked, 'Exactly when is this meeting?'

'In the boardroom at Schneiderman's law firm at six so people can stop by right after work. You'll chair?'

I looked purposefully at my watch. 'I need to get moving,' I said. 'The demonstration starts in forty-five minutes.'

'Anna... I resent your using the kids this way.'

'I'm not using them, I'm giving them a chance to join the struggle. It's called empowerment.'

'Spare the jargon. It only makes them insecure.'

'I see no harm in their participating in fighting the social-service cuts. After all, it's their fight, too.'

'What if you fail?'

'*We* can't afford to fail.'

Kids were starting to come up to the transparent wall,

signaling me; some pressed their faces to the Plexiglas. I said, 'The kids are looking forward to going.'

Toomey followed me out of my office when I went to join the kids in the dayroom. Excited about the upcoming excursion, they greeted me enthusiastically.

'The outside world. I don't know if I can take it,' somebody joked.

'Can you handle the trains?'

Everybody groaned.

'Why don't we take the van?'

'We won't be able to park,' I said.

'Father Toomey, how about a ride?' one of the kids asked.

Toomey shook his head. 'I have work to do.'

A crowd had gathered at the base of the State Office Building on the corner of Eighth Avenue and 125th Street. On the plaza the organizations had built a platform. A small, slender man was at the mike speaking to the crowd that gathered below. Around the edges of the platform various organizations had set up makeshift booths, where they handed out pamphlets and fliers.

'We've got to stick together, guys,' I warned the kids.

We all joined hands and made our way to the stage, where State Senator Montalvo was introducing a local salsa group that had written a protest song for the occasion. The event organizers had been wise enough to intersperse music and dance with the speeches, and judging by the mood of the crowd, this was working well. As the music swelled, the tightly packed crowd somehow opened to create a dance floor, and I watched as my kids gave themselves over to the beat. Someone started chanting, 'If it's good, it's good for the hood,' and other voices chimed in.

The kids formed a circle and began to dance.

'C'mon, Anna, you belong with us!'

The kids grabbed my hands and pulled me into their circle. They had taught me how to dance, to loosen up, feel the music, recognize the different beats. And now, every chance they got, they wanted to show me off. A hot salsa beat penetrated my pores, and I began to sweat. 'Like this, Anna . . . like *this!*' one of the kids shouted.

Juan put his arms around me and we danced the *merengue*, a step in which one leg is always kept stiff and just dragged along. From that the music shifted to *guaganco* and then finally to the wildest beat of all, *bomba y plena*. My hips swayed to the beat, and sweat poured down between my breasts. My heart beat in my head. Once in a while I missed a beat and stepped on Juan's feet. After a round of turns that had us in stitches, a hot light blinded me. I was looking into the eye of a news camera. I wondered how long they had been filming.

'I think we'd better stop,' I yelled into Juan's ear.

He danced me out of the camera's reach, and we stopped. The Eden House crowd applauded us wildly, and the camera crew filmed the applause.

'Ms Eltern!' The reporter pointed a mike at me. 'What is Eden House doing in Harlem?'

'We're here to tell City Hall . . .'

'*No más* . . .' some of the kids yelled. I couldn't help but smile.

'We want our money,' Juan said. 'They got money for everybody else.'

'We're sending a message that this is no time to cut services. In Hell's Kitchen there have been three unsolved murders in three months. We don't know what the police are doing. But we do know that kids need to be able to come in off the streets, where it's safe. Cutting budgets and forcing us to turn them away is leaving them out to get their throats cut.'

I saw the reporter's satisfied grin and knew I had said too much.

'That was some dance,' the cameraman said as he stopped filming.

At the edge of the crowd, O'Shaugnessy crooked his finger at me. I excused myself and walked over to him. I wiped some sweat from my forehead and turned to watch the other dancers.

'How many people can you attack in one sentence?' O'Shaugnessy asked.

'You think I was too hard?'

The music stopped. State Senator Montalvo took the mike. 'I'd like to ask Eden House to join us up here on the stage.'

'Catch you later,' I said.

'Break a leg.' O'Shaugnessy kissed his fingers and touched my cheek.

The kids and I joined hands again and pushed our way through the crowd to the stage. I stepped up to the microphone, my kids flanking me. Caught in the electricity of the crowd below and the hopeful stares of the young, I heard myself launch yet another attack on City Hall and the cops. The angrier I got, the more the crowd loved me. I finished to thunderous applause. I turned the mike over to my kids.

NIGHTSIDE

An Eden House success story named Leroy stepped up; I adjusted the mike to his height. At fifteen he was much taller than I. He began to praise the program and me. He was still talking when I descended the steps. O'Shaugnessy stood looking at me with a mixture of admiration and contempt.

'They teach you that in church?' he asked sarcastically.

'What are you doing here? Following me?'

'Don't flatter yourself, Eltern. I'm here because a lot of groups from our community board are here. I like to see the groups I deal with in action, and they like to know I take an interest.'

The crowd pushed us closer together. Our bodies mashed against each other as if we were in a subway at rush hour. My discomfort amused him. Then the crowd parted a little as the kids came down from the stage and the music started again.

'You guys were great,' I said. 'Should we be thinking about heading back?'

'Aw, c'mon, Anna,' one of the kids said. 'Lighten up. We wanna hear the other speakers, not just ourselves.'

I looked at my watch. 'Okay, but I have to be downtown for a board meeting at six.'

Leroy sighed. 'That's a thousand years from now, Annie.'

'Time is slower for the young.' O'Shaugnessy looked at his watch. 'Us old people have less and less of it. I've got to go.'

After he'd left, I sat on a bench watching the kids party. Other program heads came to discuss strategies for the coalition. It was an uneasy feeling. On one side City Hall and the budget cuts, on the other a nebulous coalition that raised more questions than it answered. I was relieved when the protest and the festivities drew to a close, so that the kids and I could head back downtown. It was five-thirty, and Toomey had already left the center for the board meeting.

Schneiderman, Seligman, and Knopf was conveniently located at Fifth Avenue and Forty-second Street. The lawyer's suite had the aura of a high-tech library, ultramodern furniture, ultrastylish receptionist, an atmosphere of sculptured ice.

'Miss Eltern, how nice to see you. Father Toomey's inside already.'

'Thanks, Adrian.'

'Will it be the usual group?' she asked.

I glanced at the list on her desk. Eight carefully selected people. Prestigious, respected New Yorkers who cared enough to attend a meeting a few times a year but not enough to interfere with the running of the program.

'Yep, that's the group.' I went inside.

Toomey was alone in the soundproof conference room, arranging perfectly aligned chairs more perfectly. On the shelves that lined the room, the case law that defined American justice was bound in the best leather American money could buy. I sat down at the head of the table. Julius Schneiderman, a partner in the firm and our board chairman, peeked in. 'All set?'

Toomey looked at me.

'Just waiting for everybody to arrive,' I said.

'Buzz me when you're ready.' Schneiderman stepped

back out. In the fifteen minutes before the meeting was scheduled to start, he could probably bill another five hundred dollars.

Toomey placed an information packet on the table in front of each chair. Eden House's financial report was on top.

'Think we'll get a quorum?' I asked.

'We don't really need a quorum. We just need a couple of generous board members to make a donation that will carry us through the next month.'

'What makes you think we'll solve our funding problems in a month?'

'You don't think we will?'

I was beginning to see what Millie meant about Toomey. The priest's manipulations were masterful. Solving our financial problems in a month was virtually impossible. But saying that now would frustrate the board, so that they might give us nothing. If I offered a pessimistic scenario while Toomey was optimistic, the board might turn against me for real this time. They wanted to help the poor, but they didn't want to get depressed, and I had played Cassandra once too often.

One by one the board members arrived. To my right sat Renée Delattre, the wife of a French executive doing a two-year stint in Manhattan. Causes and fund-raisers were Renée's entrée to New York society. Next to her sat Buzz Greenberg, a real-estate tycoon with barely concealed political aspirations. Doing good would someday do him good. On the other side of the table next to Toomey sat Arthur Baldwin, a limousine-service owner who had lost a son to drugs. Arthur's altruism sought to heal the wounds of his own past. Next to him sat Marianne Foster. She was a family-court judge who had the experience to know that without small, flexible programs like ours, too many kids fell through the cracks. Marianne had sent a lot of kids my way. I buzzed Schneiderman.

Schneiderman greeted the group warmly, then sat down across from me. I called the meeting to order. Renée Delattre read the minutes of the last meeting, and we voted to approve them. I gave Toomey the floor so that he could explain the financial report. When Toomey finished, Schneiderman folded his hands together.

'It sounds grim,' he said. He looked at me. 'What's happening with the fund-raising effort?'

'Twenty proposals are out.' I pulled a sheet of paper from my briefcase. 'You might want to see the list.'

'Any feedback?'

'Submitting proposals and getting them read is an excruciatingly slow process.'

'The program seems to be suffering in the meantime.'

Renée sighed. 'Maybe we need to do another fund-raiser.'

'I'm going to testify before the Senate Committee on Children. They have a pilot program which is funding programs like ours.'

'That sounds positive,' the judge said.

'It is. I'm certain we'll come up with something soon,' Toomey said, then looked at me.

I said, 'The immediate question on the table is next month's mortgage payment.'

'I found a wonderful new caterer,' Renée said. 'We could have a Halloween party on the Hudson.'

The group looked enthusiastic. Another chance to hobnob with the rich and famous.

'You can do that if you want to, but our mortgage payment is due now.'

Toomey gave Schneiderman a priestly look. 'How about a collection from this group? It *is* a tax deduction.'

Schneiderman sighed. 'Ahh – the voice of conscience.'

'I could throw in a thousand,' Buzz Greenberg volunteered.

'I suppose we could, too,' Schneiderman said, meaning his firm. 'But what we really need is a long-term solution. You say fund-raising is moving along, but it doesn't seem to have moved much in the last few months.'

'Maybe we need to think about hiring a professional fund-raiser,' Greenberg suggested. Renée frowned.

'With what money?' Toomey asked.

'What about the Church? You have contacts – couldn't we ask them to step in?' the judge shot back.

Toomey looked at me. 'That would be up to Anna,' he said.

I tried to hide my surprise. 'I thought you understood that it would be more than fine with me if you pitched in.'

'Well, I know your feelings about the Church—'

I cut him off. 'That's irrelevant to this discussion.'

He glared at me for the briefest moment. 'The city has asked us not to house children in the storefront. We don't have the proper permits.'

Schneiderman looked puzzled. 'That's an old issue, isn't it? You're not housing kids in the storefront anymore, are you, Anna?'

'No, I'm not.' I met Schneiderman's gaze. 'Even though I think it's pathetic to shut kids out because of some bogus regulation. I started the program in my apartment with no permits of any kind, if you remember.'

'We all know how you feel, Anna, but why tempt fate?' The lawyer's tone was either patronizing or understanding. I wasn't sure which.

'Well, if nobody minds, I'll lay the groundwork for a fund-raiser on the Hudson,' Renée volunteered. 'Perhaps on Halloween.'

After a few minutes' discussion of bills to suppliers, I adjourned the meeting. 'There's graduation Sunday,' I said as brightly as I could manage. 'You're all cordially invited.'

I knew I didn't have to worry about any of them actually showing up.

It was eight o'clock by the time I started walking home. A chill had settled over Manhattan. A small crowd entered the Celeste Bartos Forum through a side door of the palatial main branch of the public library. A warm orange light beckoned from within.

Behind the library the park was deserted except for a hunch-backed figure pushing a shopping cart. The cart overflowed with plastic and paper bags in all shapes and sizes. Under a street lamp the figure became an old woman in a cotton smock wearing cutoff socks as gloves. She reached into one of her many bags. Then she began to scatter what looked like pebbles onto some flecks on the walkway.

In the purple night air the flecks fluttered upward and separated. Luminescent in the street lamps' glow, the pigeons she was feeding wove over and under each other until they settled to cover her like a coat. Under the wings, I heard her fragile, crazy laugh.

9

'I cooked for you.'

'That's great. But this mess is awful.'

'Yes, Mother Superior.' Porsche scowled.

'Look, I won't pick on you if you don't pick on me,' I said, putting my briefcase on the chair and sitting down to unlace my sneakers.

'I'm sorry. I'm just grouchy from being cooped up all day. And you're home so late.'

'I understand. I know it's hard. It won't be for long. Still, we have to have some basic rules, rules we don't violate.'

'Violate. I thought you could only violate people.'

'You know, break, don't break the rules. Like neatness.'

'You want me to clean up?'

'Yes.'

I went to take a shower.

As I lathered my body under the falling water, I felt how tired I was. A roach with a translucent egg sac crawled from a crack in the caulking around the tub. I splashed her and watched her fall toward the drain. She struggled against the rush of the water falling from the shower, but the egg sac robbed her of all mobility. The force of the water sucked her down the drain. I got out and dried myself. By the time

I was done, the kitchen was clean and the table set for dinner. Rain battered the windows.

'Where did you learn to cook like this?' I asked Porsche after tasting her spaghetti sauce.

'Want me to teach you the recipe?'

I looked across the table at the child's face on the woman's body. She answered every question with a question. I chewed in silence. She pushed the food around on her plate. 'Not hungry?' I asked.

Fingers tapped on the door. We were both taken aback. The tapping continued. I nodded in the direction of the living room. Porsche scooped up her plate. 'Who is it?' I called.

'It's me. Colin.'

'Who else?'

'Nobody. I'm alone.'

By the time I removed the chain, Porsche was out of sight in the living room. I opened the door. The kitten meowed at my feet. Colin stood there, drenched, his guitar case in his arms as if it were an infant. 'Father Toomey threw me out.'

'I'm sorry about that.'

'I wanted to stay.'

I nodded. 'That's good, Colin. I'm glad you wanted to stay.'

'Can I stay?'

'Well, the program is full now.'

In the living room something fell. We heard a whispered, 'Shit!' Colin cocked his head. 'I mean stay *here*,' he said.

'I already have somebody staying with me.'

'But you said you were gonna get me into the program.'

I studied his desperate young face. Boys like him went to Harvard, Princeton, Yale, not the Minnesota Strip. 'All right, I'm gonna give you a break. But you better not let me down ... Porsche, Porsche. Come here a minute.'

Porsche peeked around the corner. 'What's up, Ma?'

'I want you to meet somebody.'

She sauntered into the kitchen, her hands buried in her back pockets.

'Porsche, this is Colin.'

'Hi.' He smirked. 'Your name is Porsche like Mercedes?'

She rolled her eyes. 'Yeah, like the car.'

He thumped his guitar case against his thigh.

'You any good?' she challenged.

'On the guitar?'

Porsche cracked a smile. 'Yeah, on the guitar.'

'Colin's gonna join us for dinner,' I told her. To him I said, 'I'm gonna get you some dry clothes. You can change in the bathroom.' I pointed down the hall.

As the bathroom door closed Porsche demanded, 'Why him? I thought it was only me.'

'He needs help, too.'

'But we don't even have room.'

'It's only until Monday. Colin needs help as much as you do.'

'There's something wrong with him.'

'Do you have a reason for saying that?'

'No, he's just weird.'

'Honey, there's a little something wrong with all of us.'

'Not like him.'

'You know him?'

She wove her body back and forth like a cobra contemplating a strike. 'No.'

For a fleeting moment I didn't believe her. Then I said, 'You're gonna have to trust me. I'm the adult.'

Pouting, she picked her kitten up. I set another place at the table. When Colin came back in dry clothes, Porsche warned him, 'Annie's not really supposed to take us in. She could get in big trouble.'

Colin sat down. 'I know that,' he said.

'Porsche is right,' I explained. 'There's going to have to be very strict rules, more strict even than the residential facility, because this is a small apartment.'

'Okay. I get it.' Colin winked at Porsche then looked at me. She stared at him coldly.

'I have to go to Washington tomorrow. After graduation, I'll get you both into the program officially.'

'It's your program, isn't it? I mean you're in charge, aren't you?' Colin seemed confused.

'Yes. But it's also an organization, and organizations have rules.'

'Like the Mob.' Colin smiled.

'Yeah, the Family.' Porsche sighed.

After dinner I excused myself, saying I had some work to do. I took my briefcase and descended the winding stairway. The storefront was dark and quiet. Even the neon sign in the window was off. The hotline was attached to an answering machine. I walked past all the empty desks to sit at my own. I went through my mail. On the corner across the street, kids dressed for an evil Halloween climbed in and out of cars that came and went. Some very expensive cars pulled up to the video store.

I left my desk to sit down in the window alcove, trying to escape the feeling that I was suffocating. The tinted pane allowed me to sit unseen. The window alcove itself was mirrored on both ends. The two mirrors reflected each other. As a result, when I looked up, I saw a thousand selves sitting in the marketplace of human flesh.

When I finally went back upstairs, Colin was sprawled in front of the television; the remote rested on his crotch.

'Change that to the news, please,' I asked.

'I don't like the news.'

'I always watch the news, Colin.'

'Why? It's always the same shit. People kill each other, people die.'

'Give me the remote, Colin.'

Porsche sat primly on the couch, scratching Beelzebub with her fingers. 'Enjoy the show, kitty.'

'What a tight-ass.' Colin tossed the remote in my direction. I just managed to catch it as he stormed out of the room. I heard the door bang shut. I ran into the hallway after him.

'Colin, this isn't the program. If you leave now, you can't come back.'

'Fuck you,' he yelled. 'You think you're my mother!'

He ran down the stairs, his guitar case banging against his thigh. I stood there for a moment listening to the pounding of my heart and of the rain outside. Then I went to watch the news.

Porsche knelt on the floor, playing with Beelzebub. 'See what I mean about him, Mom?' she said sweetly.

I sat down angry not just with him but with myself. Colin had behaved despicably, but had been right about the news. The telecast segments were a litany of brutality. After a while Porsche crawled over to me and slipped into my arms. I stroked the hair off her forehead. She cuddled her kitten.

'Colin's a jerk,' she said.
'Still, I feel bad.'
'You try too hard.'
'What's that supposed to mean?'
'Well, you could settle for one kid.'
'Like you?'
'Yeah.' She smiled coyly. 'Why not?'

She took the chain from her neck, opened it, removed a golden snake ring, put it on my ring finger, where it wobbled loosely, and whispered, 'Don't ever forget me, Annie.'

10

'See you tonight, darling.' I kissed Porsche's forehead. She reached up out of her sleep and hugged me.

'You gonna be okay?'

'Uh-huh.'

'There's plenty of food in the refrigerator. Whatever you do, don't go out, don't pick up the phone, and stay away from the front windows. I don't want Blue Fly to know you're up here.'

She sat up abruptly, the covers cascading around her. I pushed the hair out of her eyes. 'Go back to sleep, honey, I'll try to call later. If you hear my voice on the machine, pick up.'

She sank back into the pillows. 'I know. Anne Frank.'

I was locking the triple locks when I heard her calling after me, 'I love you, Annie.'

At the Port Authority cops were busy clearing the homeless off the wet steps of the bus terminal. Inside, I joined the sleepy line of commuters who waited for the elevator to the ramps. The elevator door slid open. I stepped into the crush of bodies and commuter smells: morning breath, anxiety, newspapers, coffee in Styrofoam cups. On the fourth floor I elbowed my way into the line for the bus to La Guardia Airport.

A few minutes later the bus descended the ramp into the city. Forty-second Street was as empty as a ghost town. Faceless bodies lay in the cavernous doorways of dilapidated movie theaters. Even on posh Fifth Avenue, the dejected were stacked on the steps of the main branch of the public library. At Grand Central, where we picked up another group of sleepy commuters, beggars crouched against the building, rattling the pennies in their paper cups.

When we arrived at La Guardia, the terminal was surrounded by protesting mechanics carrying placards. Their bleary eyes said they had been there all night. The commuters clutched their briefcases, fastened their eyes on the ground, and pushed their way into the terminal. I crossed the picket line, tossing away principle as lightly as a worn-out garment. After all, I had my own battle to wage in Washington.

On the shuttle I sat sandwiched between two men in pinstripes. As soon as we left the runway, one opened his laptop computer and the other his attaché case. I reached into my own briefcase and pulled out one of the twenty-five copies of the testimony I was about to deliver. I had adapted it from a testimony delivered before a city-council committee earlier in the month. Reading it put me to sleep.

By the time we touched down at National Airport, I was in the kind of nervous daze that comes from sleeping in the air. I grabbed a cab to the city. A pale sun glinted off the statue of Freedom perched on the Capitol dome. Freedom was bristling with lightning conductors and seemed to be wearing a bedspread. She wore a strange plumed helmet. I knew that her original cap, modeled on the cap worn by freed Roman slaves and French revolutionaries, had been discarded. The cap, President Lincoln's first cabinet was persuaded, might incite slaves to rebel.

I entered the Capitol through the ten-ton bronze doors on the east. After stopping for the security check, I stepped into the rotunda. Several hundred feet above, the Founding Fathers mingled with gods and goddesses in the fresco on the ceiling. A little farther up, a frieze depicted American history as if it had begun with Columbus. Lower down on the walls, eight oil paintings commemorated the Revolutionary War.

'The Capitol building was modeled on St Peter's in Rome and Les Invalides in Paris. The fresco on the ceiling was painted using the same technique Michelangelo used in the Sistine chapel,' a guide was telling the morning's first tourists. The tourists craned their necks and gasped.

I rushed through the rotunda, stepping over the white marble disk that was the city's symbolic center – the point zero at which Washington's street numbers and letters began. Children hopped in and out of the circle where the high and mighty were laid in state.

I reached the crowded hearing room just in time to hear the chairman's gavel signal that the hearing had begun. I signed in with a committee staff member and exchanged the copies of my testimony for an agenda. Then I found a seat.

There were nine senators up on the brightly lit dais. One woman and one African-American man, the rest well-groomed white males. James Beardsley sat to the chairman's right. The audience was packed with advocates; a handful of journalists sat in the front row. A camera crew had set up between the dais and the witness table. Klieg lights flooded the room. My name was last on the agenda. I would have to listen to six hours of speakers before my own turn. I cursed myself for coming so early. The first speaker stepped up to the witness table.

The speaker was hard to hear. I watched the back of his head. I could hear the committee's questions after the testimony but not the speaker's answers. I found myself watching Beardsley, watching the way the lights transformed him into David. By the third witness, the lack of air and the fact that I hadn't slept much the night before conspired to take me out of the hearing room and into the past.

I was in the jungle, watching David take the cleric's collar from his neck so he could breathe. We had gone up into the hills behind the village. The villagers had told us that a band of teenagers lived there and that they sometimes came down at night to steal livestock and whatever food they could get their hands on. We climbed the hill together. The dirt path ended in a coconut grove. Under the curious clicking of the palm fronds, the heat pressed in and held us like a fist.

We stepped into the pathetic collection of rags, cardboard, and tin that was the children's shantytown. They were all in one makeshift tent. The dust under our feet was covered in a thick black tar that made suction cups of my sandals. Every step released the smell of blood. I fell to my knees and retched. A chorus of insects pounded at my eardrums.

There weren't just teenagers here, but younger children, too. All dead. Small, lifeless bodies were twisted in impossible positions. Maggots crawled in eye sockets and the stumps of limbs that had been cut off. Fingers and hands with no arms clutched the earth. The boys' genitals were stuffed into their mouths. One child was slumped over, holding her intestines as if they were a long, unruly garden hose. David pulled me up and out of there. My hands and knees were coated in the children's sticky blood.

'Sorry you have to wait so long,' somebody was saying.

To hide my confusion, I bent down to retrieve my briefcase. The lunch break had begun. Beardsley stood at the end of the aisle where I sat.

'It's because I added you to the agenda at the last minute,' he said.

'It's all right,' I said, but I was annoyed.

'Please, let me make it up to you. Let me buy you lunch.'

Porsche sat on the bed by the window unwrapping a wad of bills, tens and twenties, even a couple of hundreds. 'We're leaving town, kid. We gotta. The question is where to.' The window gate rattled. Porsche shoved the bills under the bedspread. Colin stood on the fire escape. His guitar case was covered in Indian-patterned stickums. The strap was a beaded band. Porsche opened the window.

'Let me in.'

'I can't, the gate is locked.'

'So let me in the door. I gotta talk to you.'

'Talk here.'

He looked around at the windows of the taller buildings. 'Somebody'll see me and call the cops.'

'I'll talk to you later.'

'I'm just gonna stand here till somebody calls the cops.'

Porsche slammed the window shut. Colin climbed back up to the roof. Porsche hid her money in the laundry hamper. She left Beelzebub on the bathroom floor and closed the door. 'Be right back, lover.'

Up on the roof Colin stood, hands in his pockets, guitar at his feet, watching a column of mist rise from the river.

'Why are you back?' Porsche asked, coming up behind him.

'I missed you,' Colin said. 'Everybody's saying Blue Fly smacked you.'

'How'd you know I was here in the first place?'

'God used a little devil to lead me to you.'

'Do you have to talk like that?'

'It's true. I was looking for you when the cops turned me over to her. She had your cat, so I knew you had to be around. How come you pretended not to know me?'

'I *don't* know you. So what do you want?'

On the next roof over, some pigeons locked in a wire-mesh coop hid their heads in their wings.

'What are you doing in her apartment?'

'Her name is Anna. She's good people.'

'You fucking her?' Colin asked.

Porsche picked up Colin's guitar case. 'Jealous?'

'Don't touch my guitar!'

'Why are you so hung up on this guitar?'

'Just give it to me!'

Porsche danced toward the roof's edge, the guitar case

upright against her body. Colin managed to pry one of her hands loose. 'C'mon, don't make me twist it off.'

Porsche broke away by jumping across the air shaft onto the next roof. Inside the coop the pigeons scattered noisily.

'Gimme the guitar!'

'Come and get it.'

Colin's heart pounded. He felt sick. 'You know I'm scared of heights.'

'So what are you doing up here?'

'I just wanna play you the song I wrote you.'

'Why?'

'I told you. I love you.'

'Why me?'

'Can I have the guitar now? I promise to be cool.' Porsche dangled the guitar across the divide of the two buildings. The distance wasn't very far, but the drop was deep and narrow. Colin took the guitar tenderly. 'Look, I don't know why,' he said. 'You're beautiful. I love you.'

'If you love me, come over here.'

Colin dug his heels deeper into the tar.

'You're such a pussy,' Porsche taunted, and jumped back across to the roof.

'Don't you wanna hear the song I wrote you?'

'All right, then, come in – but you can't stay.'

I followed Beardsley into Statuary Hall, which was lined with bronze and marble versions of famous sons and daughters of all fifty states. He gestured at the walls. 'Here we have the good, the bad, and the ugly. Every state was asked to contribute two, and they sure as hell did.'

I let out a small, hysterical giggle, which echoed back to

us. By the time we reached the rotunda, the others had gone. Beardsley pointed at the ceiling.

'You know the poor guy who spent twenty-five years of his life painting that ceiling started the walls when he was seventy-two? Two thirds of the way done, he slipped and dangled from the scaffolding until somebody happened by. He was so traumatized, he had to let a student finish the job.'

'Serves him right. All this patriarchal self-aggrandizement. It's oppressive.'

'You just think that because it reminds you of a church,' Beardsley said.

I was afraid to look at him, afraid that if I did, I would want to undo time so that I could go back and do it all differently. In the magnificence of the empty rotunda it seemed almost possible. I said, 'I don't like it when you read my mind.'

'You should be impressed.'

A crush of reporters rushed by us to circle somebody I couldn't see. As they passed many greeted James Beardsley by his first name.

'You're a popular guy,' I said.

He smiled with just a hint of shyness. 'No more than you, I'm sure.'

His car waited at the foot of the Capitol steps. As I got in I said, 'It's funny how political types never use public transportation.'

He laughed, seeming to take no offense. 'The lunch break is short. Let's not attack each other until it's over.' He leaned toward the driver. I thought he said, 'Cramer books and afterwards.'

As the driver headed up Pennsylvania Avenue Beardsley asked, 'What did you think of the morning's testimony?'

'I couldn't hear a lot of it.'

'It's terrible how these things are staged for the camera and not people who care enough to attend.'

'Maybe that way more people get the message.'

'You think America is out there watching hearings of insignificant committees?' He gave me an amused stare.

Through his car's tinted windows, I watched the warm colors of the pruned autumn foliage. After the decay and neglect of New York, the city seemed impossibly beautiful. Tourists lined up at the wrought-iron gates of the White House. 'Why do people put themselves through that?'

'Not everybody has your aversion to history,' Beardsley answered. 'Besides, no other country in the world lets you traipse through the president's house.'

'You call that a house? Even Jefferson said it was big enough for two emperors, one pope, and the grand lama.'

'And that was before he added the pavilions.'

In Lafayette Park prochoice demonstrators carried signs that read NOT EVERY SPERM DESERVES A NAME. Beside them, homeless men lined up for a soup kitchen.

'What if she catches us?'

Porsche locked the door behind her. 'She won't.'

The hard fingers of a sudden rain tapped on the windows. Colin put his guitar down by the door, gently. 'I wanna play for you.'

'After we eat.'

'I'm not hungry.'

'Want this?' She pulled a joint from her bra. He reached

for it. She hid it behind her back. 'Uh-uh, not until we cook. Get me the spaghetti and the can of sauce up there.'

Colin obeyed.

Porsche lit the joint, and they began passing it back and forth. From the refrigerator she got two onions, two cloves of garlic, and two green peppers. Then she peeled, chopped, and diced. Colin asked, 'How come you're such a good cook?'

'I used to cook for my brothers and sisters.'

'How many did you have?'

'Two ... six ... four ... shut up and help chop.'

'At home there's me, my stepbrother, my mom, and her latest greatest husband.'

Together they turned a jar of store-bought spaghetti sauce into homemade. Porsche set the table. She even brought one of the Guatemalan candlesticks from the living room and lit the candle. Colin filled two paper cups with soda. They sat down to eat.

'This is Paris,' Porsche said, taking Beelzebub onto her lap.

'New Mexico.'

Porsche rolled her eyes. 'Okay, a toast to anywhere but here.'

They raised their cups. 'Good crystal,' she said as they listened for the make-believe tinkle.

'Quite a bouquet,' Colin added. 'Delicate but frisky.'

Porsche kissed Beelzebub on the nose. 'To the animals and to us. Okay, Noah?'

'Noah?'

'If we're gonna have a new life, you need a new name.'

'What was Noah's wife's name?'

She shrugged and put Beelzebub down next to her plate. 'I don't know. Anyway, I don't want to be the wife.'
'Why not?'
'Because nobody knows her name.'

Cramer Books and Afterwords was a bookstore restaurant. People browsed and chatted among the aisles. I followed Beardsley to the tables in the back. The people who sat alone were reading as they ate. We climbed a stairway to a loft and chose a spot that gave us a good view of the store below. As Beardsley read the menu I studied his manicured, elegant hands and decided that they were different from David's after all. David's hands were always callused and blistered. Beardsley's looked as if they had never picked up anything heavier than a Mont Blanc pen.

The waitress came. We ordered homemade soup and pasta. When she left, he said, 'I've never had this effect on anyone before.'

I felt myself blush. 'What do you mean?'

'I make you nervous.'

'Don't be silly. It's just a nerve-racking time for social-service programs.'

'And their directors?'

Was he laughing at me?

'Where were you before you became counsel to the committee?' I asked.

'I was with Mobilization for Youth in Adams Morgan.'

'That's a switch.'

'Not as big as the switch you made.'

'Not really. I went into the Church to serve in the Third World, and now the Third World has come home.'

'Touché,' he said, and broke a roll with his delicate fingers.

As I unfolded my napkin he asked, 'So who was this man I remind you of?'

The food arrived. When the waitress had gone, he repeated his question.

'I told you he was a priest.'

He reached across the table and, with his fingers on my chin, forced me to meet his gaze. 'I mean who was he to *you*?'

I pulled away. 'We worked together.'

'Did you love him?'

'I admired him.'

'I see. You admired him so much that my looking like him makes you quake in your shoes.'

Why was he doing this? I was furious. Still, I didn't dare challenge him. He held the best route to my program's salvation in his hands. As if reading my thoughts, he said, 'I meant what I said in New York, Anna. I genuinely want to help Eden House get funded by our committee.'

His eyes were like the library in which we sat, full of closed volumes. I said, 'His name was David.'

'David!' he repeated, and now he seemed flustered.

'Why are you so fascinated by him?'

He leaned forward and whispered, 'Because *you* are, Anna.'

Later, as we sipped our cappuccinos, he asked, 'Since you won't answer any questions, will you just take a tip?'

'I'm always willing to listen.'

'The committee chairman likes to hear himself talk. So in the Q and A after your testimony, give short, concise answers. Let him ask long, rambling questions. The more you let Fitzwater shine, the more he'll remember you.'

'No problem.'

'We've been here almost an hour, and I still know almost nothing about you.'

'Whereas you've entrusted to me your whole life's history.'

He laughed. 'Touché encore.'

I felt a chill just under my skin. He had that aura, that aura of being in total charge. David's aura. Except that he wasn't a priest.

'This desert is your idea of paradise?'

Porsche studied the paperback travel book Colin carried in his guitar case. A photograph. White desert. Golden shadows. Violet clouds. A finger-painted sky. On the earth below, adobe huts, sun-bleached and mysterious. In the middle distance, children playing with a spotted pony. Indian children.

'I can make a living there playing my guitar,' Colin said.

'In the desert?'

'Santa Fe. Coming with me?'

'Not without money,' she said. 'I ain't goin' *nowhere* without money.'

'Anna Eltern . . . Anna Eltern.'

The committee floated in front of me like the gods in the Parthenon. I approached the witness table. Was Beardsley my second chance? The camera's eye watched. I sat down. Adrenaline rushed through my veins. I began like this:

'In the thirty-six seconds it took me to walk up here, an American child was injured or killed by a gun. Every sixty-seven seconds a teenager gives birth. Every eight seconds a child drops out of school. Every forty-seven seconds a child is seriously abused by a parent. Every twenty-six seconds a child runs away from home. These children are not really runaways, they are *throwaways*. Isn't it time we begin to ask some questions about the adults who are running the show?

'At Eden House we've found an age-old solution, a simple solution. Christ's solution, and it's called love. Unconditional love. Human beings respond to it. At Eden House we pride ourselves on never turning a child away. But now, gentlemen, with budget cuts hitting every level of government, we have begun to violate that policy. We have begun to turn children away, to shut our doors on desperate young faces. And what's happening to Eden House is happening across America. It's an act of betrayal, and it's the reason I am here to testify to this committee today.'

I read my testimony. When I had finished, the camera and the lights turned off me and onto the dais. The chairman launched into a very long question. I offered a brief answer. Then the chairman made a few more speeches disguised as questions. I agreed with his reiteration of my testimony. He pounded his gavel, and the hearing was adjourned for the day.

As I got up to leave I was surrounded. People thanked me and shook my hand. Others gave me their business cards. Several reporters followed me out of the hearing room. I answered a few questions and the reporters moved on. As I tried to leave the hearing room Beardsley stepped in front of me. 'Like a champ,' he said, smiling. Now his eyes were almost blue.

'A certain party gave me advance warning.'

'Come back on Friday for the closing ceremony. That way I can introduce you to the chairman personally.'

I thought of Porsche, alone in my apartment. 'There's some kids in New York who need me.'

He glared at me like a father who knows better. 'Getting funded will help them, too.'

11

Just two days later, as the plane circled over the District of Columbia, again I saw the capital's special beauty. If the ancients had been able to fly over Athens or Rome, they would have seen something like this – a glistening river among lush trees, stately monuments suggesting the orderly government to which humanity aspired.

I took a cab directly to the Justice Department, which was hosting the evening's event. I climbed the marble steps to a wide sweep of doors. The receiving line was just inside the center door. The men wore tuxedos, the women evening gowns. Although I recognized none of the faces, some seemed to know me. They welcomed me with a studied kind of warmth. Then I stood in the rotunda wondering what to do next. Across the room I saw James Beardsley. He was surrounded by half a dozen elegantly dressed people. The marble floor seemed perilously slippery. I had no choice but to attach myself to his circle and wait. A discussion was in progress. A man and a woman were squabbling politely.

'The Justice Department's porn report is a travesty. The taxpayers are footing the bill for a porn catalog.'

'Well, how else do you suggest we find out what's going on out there?'

Beardsley saw me but didn't acknowledge me. I was getting angry and nervous, wishing I had never come, when he finally turned his charm my way.

'Anna. Folks, meet Anna Eltern, founder and director of Eden House.'

One of the women did a double take. 'The Eltern who wrote *One Woman's Choice*?'

The other woman took a second look at me over her champagne glass.

'That was a lifetime ago,' I said.

She said, 'I don't see how you can reconcile abortion with any theology at all.'

'And I don't see how you can reconcile children having children they can't feed or educate,' I snapped.

The women glared at me. Beardsley grabbed my elbow. 'Excuse us, ladies, there's someone I want Ms Eltern to meet.'

He leaned down and murmured in my ear as he firmly shepherded me away. 'You're here to schmooze, not alienate.'

I studied his WASPY face. Did everyone in politics speak Yiddish?

'C'mon, the chairman's in the next room.'

He steered me through an arched doorway into another smaller room, where there was a photo exhibit. 'I read your proposal,' Beardsley said. 'It needs work.'

The tiny Guatemalan worry dolls fitted neatly into Colin's palm.

'You're not supposed to crush them. You're supposed to put them under your pillow so they can take the worries out of your head,' Porsche said.

Colin dropped the many little dolls back into their colorful box. Porsche put her head on his lap. Colin leaned down and kissed her. She bit him. He yelped in pain.

'I told you I don't do that.' She struggled to sit.

'What's wrong with my wanting to kiss you?'

'I told you, I don't play that.'

Colin shoved five dollars down her T-shirt, between her breasts. 'Now will you do it?'

She reached for his eyes with her fingernails. He caught her hands. He twisted her arm back.

'Ouch. You're hurting me!'

'Kiss me.'

'Fuck you, john. I don't kiss johns.'

'I want you to stop hustling.'

'Let go of my arm, asshole!'

Colin let go.

Porsche rubbed her shoulder. 'You stupid jerk – you want me to stop hustling, or you want me to make enough money to leave town?'

'Both.'

'It can't be both.'

'Yes, it can. One big score and then no more.'

The eyes of the children in the Department of Justice photo exhibit were hauntingly familiar. Kids in the streets of urban America, black, brown, and white. Written in their eyes always the same confused innocence, the laughter of despair.

'Powerful exhibit,' I said.

'Tell me about your book.'

'It's out of print.'

'Oh, c'mon, Anna. No false modesty, please.'

Just then Chairman Fitzwater came our way. 'James ... James, help me out. Who is that over there?' Chairman Fitzwater leaned close and nodded toward the corner of the room. 'I *know* he's somebody, but I can't place him.'

'That's the under secretary of education. You met with him last month.'

'Right ... right ...'

'Senator, before you run off, I'd like you to meet Anna Eltern.'

Fitzwater took my hand in both of his and looked deep into my eyes. 'We've met, haven't we?'

'I testified on Wednesday.'

I saw a certain recognition set in. 'Ahhh yes,' he said, 'and you were wonderful.'

'I've placed Ms Eltern's proposal on your A list, Senator.'

'And rightly so.' The senator nodded. His eyes followed the attorney general, who had just entered the room. 'So nice to meet you,' he murmured, moving on.

I looked at Beardsley, wondering if he could tell how desperate I felt. Behind him was the wall of runaways. A photograph in black and white reached out to me.

She was a small figure in a satin suit, suspended from the arms of two police officers. The bend of her knees and the downward cast of her face said that she was zonked out of her mind. Her open blouse revealed a crochet top that barely covered her ribs. She had no breasts yet. Her golden African locks shone around her like a halo. A blurred slice of a third officer's hand appeared in the photo. He must have been moving when the picture was taken.

In the mirror Porsche smiled at Colin. Fresh from the shower, he stood brushing his teeth. She tried playfully to pull the towel from his waist.

'What are you doing?' His mouth was full of foam.

'I wanna see that cute butt of yours.'

'You can't kiss me, but you wanna see my butt?'

'Okay, so kiss me.'

He turned and leaned to kiss her. Quick. Gentle. Just the whisper of lips on lips. When he turned back to the mirror, she had a white foam mustache on her golden face. 'Seen my cat?'

He leaned down into the sink and splashed water in his face.

She played at pumping him from behind. 'Is that what the johns do to you?' she asked.

Colin turned and slammed her head against the door.

'Ouch, you crazy faggot!' she screamed.

'I'm *not* a faggot!'

She tried to get out of the bathroom, but Colin caught her by the arm. 'Take it back!'

'Don't you get tired of trying to break my arm?'

The pain forced her down on her knees. Under the sink she saw Beelzebub. Colin saw her, too. He let go of Porsche's arm and picked up the kitten. 'Hey, kitty, do *you* think I'm a faggot?'

'Gimme my cat. Don't hurt my cat.'

'Take it back or I'll drown this beast.' Water gushed from the faucet.

'All right, all right. I take it back!'

'Say it.'

'You're not a faggot! I'm sorry.'

Porsche grabbed a bottle of perfume and hurled it at Colin's head. 'Not my cat, not my cat! She's just a baby!'

'It's her,' I said, 'the girl you met on Forty-second Street.'

'Which one?'

'The one who was coming on to you in front of the porn shop.'

'No, it's not.' He shook his head, frowning at the photograph. 'That girl had dark hair.'

'She was wearing a wig.'

He stepped in closer, scowling at Porsche's glossy image. 'I'm afraid I don't recognize her.'

'Remember, she took the wig off?'

'If this is a test, Anna, I fail.'

'Who took this picture?'

He turned his back on the wall of photographs. 'I'm not sure. A lot of photographers contributed to this exhibit.'

He crooked his finger at an elegant woman in black standing next to Senator Fitzwater. She sashayed over.

'Anna Eltern, this is Bonnie Mullen, the senator's press aide.'

'Pleased to meet you.'

'I hear your testimony was a big hit,' Bonnie said, smiling. She was a pretty woman with gentle freckles and shining hazel eyes.

'Thanks.'

'This photograph, Bonnie. Do you know who contributed it?'

'It's a wire-service photo by a prize-winning photojournalist. The photographer's not here tonight because he's in Saudi Arabia. Why do you ask?'

Beardsley looked at me.

'The girl looks familiar,' I told her.

She studied the photo. 'It's a sad picture,' she said.

We nodded our agreement and stared stupidly at the wall where a young girl hung without the strength to look back at us.

'Will you excuse me?' Bonnie said politely. 'Nice to meet you, Ms Eltern.' She returned to the senator's side.

Beardsley studied me as if I, too, were hanging on the wall. 'The girl is special to you?'

I bit my lip. 'They're all special.'

'Then let's look at the others.' He led me expertly onward. 'And while we're at it, tell me about that book of yours,' he demanded.

'It was an adaptation of a journal I kept in Guatemala. I sold it to fund my program. But the book is out of print and the royalties have dried up.'

The truth was that I had published it as some kind of self-justification. Now, looking at Beardsley yet seeing David, I was acutely aware that I had left out the most important parts.

'Have dinner with me?' Beardsley asked.

I made a show of looking at my watch. 'I can't. I have to catch the shuttle back. Really.'

'Oh, no, you don't. You're not running out on me this fast.'

'Well, the big introduction is over, so...'

'My car's outside. At least let me give you the five-cent tour before taking you to the airport.'

When I hesitated, he said, 'C'mon, give me a little time. Fair is fair.'

A blue night had settled over the District of Columbia. Beardsley told his driver to head for the Washington Monument. There we got out to walk. He led me onto the walkway to the Vietnam Memorial. Fallen leaves scratched the pavement. A V-shaped granite wall rose before us, its surface mirror smooth except for the fifty-eight thousand names etched there. A wilted white rose and a child's photograph lay at our feet. At the wall a woman lit a match. Her fingers traced the letters of a name. The flame flickered and died. She lit another match. The black stone reflected not her face but the skull beneath.

'Do you think it will ever be any different?' I asked.

'I don't know anymore. I lost my faith,' Beardsley said softly, 'and a lot of friends, too.'

'Over there?'

'Yes. I didn't really want to go, but... family honor and all that.'

My heart traveled back to the time when David and I were so certain that the world would change. I pictured Beardsley in fatigues carrying an Uzi. I said, 'I'm a pacifist.'

'You weren't always.'

'Yes, always.'

'Not in Nicaragua. You were there when priests and nuns were running guns and marrying each other.'

'I wasn't in Nicaragua. I was in Guatemala.'

'Oh,' he said. 'I didn't hear right, I guess.'

He picked up the snapshot of a little boy that the wind had blown toward us. 'I had a brother once,' he said, and took off his glasses.

Thinking his brother had died in the war, I murmured, 'I'm sorry.'

'He was the favorite son until he refused to go to Vietnam. He was a selfish, arrogant bastard, but I think now that he was right.'

Now I was totally confused. I looked into those changing eyes for an explanation. He turned away. 'Let's go on with our tour,' he said.

As we approached the obelisk I took off my heels. The grass was icy cold beneath my stockinged feet. I craned my neck to see where the marble penetrated the sky. The sky was thick and wet, and the top of the monument blurred.

'What do you think?' he asked.

'I've been up there,' I said. 'On an eighth-grade trip. Back then I believed all the lies they told me.'

'And now you lie yourself,' he said impassively. 'Or are you different from the rest of us?'

Later we climbed the steps of the Jefferson Memorial and stood below the graceful dome. From the portico we watched the moon's sheen on the tidal basin.

'I love this place,' Beardsley said. 'What it represents, what Jefferson stood for ... He was the last Renaissance man.'

'It *is* beautiful.'

A bronze Jefferson sat on his marble pedestal flanked by the committee appointed to write the Declaration of Independence. Beardsley looked up at him and said, 'When I despair, I come here and remind myself that even the Declaration of Independence was written by a committee. What do you do when you get desperate?'

'I ask myself why the last Renaissance man had no qualms about fathering the children of a seventeen-year-old slave girl.'

He laughed. 'You don't have to tell if you don't want to.'

A powerful wind entered the colonnade, and finding itself trapped among the columns, it began to moan.

We walked to the base of the statue, where the wind's violence was lessened. 'Do you ever feel—'

'What?' I interrupted.

'That you're trapped, that you want out?' The wind nipped at my face.

'Do you?' he pressed.

I felt the texture of my trap, timeworn and secure as a prison. My eyes wandered to the frieze above us, where Jefferson was swearing on the altar of God. I read the panel aloud: 'Hostility against every form of tyranny over the mind of man.'

'The answer is yes, isn't it?' Beardsley insisted.

Suddenly there was a terrible crack in the sky. A moment later lightning illuminated both Jefferson and Beardsley. The marble around us glowed.

'The old patriarch is speaking to you,' he whispered. 'Do you still have a direct line?'

'I'm afraid it's been broken.'

I felt his fingers on my cheek, lightly. 'Let me . . .'

I stepped back. One step.

A rush of falling water surrounded the portico. Long silver slices of rain fell from an invisible sky. A chill rose in my bones and I began to shiver.

He took my hand. 'Run for it, Anna.'

In the darkness of the storm, the lawn had turned purple. Our feet sank into the soaked earth, and we ran blindly through the downpour. The limo was no longer where we had left it. We stopped running. The falling rain whispered around us like wind in jungle foliage. He pulled me to him and his lips opened mine. I dissolved, molecules to atoms, present to past; I went through the gate of the forgotten to touch the unexpected. My body clung to his, and the rain connected us like liquid skin. I pulled away.

'I don't suppose there's a chance you'd consider coming home with me?' Beardsley asked. 'I'm planning to go to New York tomorrow anyway. We could go back together.'

Two bright lights moved toward us. The driver was signaling us.

'I don't suppose there is,' I said, and climbed into the backseat.

'You can't go home like that.' He gestured at my wet clothes and hair.

'I guess I'll have to.'

'Why?'

'There's a kid waiting for me.'

'What about your staff, can't they handle it?'

'Not this kid. She's in a lot of trouble, and I promised I'd be back tonight.'

He nodded wearily. 'I have my gym clothes in the trunk. You can have my sweat suit and change at the airport.'

I opened the door onto a strange, sweet smell. The kitten meowed forlornly at my feet. I picked her up and walked down the hall to the living room. Porsche was lying on the floor in a T-shirt and no pants, her head lost between Colin's legs. His head was thrown back and I saw the whites of his eyes. Neither of them noticed that I had come in.

'Porsche!'

She turned and looked at me over her shoulder. I saw the glass pipe in her mouth and the milky-white smoke that swirled there. Her eyes were slits. Colin pulled the pipe from her mouth and sucked on it himself.

'Mom. What are you wearing?' Porsche asked with a wicked, sad smile.

'Gimme that!' I grabbed the pipe from Colin's mouth.

Colin shot up and tried to grab the pipe back. I put it behind my back. 'You bitch! That's mine!' he cried.

Porsche turned on all fours, trying to get up.

Colin balled his fist and held it to my face. 'Gimme that pipe, you crazy-ass *dyke*!'

Porsche tottered to her feet. 'Don't talk to Annie like that!'

'Fuck her,' Colin screamed. 'She's just jealous.'

He grabbed my arm. Porsche bit his hand. 'Let her go! Let her go!' she shrieked.

I dropped the pipe. It fell on the couch with a slow bounce. Colin grabbed it. 'You dames are sick.' He picked up the pipe, then pushed past me to grab his guitar case. Down the hall I saw him grab his jacket. He slammed the door behind him.

'What were you doing with him?' I heard myself yell.

'Nothing, Annie, nothing.'

Porsche held on to me with both hands. 'We weren't doing nothing. We were just smoking.'

'Crack! You're in here smoking *crack*!' I screamed. 'Get out. Get the hell out.' I was trembling with fury.

Porsche began to cry like a little girl. 'I won't do it again.'

'Get your stuff and get out.'

'Annie, please, I promise. I promise I won't do it again.'

I pulled her jeans onto her. She fought like an uncoordinated rag doll, and because her jeans fit so loosely, she lost. 'Get out,' I yelled. 'I never should have taken you in.'

'Annie, please, I'm sorry, Annie, please!'

I threw her jacket out into the hallway.

'My cat, Annie. Not without my cat,' she cried.

As she searched under the table for her kitten, I grabbed her by the arm and dragged her across the floor out into the hallway. I kicked the door shut, locked it, and sat at the kitchen table panting with rage. I ignored her pleas from the stairwell until I heard footsteps followed by silence.

12

'I wanna thank Eden House for giving me back my life.' She stopped to catch her breath. 'And, Annie, I'll never forget you.'

The lanky teenager we called Mazie raised her diploma in the air and wiped a tear from her eye. Two years ago she had been a fifteen-year-old runaway, drug addict, prostitute. Now she was accepted by Manhattan Community College.

The graduates sat in their portable chairs facing the portable podium where O'Shaugnessy, their speaker, stood in front of the microphone and played with the crooked knot in the tie that didn't really match his suit. A sudden Indian-summer heat had allowed us to have an outdoor graduation. O'Shaugnessy had orchestrated the ceremony so as to be sure everyone had a chance at the podium. One by one the kids had stepped up. Mazie was the last.

'I think you guys have said it all,' he told them. 'Thanks for choosing me to be a part of this. I know cops haven't won too many popularity contests. But if you don't like the cops the way they are, maybe you should think about becoming one.' He smiled broadly and wiped his damp brow with a handkerchief. 'All I can add is, be yourself. Because if you're not, somebody else will be.'

He was always saying stupid things like that. The kids applauded wildly, then tearfully hugged one another. Three were going off to college, three into entry-level jobs, four into the service, and two were going back to their families. I worried most for those two. Had their families changed?

Yellowing leaves shivered in a sudden breeze. As the clouds shifted, the city seemed to rise around Central Park's Sheep Meadow like a concrete fence. On the nearby roadway a roller skater danced to the soundless music in his headset. I felt autumn in my bones. I missed Porsche. As soon as the ceremony was over, I would find her and bring her into the program.

'Hey,' O'Shaugnessy said, 'wake up, smell the coffee.'

'What?'

'These kids are wonderful, Eltern. You should be very proud.'

'I am. I *am* proud.'

All around us kids were carrying chairs back to the van at the park's edge. I tried to swallow the lump in my throat.

'Give you a ride cross town,' O'Shaugnessy offered. I accepted. Riding with him would undoubtedly cure me of the desire to cry.

His car smelled of stale coffee and old shoes. A horsefly buzzed from the dashboard to the window and back again. I pushed empty paper cups and soda cans under the seat. Under my feet age and neglect had eaten away at the flooring until it was just rusty lace.

'Don't worry,' he said, chuckling, 'your foot's too big to fall through there.'

Traffic was slow. The car's air conditioner functioned more like a heater. He took his jacket off. The circles of sweat under his armpits grew. At Forty-second Street traffic came to a dead halt. The fly was getting suicidal. It pitched itself at the windshield in an ever-increasing frenzy.

O'Shaugnessy said, 'Even the weather's confused.'

We inched toward the light at Eighth Avenue. It turned red. A siren wailed in my ears. A wash of red light flooded the car. On the sidewalk a squad car sped by.

'Holy shit,' O'Shaugnessy muttered. His big body tensed, and a hard look crept into his eyes. 'What kind of stupid shit is this?'

He took his portable turret light from the backseat, reached out of his window, and thumped it on top of the car. He flipped on his siren and eased the old car up onto the sidewalk. A collection of sleepy hustlers shook their skinny fists at us. A bag lady pushed her cart slowly toward the curb. She brought her toothless face to my open window. 'You gotta *be* the *law* to break the *law*. Is that *fair?*' she shrilled.

The block between Eighth and Ninth avenues had become a parking lot for squad cars and unmarked detectives' cars. Between them a crowd had collected as if for a party. The howls of ghetto blasters mingled with hooting, laughter, and an occasional mock scream as the revelers taunted the plainclothes cops trying to canvass the scene. Colin lurked in a sex-shop doorway across the street, so washed-out I almost didn't recognize him. He was still wearing the clothes I had last seen him in. He didn't have his guitar. I reached for the door handle, planning to run over there and ask about Porsche. But O'Shaugnessy said, 'Just hang for a minute?' and got out of the car.

The commotion seemed centered in the entrance to the Empire Hotel, a five-story welfare hellhole with hundreds of occupants. Many were children. Several beefy bluecoats behind wooden horses with paper signs marked CRIME SCENE DO NOT CROSS THIS LINE blocked the doorway. They stood, legs braced wide, watching the sky or the roof across the street. None seemed older than twenty-one. A group of anxious media types tried to get their attention.

'C'mon, man, we're trying to do a job here,' a reporter complained. He was missing one arm from below the elbow. He wore his pad on a chain around his neck so that his other hand was free to write.

'I wanna talk to the captain,' another reporter demanded.

'You're all gonna hafta wait for the public-information officer.'

The reporters huddled with their photographers, then sent them off to search for some other way to get a photo of whatever atrocity the uniformed cops were guarding inside the hotel.

I tried to catch the fly in one of the empty coffee containers. When I finally got him, I brought the cup to the open window. The fly climbed to the cup's edge, rubbed its ugly legs together, and flew back into the car.

A shadow fell over me. I looked up. Domingo sat on the hood of O'Shaugnessy's car. He scooted toward the windshield and pressed his face to the pane. His small brown face flattened against the glass and became an Inca mask. In the condensation formed by his breath, he wrote my name with his finger. Then he jumped around on the hood like a baby baboon. Was he high? I took the key from the ignition and got out of the car. On the dashboard the fly was dead.

He grimaced at me. 'These reporters are so dumb, Annie.'

I hadn't seen him in almost a week. His amber skin had taken on an olive sheen, and there were deep circles under his eyes.

'What do you mean?'

He slid down from the hood and pointed to the hotel doorway, where I had lost sight of O'Shaugnessy, where cops and reporters still bickered. 'They're all trying to get in there, but she's somewhere else.'

'She?'

'The dead girl.'

'Who? Who is it, Domingo?'

He shrugged. 'Wanna see her?'

'Who is she? Do you know who she is?'

Domingo walked away from me. For a moment I stood undecided. I felt a quick, terrible stab of fear. It might be someone I knew. Then I locked the car and ran after him into the Blarney Stone. Inside the corner bar the television was the only light. A collection of workers and losers were watching a sports channel.

'Hey. Hey, kid! I told you before you can't be in here,' the bartender yelled after Domingo, who was already running out the backdoor. I chased him to the hotel's fire escape. He pulled a ladder down and began to climb. The fire escape groaned against the old brick building. Domingo was already several flights above me when I decided to follow.

From the fire escape's fifth-floor landing, we could see around the corner to the air shaft between the hotel and the tenement next door. Down there police officers milled around a plastic tarp. A line of chalk had been drawn around it. Other lines circled dark patches on the pavement. A photographer hopped gingerly between the lines, his camera pressed to his eyes.

'It doesn't matter how many pictures he takes,' Domingo said. 'She's still dead.'

A graying man in bifocals carrying a black doctor's bag approached the sheet and lifted it gingerly. I saw some red hair, but only for a moment. A moment long enough for relief to wash through me. The ME knelt, blocking my view. He seemed to be speaking into the palm of his hand. Later I saw the tiny tape recorder.

'How do you know it's a girl?' I asked Domingo.

'I heard the cops say so.'

'Maybe you heard wrong.'

The man got up and talked to the cop with the gold shield pinned to his lapel. The cop snapped his fingers; four plainclothes cops came over. I felt an uneasy touch of vertigo.

Domingo sat down on the window ledge. Folding his arms around himself, he studied his hundred-and-fifty-dollar Air Jordan sneakers. His whole outfit was new. The gray polyester suit had been replaced by cross-color jeans, one leg red, one green. The pants hung below his hips. On a ribbon around his neck, he wore one of the oversize pacifiers that were the latest fashion. He was shivering.

'You okay?'

He nodded.

'Nice clothes,' I said.

'I got me a job now.' He fluffed his pants proudly. 'Right by you.'

I was about to ask him what kind of job when his mother appeared in the unlit corridor just inside the window. She was so frail, I hadn't heard her approach. Her blazing eyes fastened on me. 'Lay offa my kid. He ain't no runaway.'

I was captivated by the purple bruise that seemed to be opening on her forehead.

Domingo said, 'Cool it, Mom. I was just looking for you.'

He slipped off the ledge into the hallway. 'Later, Annie.'

Hunched into himself like an old man, he slumped along the hallway and into the elevator. I got up to look down the air shaft again. The tarp and the body had been removed. Only the chalk line's blurred edges remained.

I climbed into the window as Domingo had done and waited for an elevator. When it finally came, it was full of children. Even unkempt, they were a beautiful bunch. The youngest was less than two years old, the oldest maybe six. I stepped inside. The children were fighting over a candy bar. The toddler screamed because nobody would give him a bite.

'Give my brother some,' a little girl who looked about four tried to persuade a three-year-old.

'No, it's mine!'

'He got money.'

'He do?'

'Yeah.' The four-year-old reached into her baby brother's

Pamper and pulled out a handful of crack vials. 'This is like money. But you can only have one.'

The door slid open. As I stepped out an angry teenager reached past me into the elevator. With one hand she slapped the four-year-old, with the other she grabbed the toddler. 'What the *fuck* you doing? I *told* you I'd kick your ass.'

She examined the toddler's diapers. 'There's one missing. Is there one missing?'

She slapped the four-year-old. The child clung to her leg, whimpering. I knew I couldn't interfere. I tried walking nonchalantly past the bluecoats guarding the door.

'Miss . . . miss, where you think you're going?'

On Forty-second Street the party was still going on. A couple of teenagers in jeans that were so baggy they looked like skirts were showing each other dance moves. At first I didn't realize that the kid in the backward purple cap was Lucky. He was concentrating intensely on sucking a candy pacifier.

'Lucky!'

He blinked at me like an oversize infant.

'Miss, I asked you where you're going,' the young cop barked nervously.

'Home,' I said.

'Home?'

I noticed the one-armed reporter again. He was still standing outside the crime-scene barricade.

'You don't live here?' the cop was asking.

'No. I'm a social worker. I was looking for one of the kids I work with.'

'You got some kinda ID?'

I pulled out my wallet, my credit cards, and my driver's license.

'Sign this, please, and put your phone number.'

At the barricade the reporter intercepted me. 'How did you get in there?'

I paid him no mind. Lucky was gone. Next to the music and the dancers, the players and their marks huddled together talking about the murder.

'Somebody got thrown out the fucking window.'

'It's the sex killer.'

'The man didn't say that.'

'Like they're gonna tell us anything.'

'You lookin' to cop or not?'

'Me and my boy are getting down together.'

'I gotta add an extra charge, all these cops are a bidness hazard.'

'Aw, c'mon, this is a hassle. *You* should be the one giving *us customers* a discount.'

'You need to quit.'

'All right, let's walk.'

The small-time dealer and two white boys from Jersey walked up the block to make their transaction. The rest of the group stood there speculating.

'Who's next? You don't know that, do you? A lot of johns going berserk out here.'

'Maybe the killer got his eye on you.'

'Shut up, fool.'

'I'd still rather die high.'

'Word.'

They slapped each other five and joined in a belly laugh. Across the street, as motionless as a cigar-store Indian,

Colin leaned on a faded poster. Would an apology get him to tell me where Porsche had gone?

'Anna. Hey!' O'Shaugnessy's frustrated face appeared over the hood of his jalopy. 'Hey, Eltern, I'd like to leave.'

'Go ahead.'

He reached a large palm toward me. 'The keys.'

I had his car keys in my pocket. 'Ooops.' I tossed him the keys.

'What happened back there?' I asked.

'Can't talk now, Eltern. I gotta check in with the captain. Get in. I'll drop you off.'

'Who was it?'

'We don't know yet. Get in,' he growled. 'I gotta get back to the precinct to deal with the press.'

I told him I'd rather walk.

13

I was having coffee and reading the *New York Post*'s early edition. At the counter the Greek owner was fighting with the Puerto Rican cook for yelling at the Pakistani delivery boy. O'Shaugnessy was in the take-out line. I spread the *Post* in front of my face. A moment later his hand came over the top.

'Don't you return your calls?' he growled.

'The day just started.'

'For some of us it's over.' He slapped the *Post*.

It dropped on the table between us. He flipped to where a headline read: AIR-SHAFT BODY UNIDENTIFIED.

'Look, I need some help and you owe me that.'

'I don't owe you anything.'

'Well, then, you owe' – he gestured toward the street – 'them.'

'What's that got to do with you?'

'The girl they found in the alley wasn't carrying any ID.'

'Most of these kids don't carry anything.'

'You know so many of them, I thought you might recognize her.'

'Why me?'

He leaned across the table and I smelled his cologne. It wasn't bad, just too much. 'You could save us a lot of time. If we knew who she was, it might help us find her killer.'

'When? When does this have to happen?'

'You know the twenty-four rule. After twenty-four hours the leads turn cold.'

'Now?'

'Just say yes or no, Anna.'

In Manhattan those who die alone, or under 'suspicious circumstances,' are transported to the medical examiner's office on Thirty-fourth Street and First Avenue, which also houses the morgue. Inside, it was like a bus depot. People sat on benches waiting to identify someone they once knew, once loved, once were married to, or – worst of all – once gave birth to. They stared at their hands, their feet, the empty air in front of them. The cop at the security desk leafed through the *New York Post*. He looked up at us, bleary-eyed. O'Shaugnessy flashed his badge.

The cop picked up the phone. 'Officer O'Shaugnessy to see the ME.' He plunked the phone down and waved us in.

I listened to my footsteps and O'Shaugnessy's in the stuffy silence. An orderly dressed in green opened a door. 'Please follow me,' he said, blowing his nose. He had a cold.

We descended a small circular stairway. At the bottom the orderly sneezed, then opened another door. I smelled formaldehyde and disinfectant. A labyrinth of floor-to-ceiling steel drawers filled a network of corridors. The orderly pulled at a drawer with his foot. It slid open to reveal a woman's torso, slim, big-breasted, no head, no arms, no legs. A mutilated wax doll. As the orderly searched over his shoulder for my reaction, his teeth sank into something soft and wet.

O'Shaugnessy snarled, 'Cool it, buddy, we're not here for a sideshow.'

The orderly blew a chewing-gum bubble. He kicked the drawer shut. The bubble popped.

The orderly pushed another swinging door with his elbow. I smelled refrigerated flesh and blood.

In the room in front of us six cadavers lay on six slabs. Each cadaver had a live companion. Dressed like doctors, wearing plastic aprons and gloves, the companions spoke to the cadavers, softly. I heard the whir of a handsaw and bones cracking. It was a moment before I realized that the assistant MEs were talking into the microphones on their lapels. I recognized the graying man from the air shaft.

'Dr Stetson, Officer O'Shaugnessy's here,' the orderly said.

'Be right with you.' The ME was concentrating on the scalpel in his hand. Expertly he cut into a young woman's chin. There was no blood. The cadavers had already been drained. He peeled the pretty face back over the skull.

'The one you want is in the back,' he told O'Shaugnessy without looking up. 'We just brought her out.'

We walked to a seventh slab I hadn't noticed before. On it a thick green plastic tarp covered a lump that was smaller than the other cadavers. O'Shaugnessy wrapped his hand around my upper arm. Across from me, on the other side of the slab, stood the ME.

'Ready?' O'Shaugnessy asked me.

I said that I was. The ME pulled the tarp down. It was too late to change my mind. I tasted blood and formaldehyde.

Her face is gray porcelain but still perfect. Not a dead child but a work of art, a statue waiting for the breath of life. I put my hand on the cheek; it is hard and solid and cold. I touch the forehead. I bend and kiss Porsche one last time.

I whisper, 'She looks so perfect.'

The way the ME and O'Shaugnessy look at each other, I know the horror she suffered is hidden under the tarp, which remains tucked to her chin.

'The killer slit her throat with a box cutter and threw her out the window,' the ME says. 'She fell on her back. That's why she looks so good. She never even lost her wig. We placed the time of death around midnight on Saturday.'

O'Shaugnessy shoots him a silencing look. We go to the forensics museum, where we can talk.

'So it's a positive ID,' O'Shaugnessy repeated.

'Yes, but I don't know her name.'

'That's as good as nothing,' he said, studying the form he was filling out. 'Was she ever in your program?'

There were no windows in the room. I wondered how many regulations or laws I broke when I took Porsche home with me.

I said, 'Not really. She was a drop-in, but she never stayed. The kids call her Porsche.'

NIGHTSIDE

'That's all you have, a street name?'
'Yes.'
'Any idea where she was from?'
'No.'
'What did you know about her?'
'Nothing.'
'C'mon, Eltern, try a little harder.'
'She'd been in the street a couple of years already. I think she was about fifteen, but she said she was older.'

On a shelf in front of me, a fetus floated in formaldehyde. In other jars, a hand, a heart, a liver, a brain. Across the room, on the floor, bones were piled next to a collection of empty boxes. I looked into O'Shaugnessy's pity-filled eyes, and I hated his guts.

'What good are the cops anyway?' I demanded.
'We do what we can.'
'No, you don't. You talk a good game, but you don't give a damn. You don't even live in the neighborhoods where you work. You don't get interested until somebody's dead.'
'Look, I know it's hard,' he said gently.
'Don't patronize me, you . . . you self-righteous know-it-all!'
'Calling the kettle black, are we?' He tucked his pen behind his ear.
'You just pretend you care about these kids, and you stand by and watch them die. You'd rather clobber them with a nightstick than do the right thing.'
'You're a little off base, Eltern.' He sounded only mildly annoyed. That made me more mad. I started screaming.
'What do you do for these kids? What in God's name do you do for them?'

'Look, we're just the front line – we don't run the show any more than you do.'

'At least I *try*. I try to make a difference.'

'I wonder,' he said. 'I wonder how many of these girls are out there facing crazy johns with no protection at all because you've talked them into leaving their pimps.'

'Now you're defending the *pimps?*' I shrilled.

'I'm not defending anybody. I just happen to accept reality.'

'Reality! A badge and a fat paycheck while these children are victimized every goddamn day.'

'It's not so fat,' he said, 'and should we be taking the name of our Lord in vain?'

I pulled myself together. 'Where do you want me to sign?'

He took the pen from his ear. 'Right here.'

I went straight to the center to talk to Toomey and the kids. The priest was in his office sorting through a stack of invoices. He looked up at me over his bifocals. 'To what do I owe the pleasure?'

'There was another murder Saturday night. I'm about to talk to the kids. We also need to schedule some additional counseling sessions, group and individual.'

He sighed. 'Do you have to tell them?'

'I'm sure they already know. I think they'll need some additional support.'

He nodded. 'Not anybody we know, I hope.'

'She was a walk-in. I think she spent half a dozen nights with us over the last six months.'

'Has the press made the connection to us?'

'Not yet.'

'Maybe they won't.'

'Maybe. I just thought you should know.'

I went to the cafeteria, where the kids were just getting up from lunch. Snatches of conversation told me that they were in an uproar. No picture had been published yet, and everybody was worried the dead girl might be somebody they knew.

'If you guys wanna sit back down for a minute, I'd like to talk to you,' I said, taking off my jacket. Some of the kids grumbled that they had homework to do in the free period that followed lunch, but everybody sat back down.

'I'm sure you've all heard there was a fourth killing yesterday. It's a hard, sad time for us, and I want you all to know the staff is here for you. We're going to have a number of groups to talk about how we feel about what's going on out there in Hell's Kitchen and what we can do to protect ourselves, not just physically but psychologically.'

'Who was it, Anna? Do you know?'

There was a moment of tense silence. 'It was a girl some of you may have seen pass through here. She called herself Porsche.'

Somebody wailed. A wave of chatter went through the cafeteria. A couple of girls started crying. I sat down and let the news sink in. Kids began calling out questions, but I knew no more than they had read in the papers or seen on television. In a very few moments the consternation turned to anger.

'Where are the cops?' somebody called out.

'They don't care about people like us,' somebody yelled back.

'We gotta make 'em care. Go out there and demonstrate.'

'I think you need to give them a few days. It only happened yesterday,' I said.

'Yeah, but what about those other girls? The one who had her throat slashed in the peep show and the one murdered in the flop-house. The cops never found those guys either. If this was Park Avenue, they'd be on the case like white on rice.'

'I'm not saying we don't demonstrate, I'm just saying we need to wait a few days and see what happens. The cops don't even know her real name yet. Does anybody here know that, or where she was from?'

Juan stood up. 'Porsche had a stack of IDs an inch thick,' he said. 'One for every occasion. You know, those IDs you buy on the Strip. We went out for about a week last year, and she wouldn't even tell *me* her real name.'

A pretty blond girl named Dina, who had come into the program only two weeks before, said, 'She was wild. She was trying to organize the working girls and get them to walk out on their pimps. The pimps were mad as hell.'

Juan sat next to me. He touched my hand. 'Can we have a service for her?'

'I think we have to wait until we know her name.'

'We don't need her name to show that we cared about her. Just something on the sidewalk by where it happened.'

I thought of Porsche's spunk, her readiness to defend the other working girls, and I choked up. I agreed to take whoever wanted to go to Forty-second Street after dinner that night. We would light candles and say a prayer. The kids went off to their classes. I went to my office. I looked up Elisabeth Kübler-Ross's stages of grief. I typed them up. I made copies. For the kids, I thought. For them.

The rest of the afternoon I spent revising the proposal for Beardsley's committee. My mind kept wandering. The moments before I had thrown Porsche out came back to me with heartbreaking clarity. If only I had listened to her pleas. If only . . . if only.

At eight o'clock on the street they call the 'Deuce,' life was bustling as if no losses had been suffered. On the sidewalk in front of the air shaft HOW MANY MORE was written in a childish scrawl. Juan and fifteen other kids placed votive candles around the question, and we joined hands. Linda, Theresa, and Dina read poems. After that we prayed. I said the Serenity Prayer because it was the only prayer left I could say. I asked that we learn to care for each other. The kids spoke more directly, as if Porsche were there and could hear them. They told her they were sorry for what happened to her, and that they were angry at her for staying out in the streets. They were angry, too, at the cops.

That gave me an idea. After we finished, I suggested the kids buy some fake IDs. Selling the IDs was supposed to be illegal. More than once the attorney general's office had tried to shut down the booths in the novelty stores that sold the laminated cards with the seal of the college of your choice. We made our way up the Deuce and on to the Strip. The kids went into the stores in groups of twos and threes, and every single one of them managed to buy a fake ID. I collected them all.

'The IDs prove the cops ain't doing their job,' Juan said.

'Actually it's not the cops who are in charge of regulating IDs,' I said. 'It's the mayor and the attorney general. The cops would probably love it if those ID booths were shut down. Fake IDs just make their job a lot harder.'

'So now that we've proved they're not shut down, what do we do? Call a press conference, embarrass City Hall into doing its job?'

'Let me think about it,' I said.

We had just turned the corner onto Broadway when Colin came running out of Playland. A plainclothes cop pursued him. Colin ran toward me. Behind me I heard the wail of a patrol-car siren. The car screeched up onto the sidewalk, its spinning turret covering the startled pedestrians in a red glow. The doors flew open, and two cops got out clutching their nightsticks. I recognized them from the precinct house, one rookie fresh from the academy and one old-timer. Russell and Jones.

Jones caught Colin and threw him onto the sidewalk. He hit him with his nightstick. Russell stood watching. The kids rushed forward. Jones pulled his gun on them.

I yelled, 'Stop ... stop ... for God's sake stop that.'

Jones picked Colin up and tossed him toward the squad car. He took Colin by the roots of his long hair and smashed his face down onto the hood.

I screamed, 'You don't have to hurt him!'

Russell cuffed Colin and tossed him into the backseat of the squad car.

'Easy does it, Miss Eltern,' Jones said. 'This kid just tore up half the machines in Playland and smashed a couple of people's faces in.'

'This is police brutality.'

'He was resisting arrest.'

The cops got into the squad car, and they sped off in a wash of sirens and lights. A couple of kids ran after them. I stood there panting, unable to catch my breath. The kids came back, demanding angrily, 'What you gonna do, Annie?'

'You've got to do something. They're fucking Colin up bad.'

We rushed to the center, a confused and angry group. The kids wanted to go to the precinct and protest.

'I'll take care of it,' I promised. 'I'll call Officer O'Shaugnessy. He's one of them. He can make sure Colin's all right.'

I beeped O'Shaugnessy, using his emergency code, and went back to the storefront. I was waiting for him behind the gate when he got out of his car and came to the door. He looked tired and mad.

'I'm off duty,' he growled.

'Two of your guys just beat up one of my kids and took him in.'

'Is this another opportunity for you to attack me?'

I ate crow. 'No – I really need your help.'

'Do I know this kid?'

'It's the preppy you gave me before.'

'Little Lord Fauntleroy?'

'Yes.'

'Was he resisting arrest?'

'They said he was, but he wasn't armed or anything.'

'Unlock the lock,' he said. 'This is no way to talk.'

'Can you come around? The padlock's broken.'

I opened the door to the hallway. With little street and no

artificial light, he looked like a grizzly giant. Hair even shadowed the back of his hands.

'I'll call in and tell them this is a kid I've got my eye on. That way you can be sure he's safe tonight. Okay?'

He stepped in. As we stood across from each other in the dark storefront, his eyes said that he felt the emptiness, the absence of kids, and the knowledge that at least one would now never come back.

'You all right?' he asked.

'Yeah.'

'You want me to get that broken lock off?'

I nodded stupidly.

I sat in my window alcove as he went to the trunk of his car. He came back with a triangular steel file. He sawed at the lock until it opened.

'Thanks a lot,' I said. As I pulled the gate back I asked, 'So you'll call about the kid?'

'Isn't that what I just said?'

Inside the storefront the phone was ringing. 'Go ahead,' O'Shaugnessy said bitterly. 'I'm outta here.'

As he pulled out I picked up my phone. The voice on the other end made my heart flutter.

'Hi, it's James. I just wondered how you were doing.'

'There was another murder.'

'That's terrible,' he said. Then, after a pause, 'You working on the proposal?'

'Trying to.'

'The committee's bringing hearings to New York soon. I'll be in and out of the city to set up the office. Maybe I can stop by.'

'That would be good.'

'When the hearings get going we'll light a fire under the NYPD and get some action on these murders. What do you think?'

'I suppose,' I said. The hollowness of my own voice was very scary.

Later that night I went down to criminal court on Center Street to see if I could get Colin remanded to the program. He wasn't on the docket yet. After a sleepless night I tried again. In 1991 the Court of Appeals, New York State's highest court, had ruled that a defendant must appear in court for arraignment within twenty-four hours of being arrested. But the law didn't always work. Colin was lost in the system.

14

In the gutter the wind played with an empty soda can. It scratched a hollow tune over a sprinkling of crack vial caps. I climbed the steps into the grim bulk of the criminal-court building. With its ziggurat-shaped towers and cast-aluminum detail, it housed all the misery of the world's largest round-the-clock criminal court. I stepped into the revolving door.

Shifts were changing. Weary defense lawyers, prosecutors, cops, court officers, stenographers, and Spanish-English translators staggered toward the exits. The art-deco lobby towered over prostitutes in Spandex and spikes. Teenage token suckers propped baggy limbs on the grime-engraved marble walls. Pickpockets, three-card monte players, and small-time shoplifters lurked among the pillars. At the concession stand that offered newspapers and sweets, a man in a robe and fez purchased a candy bar for his veiled lady. A pimp with pomaded curls rocked on his heels, watching them.

I stepped up to the metal detector and placed my purse on the conveyor belt. The uniformed guard fingered around inside it. A female court officer patted me down, then waved me through. I headed down the hall toward the arraignment court. Ahead of me a cop shuttled a greasy, cuffed prisoner toward the holding pens behind the courtrooms. Defense lawyers and prosecutors haggled over plea bargains. The place seemed oppressively silent. I tasted the mixed emotions of helplessness and hope.

Outside the courtroom women young and old checked the list of cases taped to the wall. Women dressed in their best, women holding crying babies, women chasing restless toddlers, bleary-eyed women preparing to fight a system they didn't understand on behalf of loved ones they couldn't keep in line. Colin's name was on the list. I was happily surprised.

Nervous human hands had oiled the padded courtroom door in sweat. I pushed it open. In the light that filtered through windows opaque with soot, the room seemed as two-dimensional as a faded sepia photograph. The floor stuck to my feet. I sat down in a pew. Ossified chewing gum decorated the wood where the faithful had used penknives to etch their names.

Spectators and perpetrators were separated by a wooden balustrade. A cardboard sign warned:

> BEYOND THIS POINT OFFICERS
> MUST SHOW SHIELD AND ID.

The other side of the balustrade was heavily populated by court officers, legal-aid staff, police officers, district attorney's staff, the court reporter, and the official court interpreter. At a podium in front of the bench, a stately black woman in a red power suit studied the contents of the folders that represented the morning's cases. Her concentration was intense.

The legal-aid desk was more casual. Seven men and women in corduroy and tweed restlessly waited for the court day to begin. The men invariably wore their top shirt button open, and the women in cheap suits wore no makeup. I went up to the balustrade.

'Excuse me . . . I'd like to speak to Colin Winklesworth's lawyer.'

'The cases will be assigned as they come up, ma'am.'

'When do you think he'll come up?'

'There's no particular order. Take a seat. We'll let whoever catches the case know you're waiting.'

I sat down again in the second row. The first row was reserved for attorneys and police officers. Except for a young wife mutely rocking on her heavy haunches, the pews were still empty.

I watched the ADA's hands open and close the folders that were the heart of the proceedings about to commence. Yellow covers for felonies, blue for misdemeanors. I wondered which folder was Colin's. It would be thin – his paper trail had just begun. Each folder had a companion folder on the legal-aid table. If the case was big enough, legal aid might actually spend five minutes with the defendant. But the assistant district attorney had only one job – reading the charges. She would lay eyes on the defendant only once. Prosecutions would be assigned to other assistant district attorneys later.

In front of me three female police officers flexed their muscles, examined their manicured fingernails, and traded courtroom gossip as they unwrapped their bagels and Danish. The young woman next to me wiped a tear from her cheek and leaned forward. 'Please – where will I be able to pay the bail bondsman?'

'Honey, do you know your man is gonna make bail?'

'It's his first offense.'

'Well, don't be jumping the gun. Wait and see what happens.'

Mothers, sisters, girlfriends, and children began to stream through the big oak doors at the side of the room. They crowded the pews. Soon we were joined by police officers, detectives, defense lawyers, and the reporter with the missing arm. What was he doing there?

At nine forty-five the judge appeared from the robing room behind the courtroom. It had been a long time since his tired but kind face had seen the sun. His robe flowed around him like black water. Two armed court officers accompanied him to the bench. He sat down in front of the soiled American flag. Over his head gold-leaf letters proclaimed IN OD WE RUST.

The court officer began his chant: 'All rise! All persons having business before this Honorable Court draw near, give attention, and ye shall be heard. The Honorable Judge Saul Abramson presiding. Take seats, put away all reading material. There will be absolutely no talking. AR-one is now in session.'

The courtroom quieted. A door in the wood paneling behind the bench opened. For an instant I saw the green walls and the prison bars of the holding pens. A court officer brought out the first group of prisoners. They sat on a bench along the wall. Colin was not among them.

Another court officer called the first case on the docket. A frail old man was brought to stand before the judge.

The ADA snatched a file and began reading the charges.

'The defendant was charged with stealing an oat-bran muffin from Zaro's in Grand Central.'

Legal Aid rubbed the stubble on his face. 'Your Honor, this man was hungry. His only crime is poverty.'

The defendant pleaded guilty to petit larceny and was sentenced to time served.

For the next few hours this three-minute scene was repeated endlessly. One by one the court officers succumbed to the monotony and nodded out. I had just caught my own head falling forward when I saw Colin in the group of prisoners shuffling out from the holding pens. He was barely recognizable. In his bruised face his eyes were slits. His clothes were ripped and vomit-splattered. One of the legal aids leaned toward me over the balustrade. She was somewhere in her twenties, but her long hair was striped gray. The cheap rings on every finger set off the plastic Swatch around her wrist. She held an open folder.

'My name is Rhoda Bluestone. I represent Colin . . . I understand he's with your program.'

'Yes, he's a client of mine, and I'm willing to take him back if you can get the judge to agree.'

She pushed the hair off her face to see me better. 'Are you sure this is the kid you hope to walk out with? There's no mention here that he's a client of yours.'

'He had just been remanded to me by the public-affairs officer in Manhattan South. We hadn't even had time to process the paperwork when this happened.'

'The community-affairs officer *said* you could have this kid back?'

'Not exactly.'

'Well, what exactly *did* he say?'

The bridge officer called out, 'Colin Winklesworth.'

'We'll talk later.' She headed for the bench and stood next to Colin. I could no longer see their faces. The ritual began.

'Docket ending in three seven three, Colin Winklesworth the Third charged with one twenty-five twenty-five on the presworn affidavit of Officer Jones. Counsel waives reading of the rights and charges?'

'So waived.'

One twenty-five twenty-five was not a charge I was familiar with. It was a while before I began to understand what I was hearing.

'Notices by the people.'

'Your honor, grand-jury notice and statement notice. In substance the defendant stated to the police officer before rights in the radio car, "I'm sorry, I'm so sorry. She didn't have to die. I loved her." Later, in the precinct house, he signed a confession.'

The judge's eyes rested on the ADA. 'I'll hear you on bail.'

'Your Honor, this is a homicide case. Deceased was raped and thrown from a five-story window. This is an extremely heinous crime. The defendant has made an admission of guilt, and we're asking for the defendant to be remanded.'

The judge's eyes moved to the legal-aid attorney. 'Counsel, I'll hear you.'

Rhoda Bluestone tossed her hair back. 'Your Honor, my client has never been arrested for anything before but loitering. He grew up in the city. He lives with his family here, a good family. He has never had any serious conflicts with the law. He knew the deceased, but he did not commit this crime. We're sure he'll be vindicated, and we would ask you to set bail in this case and not remand my client. The family would be able to post substantial bail here should the court be inclined to set bail. The only evidence appears to be my client's statement in the radio car that he loved the deceased, and a coerced confession. As Your Honor can see, an eight-hour interrogation without the advice of counsel makes this confession highly questionable.'

'Your Honor, that's not the only evidence. There's a palm print, and the defendant was seen exiting the building. He cold-bloodedly watched from across the street as the dead girl's body was carried out of the alley.'

'Your Honor, these witnesses were not witnesses to the crime, and according to the information we have, they did not see the crime being committed—'

'I've heard enough argument,' the judge interrupted. 'Ms Bluestone, I'm going to remand your client to Part F for this Friday. That's one eighty eighty.'

The officer standing behind Colin put his arm on Colin's elbow. As Colin turned to go his eyes met mine. He rushed toward me. The officer grabbed him by the shirt. Colin reached across the balustrade. Thick tears rolled down his bruised face.

'I'm sorry,' he cried. 'I'm sorry.'

The court officers grabbed Colin. Horrified, I watched them disappear into the pens behind the wall.

'Hey, hey. What did he say to you?' I heard somebody ask.

It was the one-armed reporter with the pad around his neck.

'My name is Mike Taylor. I'm covering this story for the *Post*.'

I got up and headed for the exit. Rhoda Bluestone followed me. 'I thought you said you were here to help this kid.'

'I don't see how I can. I thought he got busted for breaking some video machines.'

She smacked the courtroom door with her palm. It swung open. Someone else was keeping pace with us. Something fleshy bounced between us. The faster I walked, the faster it bounced. Once or twice it hit my arm.

'I heard you say that Colin Winklesworth was enrolled in your program,' Mike Taylor said.

I didn't stop.

'Call me later,' the legal aid said, shoving a card at me. I took it. She went back to the courtroom. I continued toward the exit to the street.

In the pandemonium of the hallway, B-boys swaggered, pimps squabbled with their whores, ambulance chasers searched for misery that could afford them, and mothers wept. O'Shaugnessy stood talking to a reporter. As I passed by him I whispered, 'You could have told me.'

'What were you doing at the crime scene?' Taylor demanded, sticking close.

'I'd be happy to answer any questions about the case,' O'Shaugnessy told Taylor.

'I'm asking *her*.'

I pushed my way through the parade of losers and hangers-on that crowded the hallway. Taylor stayed on my heels.

'If you have any questions about Manhattan South cases, that's what I'm here for,' O'Shaugnessy called after him.

'Why won't you talk to me?' Taylor asked.

'These kids are underage,' I said. 'Our records are confidential.'

'Colin is eighteen,' he said.

I left the building by the backdoor. Taylor followed. I stood for a moment watching the bustle of Chinatown. Taylor ran in front of me.

'Just tell me what kind of kid he is—'

I walked around him.

He called down the steps after me: 'Hey, Eltern – is that a no-comment?'

15

'That's nuts.' Juan shook his head. 'Colin's an asshole, but he's no killer.'

'He confessed.'

'Sure, after they beat the shit out of him.'

In the center, opinions were divided. The guys agreed Colin was innocent. But some of the girls who had seen his violent outbursts weren't so sure. Maybe Colin blew up only around those who were weaker than he was.

'We have to help Colin,' Juan said.

'What if he did it?' Dina said angrily. 'He smoked a lot of crack. He mighta did it.'

The kids ambled off to class, still mumbling among themselves. They were confused.

Juan lingered after the others. 'We miss you, Anna,' he said. 'It's different when you're not around. We're always writing reports.'

Father Toomey stuck his head in. 'Your group is waiting for you, Juan. Being on time is part of being responsible.'

'See you later.' Juan smiled at me and backed out the door. Toomey stepped in.

'Juan complaining about the new progress reports?' Toomey asked casually.

'Are they really necessary?'

'We're going for a broader funding base. We have to generate some paperwork around here.'

'It's humiliating to ask a kid to write when he hasn't learned yet. Wouldn't it be better to teach him rather than to discourage him?'

The intercom buzzed. I picked up the phone. It was Danielle, one of our graduates. We had hired her as our receptionist while she went to City College at night.

'Anna, there's a Ms Bluestone for you. She said "Ms," *not* "miss."'

'Thanks, Danielle. Tell her I'm in a meeting.'

I slammed the phone down harder than I meant to. Then I told Toomey about Colin's arrest, the murder charge.

'Well, that's a relief,' he said. 'At least the police won't be poking around here.'

'A lot of the kids don't believe he's guilty.'

'Oh, so now we're in the business of second-guessing the police, too.'

He stepped out of my office as casually as he had stepped in. I remembered Colin's tearful face in the courtroom. I remembered his rage when I had asked him to change the television channel. Had he killed Porsche in a fit of rage? All that day I turned that question over and over in my mind. I was still running that mental treadmill later that evening when James Beardsley knocked on the storefront door.

'I'm in town to set up for the hearings. I hope you don't mind my dropping in.'

'Come in.'

We sat together in the storefront's small reception area. I

couldn't think of anything to say. He opened his briefcase combination lock. It clicked loudly. 'I brought you a sample proposal,' he said. 'The deadline is this Friday.'

'Coffee?' I suggested.

'That'd be great.'

'Come inside. I'll show you the changes I've made on my proposal.'

We had barely started our coffee when O'Shaugnessy tapped his fingers on the windowpane. I opened the door. 'I'm closed,' I told him.

He stepped past me. 'Your lights are on.'

In his hands he held a rolled piece of paper. I whispered, 'The guy inside is from the committee in Washington. Watch what you say.'

Beardsley was reading the newsletter written by the kids. He got to his feet when we came in. O'Shaugnessy glared at him until I said, 'James, meet Officer O'Shaugnessy, the precinct's community-affairs officer. He's sent quite a few kids our way.'

'James Beardsley. Pleased to meet you.'

O'Shaugnessy sat down, ignoring Beardsley's outstretched hand. 'I hear your committee's coming to New York.'

'Yes. Yes, we are.'

'That should be a media circus.'

There was an uncomfortable silence. I told O'Shaugnessy, 'Mr Beardsley wants to understand our problems here in this community. Last week I gave him a tour of Times Square and the Strip.'

O'Shaugnessy ignored what I had said and unrolled the paper in his hand. 'I just came by to bring you this. Our artist did a pretty good job, I think.'

It was a drawing of Porsche. O'Shaugnessy put it into Beardsley's hand. It seemed to tremble there.

'The mystery girl?' Beardsley asked.

'I see you're informed.'

'Am I right that this is the fourth murder since July?'

'You're right.'

'Is the NYPD too busy to clean up Times Square?'

'Is that a rhetorical question?'

'You don't have to be rude, O'Shaugnessy. Mr Beardsley is professionally concerned.'

'No offense, but everybody's an amateur detective and it's rarely helpful.' O'Shaugnessy's face was red. 'But this drawing could help us learn who the victim was.'

Beardsley gave the drawing back to O'Shaugnessy. 'I'd better be going.'

'You haven't had your coffee,' I said. 'We haven't looked at the proposal.'

'You're busy. We'll talk.'

'Thanks for stopping by.'

'I'll fit you in Friday at one o'clock, Anna. Bring your disk with you in case we need to make any last-minute adjustments. Deal?'

'Great.' I smiled, anxious for Beardsley to leave before O'Shaugnessy attacked him again.

O'Shaugnessy gave Beardsley a casual salute. I stepped out to the sidewalk with him. His car and driver waited at the curb. I watched them pull away before going back in. O'Shaugnessy hadn't moved. I went past him to the kitchen and started rinsing the coffee cups Beardsley and I had used. He got up and followed me.

'You got something against me?' he demanded.

'Of course not.'

I rinsed the few dishes in the sink.

'Why so angry?' O'Shaugnessy asked.

There were no dishes left to wash. I started scrubbing a pan that wasn't dirty. Behind me he began slapping the drawing of Porsche into his palm.

'Could you stop that?' I snapped.

'I'll stop if you stop.'

'What exactly is it you want?'

'I'm concerned about you, Eltern. You seemed awfully frantic down at Center Street today.'

'A *Post* reporter was hounding me. If you had told me the kid was charged with murder, I wouldn't have been there in the first place. It's bad press for the program.'

'Nobody expects you to succeed with every kid.'

Right then and there I should have told him what was really bothering me. That the very night of the murder I had thrown both these kids out. But I didn't.

'You should be breathing a little easier now that there's been an arrest,' he said.

'I'm not so sure you've got the right guy.'

'Don't be ridiculous. *We* got the right guy.'

To get away from him, I sat in the window alcove. Millie had put a lace curtain over the window as if we were back in the Poland of her youth. We watched the activity across the street. Kids were getting in and out of cars with Jersey plates.

'So much blind self-abuse,' he said.

Feeling his eyes on me, I folded my arms over my chest.

Across the street, business had really picked up. The

video store had added a motor-scooter delivery service. Probably to the hotel trade.

'Why doesn't New York's Finest shut that place down?'

'Is Mr Ivy League your type?'

'Don't be ridiculous. Our relationship is professional.'

He sat down next to me. 'What profession?'

I reached over to slap him, but he caught my hand midair. A controlled anger sparkled in his pupils. 'I thought you said you were nonviolent.'

I whispered, 'I'm sorry,' and fought back tears.

I was falling apart, and there was nothing I could do about it. He released my hand and got up.

'You're just like these kids, Eltern. He's rich, that makes him *nice*.'

'Your mind is in the gutter.'

'We work in the gutter, you and I. And we've been doing it a long time. Let's try to get along.'

'*We* don't work together. We're on opposite sides of the fence.'

He stroked the shadow of a beard that always seemed to be growing on his face. 'The kids you've had the most success with are the ones you got from me.'

'Only because they've seen the inside and it scares 'em.'

'Like I said, we've been successful together.'

'I'm not successful. I'm sinking. James Beardsley can get my program federal funding. James Beardsley can save my kids.'

'So you gave the bastard the tour. They love stuff like that. Him and all the other voyeurs in Washington.'

'What's that supposed to mean?'

'All these DC types are alike. They love an issue till they

get a media hit. Then they're gone. But you don't see that, of course. You don't see past the Boston accent and the thousand-dollar suit.'

'James Beardsley is just as sincere as I am . . . as you used to be.'

With three fingers O'Shaugnessy pulled the curtain back to expose the action in the street. 'You're always setting yourself apart from me.' He pulled the .38 from his shoulder holster. 'Is it because I carry this?'

'Cut the dramatics, O'Shaugnessy. I'm just tap dancing to raise the funds to survive.'

'That makes you a lot like these kids,' he said, gesturing at the scene outside the video store. 'They're just dancing as fast as they can.'

16

The next morning there was a clunker not unlike mine parked in the no-parking zone in front of the storefront. As soon as I stepped onto the sidewalk, the driver jumped out.

'Can I talk with you?' It was Rhoda Bluestone, Colin's legal-aid attorney.

I nodded at her car. 'They'll tow you.'

She said crisply, 'Not if we're in it,' and opened the passenger door. I slipped in next to her. Several newspapers lay on the floor. Colin was on the front page of most of them.

PREPPY RUNAWAY CHARGED WITH MYSTERY GIRL'S MURDER

A prep-school dropout was charged today with the brutal murder of a teenage runaway whose identity remains unknown, according to authorities. Colin Winklesworth III has been disowned by his well-known family. The eighteen-year-old was represented at his arraignment by legal-aid attorney Rhoda J. Bluestone.

'Winklesworth refuses to talk to me,' she said.

I shifted my briefcase off my foot. My head was throbbing.

'Maybe you could get him to open up,' she said.

St Christopher, dangling from her rearview mirror, twisted around himself. I unwound the string from which he hung. 'You Catholic?' I asked her.

'Jewish. I don't have the heart to get rid of him. He came with the car.'

'Superstitious?'

'This case is a bitch,' she said.

There was a long silence as she tortured her lower lip with her sharp little teeth. 'Look,' she said, 'I got you a temporary ID. If you're willing to say you're my assistant, I can get you into Rikers. I think he'll talk to you.'

'Isn't that illegal?'

'You don't help people by sticking to the rules.'

Even though I was no longer sure that was true, I said I would go with her.

When his fingers touched mine, he dropped forward onto the table, trying to swallow the sobs that shook him.

Rhoda watched him for a moment, then said: 'Colin, I can't defend you if you won't talk to me.'

Through a window in the door, the guard watched dispassionately.

'What happened that night?' I asked him.

Nearby some bars clanged shut. I recalled Porsche, just a young girl covering her terrible need for love and acceptance with a brashness that wasn't always pleasant, caring for small, helpless creatures the way she desperately wanted to be cared for.

Colin raised his tearstained face. 'I don't know why I did that to her.'

Rhoda shook her head. 'I want to help you, Colin. But I can't help you unless you help me. What happened the night the girl was killed?'

'It's hard . . .' he said.

Rhoda lit a cigarette for him. 'Walk me through it,' she said.

He wiped his face on his sleeve. 'We were hanging out in Lucky's apartment.'

'Lucky who?' Rhoda asked.

'Irish Lucky. Anna knows him. She introduced me to him that night at the storefront. The night you brought Porsche's kitten to the precinct. You still got that kitten?'

'Yes, I do.'

He swallowed a whimper when I said that.

'Then what?' Rhoda asked gently.

'When Toomey threw us out, we all snuck into Lucky's grandmother's apartment. She's in the hospital.'

I asked, 'Who's "we all"?'

'Lucky, Eclipse, me.'

'What about Porsche?'

'She wasn't in the storefront that night.'

'How did she wind up at Lucky's apartment?'

'I introduced her to Lucky the night you threw us out. She paid Lucky a few dollars to let her use the place to meet a john. Some regular of hers. Then me and her were gonna use the rest of the money she made to go to New Mexico.'

'New Mexico?'

'It was my idea. She said she'd go with me, but only if we

had a wad of cash to start out with. She said she couldn't go without money.'

'Who was this john?'

He shrugged. 'She wouldn't tell us. It was private, her private thing. She told us she'd meet us at the park when he left. Me and Lucky went to Forty-seventh Street and got down on some crack. After a few hits I started to get crazy jealous of whoever this guy was. I went back to Lucky's building and hung out across the street waiting for him to come out. But he didn't come out. A long time later I went up. I thought it was a long time, but Officer Green said it was just a coupla minutes. I don't remember killing her, but the polygraph said I did.'

He stared down at his hands. 'Do you know what happened to my guitar?'

'I'll find out ... Colin, the cops are saying you confessed.'

'I do remember there was a lot of blood, but I didn't see Porsche.' He rubbed a finger across his brow. 'Officer Green told me I probably blacked out from the crack, and that's why I don't remember what I did to her. He said if I could remember, they could get me help. I need help.'

'I know you do, Colin.'

'Does my mom know I'm here?'

'Do you want me to talk to her?'

'I don't know how I could do that to Porsche. I don't know if they can help me. Maybe they should electrocute me.'

Rhoda and I followed the corrections officer through hallways, checkpoints, guard huts, electronically operated bars, and finally we came to the exit gate. A silent prisoner traveled with us, pushing a food cart. On his head he wore the thigh portion of a pair of panty hose.

Back in the car Rhoda turned the key in the ignition, then leaned back and sighed. 'They interrogated that kid for something like eight hours. They gave him a polygraph and said it showed he was lying. He doesn't know whether he's coming or going.'

'How could they get away with that?'

She shrugged. 'His parents hung up on them, and he didn't ask for counsel.'

'Did they give him Miranda?'

'Oh, yeah. They're not crazy.'

'Do you have his parents' address?'

'Of course, but they won't talk to me either.'

'I want to give them a try.'

'His mother's name is Bendix now. She remarried when Colin was about four.' Rhoda drove me to the address and dropped me off.

I climbed the steps. There was only one name over the bell – 'Bendix,' in beautiful gold script. I rang. The chime echoed back to me from deep within the house. An elderly Latina opened the door.

'Mrs Bendix, please.'

She stepped back, letting me into the vestibule with its ceramic umbrella stand. The hardwood floor gleamed beneath my feet. 'Are you expected?'

'Yes,' I lied.

'Mrs Bendix will be back from the hair salon any moment. Come in, please.'

I followed her up the narrow stairway with the rosewood banister. The wood was so soft, a fingernail could leave its mark. Still, its sheen was immaculate. We came to two large rooms divided by columns. The ceilings were as high as a temple.

'Can I get you something to drink?'

'I'm fine, thanks.'

'Please sit down.' She pointed to the enormous art-deco couch. I sat. She left. A million dollars in modern art hung on the walls. I got up and walked to the wide expanse of windows that opened onto a wrought-iron balcony. In the courtyard below, a statue stood in the center of a fountain. I watched the water cascade until I heard footsteps behind me.

She was a small, well-manicured woman wearing a black Chanel suit and shoes that cost more than my entire wardrobe. Her short blond hair fell into a pageboy, and her makeup was so perfectly applied, you couldn't see it. You just knew it was there. A French manicure outlined her fingernails. She exuded a fragile sexuality. Colin was a taller male version of her.

'Doris tells me I am expecting you?' she said sharply, but her voice was too thin to be intimidating.

'I'm sorry. I lied. I just wanted to be sure you'd see me.'

'Why?' She took a cigarette case from her Gucci bag. 'What charity do you represent?' Obviously this had happened to her before.

'My name is Anna Eltern. I have a program for runaways.'

She studied the clasp on the case. 'Is this about Colin?'

'I'm afraid it is.'

'You have no right to barge in here, Miss Eltern. Please leave.' Even angry, she stayed polite.

'If I could just talk to you—'

She picked up an intercom phone. 'Jack, can you come down here? We have an intruder.'

An attractive man in an elegant hand-sewn Italian suit came into the room. He studied me as if I were a rodent. She lit a cigarette. 'Honey, this is Miss Eltern. She's here about Colin.'

He inserted a finger under his collar.

'Ms Eltern, this is my husband, Jack Bendix.'

Bendix's blue eyes were hard as marbles. 'What exactly does it have to do with you?' he asked.

'The truth is I threw Colin out of my program and I feel terribly guilty. If I hadn't put him back out on the street, he might not be in this trouble now. I just saw him an hour ago at Rikers Island, and he's in bad shape. He asked for you.'

Jack Bendix raised an eyebrow and sighed. Then he headed for the bar and began to make himself a martini. He looked at his wife. 'What are you having, sweetheart?'

Their eyes met in a moment of anguish that all the glitter in the room did not overshadow.

'Surprise me,' she said weakly.

'If you were behind Colin, he could probably get bail and get help,' I offered.

'Why are you do-gooders always so pushy?' Bendix slammed his glass on the bar and stalked out.

Mrs Bendix dragged on her cigarette nervously; her eyes were moist.

I said, 'This must be awfully hard for you.'

When Bendix came back, he had taken his jacket off. In his hand he carried a bulging manila folder. He dropped the folder on the couch next to me. 'Here are the bills and correspondence from therapists, teachers, and institutions that felt compelled to throw Colin out, Ms Eltern. You weren't the first. He went to the finest schools, the top rehabilitation facilities, you name it.'

'We tried everything.' Colin's mother picked up the drink her husband had mixed.

'Mona's health was almost wrecked. We have two other children. I refuse to let Colin destroy this family.'

A boy about Domingo's age came running up the stairs. 'Mom, Mom, I got the part in the school play!' He stopped when he saw me. 'Oh.'

'Danny, this is Ms Eltern.'

He came toward me to offer his hand. We shook formally. That obligation fulfilled, the boy turned to his father. 'Dad . . . Dad, it's the lead.'

'That's great, son. As soon as Ms Eltern leaves, we'll celebrate with an ice-cream sundae. How does Rumpelmayer's sound?'

Danny's face lit up; he looked at me hopefully.

At Eden House Mike Taylor, the *Post* reporter, was leaning over Rich Cannon's desk when I walked into the recreation area. 'Well, when do you expect her?' he was asking Rich.

I was contemplating my getaway when he turned. 'Well, well,' Taylor said. 'Speak of the devil.'

I tried walking past him, but he stepped between me

and the inner door. 'We have it from two independent sources that the mystery girl and her killer were in your program.'

'You can't keep harassing me like this. I have a job to do.'

'So do I.'

Curious kids were casting glances through the Plexiglas wall.

'You're upsetting our kids.'

'I'm just asking for your comment.'

'We abide by the confidentiality rules that apply to minors. And I told you that before.'

'Winklesworth is eighteen, and nobody knows how old the girl was.'

I pushed past him into the dayroom, where he couldn't follow. As soon as I got inside, I was surrounded by kids. They were in an uproar. For a moment the reporter stood there watching me through the transparent wall. The kids stared him down. They pushed their noses against the Plexiglas and made monkey gestures. Taylor's face reddened. Finally he gave up and walked out. Rich Cannon was trying not to laugh.

'I hope you know what you're doing!' A furious Toomey emerged from his office.

The room fell silent. The priest, who was usually smooth as ice, was ruffled.

'You can't alienate the press and expect to survive,' he snapped.

I walked into his office and gestured him inside. When he followed, I closed the door.

'You have to blow up in front of the kids?'

He sat down behind his desk to reestablish authority and fingered his paperwork nervously.

'Relax,' I said. 'I had nothing to say to that reporter.'

'I saw the circus out there.'

'That couldn't be helped. The kids are anxious. They're gonna act out.'

'You encourage that, Anna. How many times has the board asked you to observe some clinical protocol rather than this intensely personal approach, which can only backfire? And believe me, it will backfire.'

'Both those kids were turned out by us when Open Intake was suspended.'

'Does the media know that?'

'Is that all you're concerned about?'

'What kind of documentation is there?'

'Just our own and the memories of the other kids, of course.'

That calmed him. He said, 'I'm not letting the press at these kids. When and if we do decide to talk, I can defend suspending Open Intake. Given the budget cuts, we had no choice.'

I went back to my office to put the finishing touches on the proposal revisions for the committee in Washington, but I couldn't concentrate. Why did I keep antagonizing Toomey when I was so vulnerable myself? Why hadn't I told him the truth? How long before Colin told? I pushed the proposal aside. It was four-thirty. O'Shaugnessy would be in his after-hours office at the Blarney Stone. I decided to tell him what had happened that night when I threw Colin and Porsche out of my apartment.

The bar brimmed with people, chatter, music, laughter,

cigarettes, and booze. O'Shaugnessy sat by the phone in the back. As I approached him I was struck by his attempt to hide his surprise. His friends at the bar were surprised, too. O'Shaugnessy introduced me.

'Gentlemen, this is my friend Anna Eltern.'

A cluster of friendly Irish faces greeted me. They seemed to assume that I was his girlfriend, so they left us alone.

'Buy you a drink?' O'Shaugnessy asked.

'Thanks.'

'Have a seat. Stout okay?'

'Fine.'

O'Shaugnessy flagged the bartender.

I had never visited him here before. He didn't know what to say to me, and I didn't know where to begin. After a few tries that led nowhere, he started talking to his buddies again. By the time my stout arrived, he was leading a chorus of 'Danny Boy.' I sipped my stout, watching him in the mirror behind the bar. In the mirror's angle his features softened and he became good-looking, in a crazy way.

'How we doin'?' he asked, when the ballad was done.

'I have to talk to you.'

The guy on the next bar stool listened intently. O'Shaugnessy picked up our glasses and led me to a booth. 'Did you know about the eight-hour interrogation?' I asked.

'Not while it was happening. I was off.'

'I haven't seen anything about the interrogation in the papers.'

He smiled. 'I'm good at what I do. If they don't ask, I don't tell them. It's sure to leak any moment now.'

'Colin is in very bad shape.'

That seemed to interest him. 'When did you talk to Colin?'

'Earlier today. His legal aid got me into Rikers.'

'How smart is that?'

I shrugged. 'She asked me to help her out.'

'And, God knows, that's a role you can't resist.'

I ignored the sarcasm. 'How could the department get away with an eight-hour interrogation?'

He pulled out his wallet. 'Do me a favor, Eltern, don't ask me any more questions.'

As he extricated a bill I saw a picture of a boy that looked about fifteen.

'Yours?'

'Yep. He lives in Puerto Rico with his mother.'

'Too bad.'

'I don't know about that. I see him every vacation. She's a teacher down there. They have a good life.'

In the moment that he glanced at the five-and-dime snapshot, his face was transformed by love. I suddenly remembered another picture. Porsche's picture at the Department of Justice exhibit. A wave of self-pity swept over me.

'I think you were right about me,' I said. 'I do more harm than good.'

'I didn't say that.'

'Porsche met Colin at my program.'

'What's that besides a coincidence?'

The lump in my throat made it hard to breathe. I wanted to say more, but the words didn't come.

'I think it's time you call me by my first name,' he said. 'I don't call you Ms Eltern.'

'You mean Jesus?' I asked.

'That *is* my name.'

'It's just that . . .'

'Too good a name for me?'

'No . . . no.'

'Too sacred?'

'Maybe.'

'You gotta loosen up, Eltern. It's just a cultural difference.'

The conversation died. He put some money on the table and ordered another round.

'Try it,' he said. 'Say Hey-Zeus.'

He was trying to get me to laugh. If I did, I knew tears wouldn't be far behind. So I worked on my blank stare. At the bar his friends were bellowing Irish freedom songs. O'Shaugnessy started to sing along, his voice unexpectedly deep and sweet. I studied the bottom of my emptying glass. Down there was the pit of memory. I began telling him about throwing Porsche and Colin out, but he cut me off.

'You need to eat something,' he said. 'I'm gonna order us a burger.'

I realized how badly I had to go to the bathroom. 'Excuse me a minute?'

The way to the bathroom was not a straight line.

Pulling down my jeans, sitting, then getting back up were not easy in that small room that kept swaying. When I got back to the table, O'Shaugnessy was soaking a hamburger in ketchup. There was a hamburger in front of me too.

I bit into my burger. It tasted as if it had been cooked last week. I picked at my french fries. A short, bald man slipped into the bench next to O'Shaugnessy.

'Anna Eltern, meet Bobby Day. He owns the joint.'

Day reached a hand across the table. 'Nice ta meet ya. Hey, you think that kid killed the others, too?'

O'Shaugnessy stopped chewing. 'C'mon, Bobby.'

'Not knowing is bad for business. I got no women in here.'

'I'm eating, Bobby.'

Day got up. 'The thing is, you won't tell me nothing.'

Somebody put a quarter in the jukebox, and suddenly we were in the seventies. I tried to figure the year. O'Shaugnessy was enjoying his burger. I remembered the year. It was the year I had entered the convent.

'C'mon, eat,' O'Shaugnessy said. 'You need it.'

'I'm not hungry.'

The lettuce in my burger was limp as old dollar bills.

'You're a crusader, Eltern, and that makes you dangerous, dangerous to yourself.'

'How so?'

'No crusade, no self . . . it's how you define yourself.' His eyebrows met in a scowl.

'What are you saying?'

'You think it's not working, that the world is getting worse and everything you're doing is a waste.'

The music beat against my ears; I began to feel nauseous. 'It's worse than that.'

'No, it's not,' he said.

He finished his burger and dabbed the corners of his mouth with the cheap paper napkin. 'It's a crisis in confidence. If you didn't have 'em, you'd be dead.'

I kept chewing.

'I've been there,' he went on. 'When I first came on the job, I thought I could single-handedly change the world.'

'And now?'

'I do what I can. And if you really want to do something, use your network to find out that girl's real name. We don't want to bury her in potter's field as a Jane Doe.'

'Jesus,' I heard myself whisper. But I didn't mean his name.

'Yeah?' He smiled. 'What is it?'

The bar around us seemed to slow down. My words melted into the beat of the jukebox. 'I'm not who I thought I was.'

'You're smashed is what you are. Lemme take you home.'

I shrugged as if it didn't matter either way, but suddenly I wanted like hell to get out of there.

To get to his car, we walked past Holy Cross Church. A locked iron gate protected the church. Behind it rose the steps to the entrance. Two kids lay there clutching each other. I rattled the gate. I rattled it with both hands. A young head turned. 'Lady, we're trying to sleep.'

My heart beat frantically. O'Shaugnessy pulled me around to face him. 'Anna,' he said, 'we're going to my place.'

I remember climbing down to his basement apartment. The underside of the sandstone steps that led to the building's main entrance rose above us. He unlocked a wrought-iron gate. Only one of us fit in the alcove in front of the door with the cornucopia knocker. I waited as he unlocked his three locks.

'I don't have much company,' he said, and we stepped into a tiny newspaper-filled vestibule.

A creature with fluttering ears and tail was jumping up to kiss me.

'Down, Sophia, down!' O'Shaugnessy patted a dog, who shivered with excitement. The dog led the way down a narrow hallway where picadors, a matador, his fluttering cape, and *el toro* were painted on black velvet. The hallway led to a living room, where books and magazines littered a coffee table and a plastic-covered green velvet couch. O'Shaugnessy opened the shades onto the sidewalk. A meat truck made its way to the packing plant by the river. From across the street, a flood of white neon came and went.

'Your apartment is like your desk. Messy.'

'That's right,' he said, 'because I live here.'

I sat down. My head was so heavy, I put it in my hands. He sat down next to me.

'Don't fall apart on me now, Eltern.'

I felt cold, cold enough to die. He took my head into his huge hands. 'C'mon, cry,' he said.

But I didn't want to cry. My hands started to unbutton his shirt buttons. His chest expanded. I heard him sigh. He caught my fingers in his. 'Don't,' he said hoarsely.

I pulled my hands out of his. 'I just wanna be near you.'

'You're stewed. Completely stewed.'

I kissed him. He shifted on the couch. The plastic squealed. He pushed me back. In front of my face, St Jude danced between the hairs on his chest – St Jude, the patron saint of lost causes. I pulled O'Shaugnessy's lips to mine and whispered his name. Jesus.

17

In the crack of light above me, I saw some feet pass by. I sat up and banged my head. I lay back down and took stock. I lay under a coffee table, wrapped in a sheet. O'Shaugnessy was sprawled on a couch in boxer shorts and a T-shirt, snoring. I crawled toward the neat pile of my clothes on the rug, took them to the bathroom, and got dressed. Then I tiptoed to the door, unlocked the three locks, and slipped out.

The night was just ending on Eleventh Avenue. It was Friday, and I was due in Washington at one o'clock. In front of the gay bars, the last stragglers of the night waited for a stranger to go home with. A car cruised by, a driver yelled obscenities. There were no cabs. I decided to walk. As my head cleared, last night's insanity came back to me. Instead of talking to O'Shaugnessy, I had gotten drunk and gone to bed with him.

By the time I reached Thirty-fourth Street, traffic had picked up. A few leather boys shared a cigarette. They studied me as I passed by. I was no less strange to them than they were to me. I wore a wrinkled skirt and blazer, and I clutched my purse as if it were a shield.

The Department of Sanitation parking lot was quiet. The

mountain of rock salt stored in the enormous beveled shack gave this lot its name: the Salt Mines. Here among the garbage trucks homeless kids were bought and sold. During one of last winter's coldest nights, two kids had climbed into the back of one of the trucks to sleep. They were so exhausted, they didn't wake up when the truck took off the next morning. They were crushed to death in a load of garbage.

A lonely figure crossed the wide, empty avenue toward me. We met in the middle of the street. He wore a lime-green wide-lapelled suit, a beige cashmere coat, and matching hat. Chestnut eyes sparkled in his purple-black face. A newspaper was tucked under his arm. We stopped to stare at each other. Someone moaned. An old woman sat up from her bed of newspapers, boxed the air, and lay back down in the doorway that was her room. I said, 'You crawled out from under your rock kind of early, Blue Fly.'

'I'm just wrapping up.'

He moved his hand a fraction of an inch. Just enough to extract the newspaper that his arm pinned to his body. It was yesterday's late edition of the *New York Post*. Porsche was on the front page. The drawing.

'You could be next.' He grinned.

'Her killer's been arrested,' I said hopefully.

'Oh, that's right.' He winked at me. 'That Colin is bad to the bone. I guess he killed 'em all. I guess it's all taken care of now.'

'What's that supposed to mean?'

'Don't get hot, honey. It means jack shit. It's kinda chill the way the trash takes out the trash.'

Down the avenue two cars careened toward us. The

drivers seemed to be drag-racing through the emptiness of the morning. We barely had time to get out of the way. He crossed the avenue to his car. As he opened the door I followed him over.

'What was Porsche's real name?' I asked him.

He floored the pedal, but the car was still in park. The engine roared. He said, 'She had a lot of names, babe. None of 'em matter now.'

I arrived at Beardsley's office an hour late. I apologized to Dottie, his secretary. She said, 'Mr Beardsley couldn't wait. He had an appointment on the Hill.'

Dottie was a stately gray-haired woman with a trim figure. Her office was just a tiny anteroom to Beardsley's. Virtually all the floor space was taken up by machines: computer, printer, copier, fax.

'Make yourself comfortable.' She opened the door to Beardsley's office to show me the couch where I could wait.

It hadn't been ten minutes before she returned. 'Pardon the intrusion, Ms Eltern,' she said. Two workmen came in behind her pushing handcarts loaded with boxes. 'Today is hectic around here. Right here in the corner,' Dottie told them, then turned to explain. 'Our office is the clearinghouse for returning the pictures that were donated for the exhibit. Poor James never says no to anything.'

'Could you stack them next to each other, not on top?' I heard myself ask. In a fraction of a second I had formed a plan.

Dottie frowned. 'We don't have room for that . . .'

'It's just that as long as I'm here, I'd like to look for a picture I saw the night of the exhibit. I'll stack the boxes when I'm done,' I promised, seeing her hesitation.

'All right, then,' she said with reluctance, and gave me a pair of scissors to remove the masking tape that sealed the boxes. As soon as she left, I began my search.

The photographs were still framed and folded in bubble wrap. Many I could determine through the wrap were not the photograph I was looking for. Others I unwrapped and carefully rewrapped. In picture after picture, old accusing eyes in sad, young faces called out for help. I had only two boxes to go when Beardsley finally returned.

'Taking over my office?' he asked as he stepped in. I couldn't tell if he was joking or not. His eyes were hidden behind designer glasses.

'Just temporarily.' I smiled. 'I put the proposal on your desk.'

'I'll look at it later.' He sighed, loosening his tie, then buzzed Dottie to bring him his call sheet.

As I kept pulling out the photographs I listened to him negotiate with senators, congressmen, and a lobbyist. In a subtle way he changed personalities with each call. Half an hour later he came over and knelt beside me. 'Want some help?'

'I couldn't resist the opportunity to look for Porsche's picture.'

'Dottie tried to tell me what you were up to, but I still don't understand about the picture.'

'The one I showed you at the Department of Justice exhibit. The picture of the girl you met when I gave you the Times Square tour.'

'You didn't introduce me to anybody in Times Square.'

'The kids in front of the porn shop . . . the one that flirted with you.'

'We've had this conversation before.' He took his glasses off and rubbed his eyes, bored. 'How about a coffee break?'

'I'd rather just get it over with.'

'When you get back from getting us some coffee, I'll pitch in.'

'Get back?' Was he going to make me his errand boy?

'I told Dottie she could call it a day, and the truth is I have to make a couple of confidential calls, Anna.'

My calves ached from so much kneeling. I stood up. 'Okay, I can take a hint. My treat. What'll you have?'

'Just coffee. Black.'

It was the end of the day, and seven floors of support staff were leaving at once. I waited ten minutes for the elevator, then headed for the nearest coffee shop.

When I got back, the corridors and offices had emptied out. Beardsley's office was locked. I knocked. No answer. One of the coffee containers was leaking through the bag in my hand. I knocked again. I kicked the door gently with my foot. Beardsley opened the door a crack. 'Anna . . . sorry. I didn't realize Dottie locked up when she left. How long have you been standing here?'

'It's okay,' I lied, but I was tired and frustrated.

'Come in.'

He opened his coffee container, took a sip, placed it on his desk. 'You *were* over an hour late. Let's see the proposal.'

As he read the rewrite of my proposal I sat down on the

floor and opened the last box. This box contained pictures that were not framed. I flipped through the faces.

'It's not here. Where could it have gone?'

He looked up, his pencil poised over my proposal. 'It could have been picked up by its owner directly from Justice. What about fingerprints and dental records? Couldn't they be used to identify this girl?'

'They tried that – apparently she was never printed.'

'Dental records?'

'You have to have a dentist to show them to. One who treated her.'

'We're bringing the hearings to New York City, did I tell you? You'll have another chance to show off for the boys. That should guarantee your funding.'

'Yes, you told me.'

'I'm excited. It'll be good PR. Maybe you can give the members of the committee the tour you gave me.'

'Great. If it'll help, great.' I started flipping through another box.

'Didn't you do that one already?' Beardsley seemed annoyed.

At that moment my hand found the photograph. Triumphantly I held it up to show him.

He didn't seem surprised. 'You'll do what you have to, of course,' he said, shaking his head. 'But I'd advise discretion, Anna. The committee won't want to come to New York with bad publicity.'

I got up, barely hearing him. My feet had fallen asleep. 'I don't know how I missed it.'

I extracted the photograph from its frame. There was a UPI stamp on the back.

'Who took it?' he asked.

'A UPI photographer.'

'That's actually good. It means it could have surfaced anywhere.'

I knew what he was saying, but I chose to ignore it. Instead I said, 'So you think the proposal is good.'

'I'd like to say differently but it's great. Will you come back to Washington anyway just to visit with me? I'd love to spend some time with you.'

Before I could answer he added, 'Just think about it. Whenever you feel like it, we could make a day of it. Get to know each other a bit.'

18

I sat in the storefront window studying the photo of a limp Porsche being picked up by a couple of cops. Across the street Domingo stood in Samsara's doorway, looking left then right. I went outside to call him over. He walked around the corner. I went back inside and studied the photo some more.

Then it dawned on me. The thing the picture had been saying all along. Porsche *had been picked up* by the cops, at least this once. Even if this had not been an arrest, she was obviously underage. That meant the cops could not simply have released her. Either they had sent her back home or, if they had not been able to locate a family, they would have placed her in a 'nonsecure facility,' shoptalk for a foster home. If she had actually been arrested, she would have been placed in a 'secure facility' – a children's prison – like Spofford. That would mean there were records.

I heard Domingo calling at the door. I put the photo down and got up to let him in.

'Sorry about the cloak-and-dagger shit,' he said. 'But those people don't like you and I don't want to lose my job.'

'You work there?'

'It's a good job,' he said defensively, 'I develop pictures in the darkroom in the back. For the twenty-four-hour photo pick-up, you know.'

I remembered the night Blue Fly had followed me into Samsara. 'What else goes on in there?' I asked. 'Does Blue Fly pimp from there?'

'He comes around. They have telephones in the back. He sends girls to hotels to deliver tapes and drugs and ... You're not gonna make me lose my job, are you?'

He scuffed the floor impatiently while I debated my dilemma. I wanted his trust back. Dealing with the video store would have to wait.

He spotted Porsche's photograph. 'Where'd you get this?'

'I'm giving it to the cops. Maybe it will help them find out who Porsche really was.'

'I could make you a copy. That way I can have one, too.'

'You sure it would be all right?'

'I'm alone in the darkroom. They don't come in.' He looked at his watch. 'I work till eleven. I just came out for a sandwich. I could bring a copy back when I wrap up.'

We went to the kitchen. As I made Domingo a sandwich he cuddled Beelzebub. 'Is Porsche gonna have a funeral with flowers and a church?'

'First we need to know who she was.'

He looked confused. 'I *know* who she was. She was my friend.'

Domingo took his sandwich and Porsche's photograph

across the street with him. Two hours later he was back. In one hand he held the envelope I had given him, in the other a pink-and-black plastic bag from the video store. He had enlarged the photo, so that in the copies Porsche's face blossomed against the blur of hands and arms.

'Thanks, Domingo.' I kissed his cheek. 'Tomorrow I'm gonna take this to the runaway squad and see if it matches any picture they have.'

He handed me the pink-and-black bag. 'Will you help me put these up?'

Inside was a stack of fliers. I took one from the top. It was a photo offset of Porsche's face, taken from the photograph he had just duplicated. Under it he had neatly printed:

> CASH REWARD
> IF YOU KNOW HER REEL NAME
> CALL 555-HELP

'Wanna help me put them up around the neighborhood?'

'How did you make these?'

'From the photo. I made a negative first. Then I blew up her face. I figure the kids out here won't talk to the cops. But they might talk to you.'

We headed into the night together. At the nearest street lamp, because I was taller, I taped the first flier. Porsche's face danced in the play of light and shadow.

'I called the police,' Domingo said, 'but don't tell anybody.'

'What?'

He shrugged. 'I dropped a dime, anonymous, you know.'

'Domingo, did you see anything that day?'

'Just her in the alley when I was sitting on the fire escape. But I didn't know it was her, cuz it looked like she had red hair.'

He shoved his hands deep into his pockets and walked with me up the street, kicking the pavement in a sad little shuffle.

'We called her the animal girl. She was good people.'

'Animal girl?'

'Yeah. She was always saving things, you know, birds, cats.'

'Blue Fly beat her up pretty bad the week she was killed.'

'Blue Fly hits a lot of girls. He don't kill 'em.'

'What about Colin? You think he killed her?'

'Why? Cuz he was sweatin' her?'

'He was?'

'Yeah, he was *loco* in the *coco* for her.'

I remembered the night I met Colin. How he had decided to come with me only after quizzing me about Beelzebub's owner. How he had named the kitten Little Devil. And thus it dawned on me that Colin and Porsche had known each other before I introduced them.

We walked to the parking lot in silence. I taped a flier to the door of the attendant's shack. Domingo scrounged the pavement for a cigarette butt. I stepped back to see my handiwork. He lit his butt.

'How did they meet?' I asked.

'I dunno. Colin was always following her around. She couldn't stand him, but he kept kicking it to her. She couldn't get rid of him.'

NIGHTSIDE

'Why?'

'He gave her drugs, wrote songs for her and stuff.'

'Domingo – do you think he killed her?'

He sucked on the cigarette. Smoke veiled his Indian features. 'I dunno. Maybe if he was high on crack. But I don't think so.'

We left the lot. I taped a flier over a gangster-movie poster. On Forty-fourth Street Domingo taped fliers on the doors of the Actors Studio and Playwrights Horizon. We decided to hang some in the park.

The menacing shapes that lurked in the shadows of the park were just a homeless man and his dog. The man slept on a broken bench. The dog sat in a shopping cart in a Zorro hat and plastic cape. His big sad eyes with the crusty corners blinked as we passed. Then he growled to alert his master. The old man didn't stir. The mural that was last summer's Boys Club project writhed like a pocket-park *Guernica*. Glass sparkled magically on the pavement.

'Let's put it on the baby,' Domingo said, pointing at the mural. 'Everybody sees that.'

The baby's bright yellow hair almost fell over its eyes where a fat tear rolled down. A collection of red-top crack vials filled one plump little hand; in the other, milky crack smoke swirled inside a glass pipe. HELL'S KITCHEN was scrolled in red flames that devoured the baby's alphabet blocks and threatened the New York City skyline in the background.

'A cop killed her,' Domingo said abruptly.

'What makes you say that?' I asked, keeping my voice casual.

'The grapevine.'

Like the other kids on the Strip, Domingo blamed the cops for all his misery. He crushed his butt under the heel of his new hightop sneaker. 'You should be more careful, Annie. Everybody hates you.'

'Everybody?'

'The pimps, the cops, even my moms.'

'Where is your mom?'

'Hustling the Strip.'

'Your mom hardly knows me. Why should she hate me?'

'She says I love you more than her, but it's not true.'

We walked and put up fliers without talking until he said, 'She got AIDS.'

Our footsteps echoed like a slow tap dance.

'It's you I worry about,' I said after a moment.

'No sweat.' He winked.

'You know Irish Lucky, right?'

'Yeah.'

'Have you seen him around lately?'

'Why?'

'Because Porsche was killed in his apartment, and the cops can't find him.'

He took another flier from the bag. 'It's his grandmother's apartment, but she's in the hospital.'

'You've seen him?'

'Nope. Me and him don't get along. What's gonna happen to Colin?'

'He'll be in court again on Tuesday.'

We both stepped back and studied the last flier we had taped up. 'That should do it,' I said.

'I gotta be going. If you see Colin, tell him I said hi.'

I offered Domingo a five-dollar bill. He didn't take it. 'For helping me,' I said, and shoved it into his shirt pocket.

He pulled the five back out. 'I don't need this.' He took a wallet from his back pocket and sorted the already sorted bills.

'Just the same,' I said, 'I want you to have it.'

Silently he added it to his stack and flipped the wallet shut. Then he gave me the palm of his small hand in a high five and headed rapidly in the direction of Times Square and the Strip.

Before going home, I stopped by the local grocery store. From the orange glow of the *bodega's* window, plantains, guava, mavi, bananas, yucca, and yautia beckoned like an oasis. The *bodega* never closed, and everybody from pimps to cops bought cigarettes and soda here. Pedro, the *bodegero*, stood by the cash register, behind the cellophane-wrapped snack foods and the other items small enough to pocket unseen. He was counting foodstamps.

'*Cómo va la cosa?*' I asked.

'*Allí, señorita, allí.*'

I offered him a flier. 'Did you know this girl?'

He turned the paper this way and that. 'Very bad picture,' he said.

My heart leaped. 'You knew her?'

A sucking sound raised the hair on the back of my neck. Behind me Blue Fly leaned on the wall in the niche by the noisy cooler with the glass door. A touch of gold gleamed from his open mouth. When he smiled, I saw the reason why. He had a new gold cap on his right front tooth. A golden letter *P*.

He grinned wider. 'I eat little girls and their initials get stuck on my teeth.'

The facets on his pinkie diamond could shred a cheek with one backhand slap. His tongue flicked over his lips. 'C'mon, babe, you just gotta quit.'

I turned to the *bodegero*. 'If you didn't know her, how do you know it's a bad picture?'

Pedro handed the flier back to me. 'So many little spots,' he said. 'Eyes hurt.'

'Dots,' Blue Fly corrected his English. 'Those things are dots, like what makes a TV picture. Get the picture?'

I suggested: 'Maybe she bought cigarettes in here.'

'I don't know.'

'Could I put this in the window?' I raised my hand to show him the masking tape.

'I do myself,' Pedro said. 'You leave it.'

'You're so busy, Pedro, you'll forget. You have daughters – don't you worry about them?'

'My girls good girls. Every Sunday they in the church.'

'Just the same' – Blue Fly glared at Pedro – 'girls is girls.'

The next morning I took the subway downtown. The runaway-squad headquarters was on an elegant residential block across from an antique store and next to a pool hall, where tables were interspersed among cast-iron pillars. The Police Athletic League was housed on the first floor of the hundred-year-old building; a bulletin board listed a schedule of activities.

The words 'Runaway Squad' were stencilled on a piece of white cardboard in red Gothic lettering. Because Times Square is the national mecca for runaways, worried parents from across the country send this squad snapshots of their missing children. When an underage kid is picked up, these shots are often a cop's best tool to find out who the kid is. I knew several of the officers who worked here well. That day Feldman and Szabo were on duty.

I got along with Sergeant Feldman. His boss, Lieutenant Szabo, would be a problem. What Szabo lacked in smarts, he made up for in obsessiveness. Szabo never listened. He answered every question with the question 'Have you checked the morgue?'

These days I let Toomey deal with the runaway squad.

Feldman was at the desk. I figured Szabo was in his office, because Szabo was never not there. I hoped he stayed put. I didn't feel like tangling with him today.

'Can I help you?' Feldman's tone said that I shouldn't come any farther into the room until I had explained myself. Then he did a mild double take as he recognized me.

'Anna, you look different. You cut your hair.'

'You're the same, Feldman.'

He chuckled. 'So is my life. You don't get downtown much anymore, do you?'

'Unlike some people, I delegate.'

His eyes wandered toward Szabo's door. We both chuckled. 'This must be big,' he said, 'to bring you down personally.'

I opened the envelope I was carrying and slid the picture out. I turned it to face him. 'I'm looking for this girl's family. I have no name. She's a Jane Doe.'

'Ah, the mystery girl. Where'd you get this?'

Feldman studied the picture for a moment. Then he turned it over to the UPI stamp and date on the back.

'From the date I'd say this was taken during the last mayoral election. You know, after Hizzoner had Times Square cleaned up.'

'Do you think this was an arrest? The photographer who took it is in Saudi Arabia now.'

He turned the photograph faceup again, then shook his head. 'Probably not. Probably these guys were just moving the riffraff around.'

'What if it *was* an arrest?'

'There'd still be no point looking for her prints. You know, if a kid is underage, we clean the prints out at the end of the year. The law says we have to. Anyway, I know for a fact the department ran her prints after the murder, and came up with nothing.'

New York State had a computer in Albany that could, in a few hours, match a set of prints against any other set taken in the state. That year no other state could make that claim.

'Can I look through the picture file for a matchup?'

He shrugged. 'Sure, but the department's already doing that, Anna. There's somebody in there now. Second guy they've sent.'

Still, Feldman led me to the inner room. 'You two know each other?' he said by way of introduction.

O'Shaugnessy had his back to me when I first saw him, so I had a few seconds to prepare myself. When he turned, his grin became a grimace. 'Sure thing,' he told Feldman.

I said, 'Hi.'

'You don't mind if Anna joins you? You two are looking for the same girl, anyway.' Feldman handed O'Shaugnessy the photograph.

'Sure thing,' O'Shaugnessy said again.

'Let me know if you find anything.' Feldman walked out.

For a moment we were silent; then O'Shaugnessy whistled. 'This *is* a find.' He pointed at the two cops in the photograph. 'That's Sanchez and Pinter. You couldn't have brought this to me?'

'I . . .'

'What?'

'I . . . look, the other night, let's forget it.'

'What are you talking about?'

'I want to go back to the good professional relationship we had.'

'I thought you said we were on opposite teams.'

I spread my hands lamely. 'I was wrong.'

His eyes stayed on the photo. 'Why are you so obsessed with this girl? Why do you keep meddling?'

'I want to help.'

'Where'd you get this?'

'I told Feldman that it's a UPI shot.'

'What is it really?' His voice went up an octave.

'It *is* a UPI shot, but it was in the Committee on Children's exhibit at the Justice Department. I wanted to keep them out of it.'

'Since when do you do the committee's PR?'

'They didn't have to give me the picture. It's hard enough to get the press to look at this issue on the merits, and the committee is bringing hearings to the city in two weeks. They can do a lot of good, but not if we get them mixed up in—'

'I see,' he said. 'And just what part of the other night did you want me to forget?'

I was silent.

He set the photo down. 'There was nothing memorable enough to forget.'

'You don't have to insult me.'

I sat at the table where hundreds of files were stacked in boxes. Each folder had a snapshot stapled to the front. O'Shaugnessy sat across from me. I remembered the feeling of trying to get under his shirt, next to his warmth.

'What else is the department doing to find out who she was?' I asked.

'We're circulating dental records and footprints to hospitals around the country. I just came here to double-check.'

'On your own time?'

'Yeah. On *my* clock.'

'So what's *your* motivation?'

'My motivation?' He looked bleakly around the bare government-issue room. 'Who knows, Anna?'

We began searching for a snapshot that resembled Porsche. The stacks seemed endless, the room stuffy. Grime crept under my fingernails and dust into my nostrils. I started sneezing.

He asked, 'How's your proposal coming?'

'It's finished, turned in.'

'If you plan to see Mr Ivy League again, just remember this is the age of AIDS, Eltern.'

'What's that supposed to mean?'

'Well, the other night I could have gone ahead without protection. You didn't care.'

'I thought we agreed to forget it.'

'We did and we are. But right now we're just us talking

between us. The point is you left yourself wide open the other night. That was stupid.'

'I don't usually drink.'

'It only takes one time.'

I said, 'That night will never happen again.'

His complexion flushed darker. He looked down at his hands. 'Too bad.'

I stopped talking to him. As I went from snapshot to snapshot I wondered how many of these children were living and how many were now dead. How many were just barely surviving in the loveless purgatory of the homeless? After a while I realized that O'Shaugnessy was staring at me.

'What do you think?' He pushed a folder across the table.

Even in the faded Polaroid, the unique beauty of her features and the wildness of her hair were unmistakable. She was holding her gerbil and smiling a nine-year-old smile.

The thin folder held only one routine form. The Baltimore Department of Human Services had sent this form to runaway squads across the country because a 'dependent minor' had run away from her foster home.

'If we hadn't done this, the department would have missed it,' O'Shaugnessy said angrily. 'Boy, are they gonna be pissed that I found this. I'm not even on the case.'

'You could say I found it.'

He shook his head. 'Naaw, I don't mind a little heat.'

We fell silent. I felt his eyes on me as I studied the Polaroid. The innocence of her smile caught in my throat. 'Charmaine Jefferson,' I read. 'She was barely fifteen.'

'I'm gonna request her file from Health and Human Services in DC,' O'Shaugnessy said. 'The file will tell us who her parents are. I'm gonna hang on to this UPI shot. I wanna show it to Sanchez and Pinter. Not that they'll remember anything.'

I shrugged. He slid the photo into the folder and the folder under his arm.

On the long stairway down to the first floor, he said, 'You came to my apartment, you kissed me once, and then you passed out. But not before you threw up on me. I did manage to get you out of your clothes and into the shower.'

'That's it?'

'Yeah,' he said. 'Real erotic.'

19

A couple of days later Colin's case arrived in Part F, felony court. The law said he had to be indicted or released. Since grand-jury proceedings were secret, nobody knew which it would be. The courtroom was packed. In the front row O'Shaugnessy and the DA's press officer sat with the criminal-court press corps. Mike Taylor was there, too. All the benches were full; spectators lined the side walls. I found a spot near the door.

The judge sipped his water. The assistant district attorney grimly fingered a three-foot stack of folders. The legal-aid attorneys made notes. Court officers in gleaming white shirts escorted prisoners in and out of the holding pens.

Defendants who had made bail or been released on their own recognizance sat with long-suffering mothers and wives. By New York City standards these were all small-time offenders: shoplifting, harassment, token sucking, resisting arrest, possession of narcotics, assault, and trespassing – which could mean anything from drug possession to prostitution or shooting up in an abandoned basement. When the defendants' names were called, they crossed the balustrade to stand before the judge. There was never any warning as to who would come next. Heavy offenders like

Colin were warehoused in the holding pens until their names were called.

An indictment is a three-minute procedure. A piece of paper – a list of charges – changes hands. The case is adjourned. In three weeks the defendant will be arraigned again, this time on the indictment. At this second arraignment, a trial judge is assigned by lottery.

I was looking for Rhoda Bluestone when I saw Colin's mother elegantly planted in the second row. The man next to her turned to whisper in her ear. I recognized Mitchell Thomas, one of the city's top criminal lawyers. The lawyer's superbly styled and blow-dried graying hair offset a deep navy pinstripe suit and understated silk tie. So she *had* responded to my plea.

A dozen defendants came and went. The air in the room grew increasingly stale. The proceedings up front were a monotonous drone that mingled with the spectators' coughs and whispers. Suddenly the sleepy courtroom woke up. I hadn't even heard Colin's name being called. He looked bleary-eyed and desperately confused. He wore a brand-new suit.

'Colin . . . Colin!' a young voice I recognized called out.

The judge rapped his knuckles on the bench and yelled, 'Order in the court.'

Eclipse and Domingo pushed to the front of the crowd clustered along the wall. Two feet shorter than everybody else, they held hands and watched in wide-eyed absorption. I waved at them. Domingo winked back. It took guts for kids who hated the system as much as they did to show up in a courtroom.

Colin's lawyer joined him in front of the judge. I was too

far back to hear what they were saying. But I saw the DA give the bridge officer a piece of paper. I watched as the officer handed that same piece of paper to the judge. I knew that meant the grand jury had voted a certificate of affirmative grand-jury action – the indictment. What happened next I couldn't interpret. A man I didn't recognize joined the parties in front of the judge. He, too, presented the bridge officer with a piece of paper, which was then handed up to the judge. In the hush that fell, I tried to read the judge's lips. Reporters began to head for the exit, walking fast. Taylor lingered the longest. O'Shaugnessy and the DA's press officer came my way, too.

A collective sigh rose from the spectators as we realized Colin Winklesworth III was about to walk out of the courtroom, free for the moment. Flanked by his mother and his lawyer, Colin came toward the exit. Domingo and Eclipse followed. The judge rapped his knuckles. 'Order, order in the court.'

I stepped into the hallway.

As O'Shaugnessy passed by me he whispered, 'They must have some pull to keep it quiet that Thomas was granted a bail application on the eleventh floor. He's walking on a quarter of a mil.'

Reporters and cameras circled the courtroom door. The glare of klieg lights snared Colin and his entourage. Colin's eyes narrowed at the barrage of questions. His mother grew pale. This was a situation in which she had never expected to find herself. Mitchell Thomas, however, basked in the attention.

'When was the defendant granted bail?' a reporter demanded.

'Yesterday.'

'Why wasn't the press informed?'

'We're not trying this case in the media.' Thomas smiled graciously.

'What's your defense strategy?'

'We're not going to discuss the case now. Obviously we're gratified that the court granted bail,' Thomas answered smoothly.

'Any chance you'd wanna give me an interview?' Taylor asked Colin.

'Back off,' Colin's lawyer barked.

'What kind of a case can you build when your client has admitted he killed her?'

Thomas's expression did not change. Firmly he said, 'The statements of a frightened and confused young man after a brutal eight-hour interrogation can hardly be construed as a legitimate confession.'

Domingo and Eclipse pushed their way forward. 'Colin, Colin . . .'

The boy's face brightened. 'Eclipse. Where's my guitar?'

The reporters had turned to Colin's mother. 'My son is innocent.' Her discomfort only served to whet their appetite.

'Any proof?' Mike Taylor demanded.

'You don't have to take my word for it. Ask Ms Eltern, she knows my son. Colin was in her program.'

The microphones turned to me. In the white heat of the klieg lights I saw only Colin, Domingo, and Eclipse. Trusting eyes waiting for a response. I said, 'I don't believe Colin is a murderer.'

'Are you saying this is a faulty indictment?'

'There's a lot of political pressure to do something about the violence in Times Square. Maybe in this investigation the system moved too fast. Maybe all four recent Times Square murders should be investigated by a special prosecutor.'

'What's up, G?' Domingo grinned at Colin.

'Come with me, Colin, the car's outside.' His mother grabbed his hand.

'He's my friend,' Colin pleaded.

'I said stay away from him.' Colin's mother positioned herself fiercely between Domingo and Colin.

'He's my boy,' Colin whined.

She pulled him forward. The reporters followed them into the crowded hallway. Domingo and Eclipse looked up at me expectantly. 'Is he gonna be okay?'

'So you finally admit that he was in your program.' Taylor stepped between us, his face greedy for detail. 'You could have told me days ago. I would have had an exclusive.'

I took one kid by each hand and pushed away in the other direction. The front door is not the only way in and out of the criminal-court building. The side entrance, as unfriendly as the front, also leads to the district attorney's office. The backdoor is my favorite. Domingo, Eclipse, and I had made it to the steps that overlook the vibrant, narrow, crowded streets of Chinatown when O'Shaugnessy came out the revolving backdoor.

'Hey!' Domingo slapped him five.

O'Shaugnessy was wearing a suit that fit too snugly and carrying a canvas briefcase. This was as formal as he got.

'I've got to talk to the lady,' he told the kids. 'Do you guys have carfare and lunch money?' He didn't wait for an answer, but handed each a five-dollar bill. 'See you in the neighborhood.'

'Later,' they chimed.

Domingo grabbed Eclipse's elbow and steered her back into the building. The front exit was closer to the subway. 'And don't talk to any reporters,' O'Shaugnessy called after them.

We walked down the steps and into the fragrances of the Orient. He led me to a dim sum parlor as large as a cafeteria. Except for the mirrored walls it was unadorned. Everyone in the restaurant was Chinese.

'Why'd you get into all that just now, Eltern? I thought we were finally on the same wavelength.'

'I said more than I meant to. But you don't have to take it personally.'

He shook his head. 'The brass will take it personally. Then guess who the heat will come down on?'

I hadn't bothered to think how my words would affect him. 'I'm sorry,' I whispered, 'I didn't think about you.'

'What else is new?'

A waiter set two plates, water, napkins, and silverware in front of us.

'Chopsticks, please,' O'Shaugnessy asked. The waiter smiled.

'I really *am* sorry,' I said.

'That's okay. I'm a big boy. I can take the heat. The question is, can you?'

'What do you mean?'

'The feeding frenzy on this case has just begun. You

don't know how it's gonna go. Do you need this kind of attention? Can you afford it?'

'I'm not worried about myself.'

'Maybe you should be.'

'Where's the menu?'

'There's no menu. The waiters will come around with trays. You just point to what you want.'

Dim sum is an assortment of dumplings wrapped in a delicate noodle dough. Inside are shrimp, pork, vegetables. The challenge was actually getting them into my mouth with the chopsticks. Only when we finished did O'Shaugnessy unzip his canvas briefcase. 'This is the DHS file. Read it and weep.'

The waiter brought us a pot of tea. O'Shaugnessy filled our cups. I began to read.

The chronology began Christmas morning five years ago. A week before Charmaine Jefferson had turned ten. That Christmas morning her mother, Lydia, had dropped her off at an emergency shelter. The report filed by the social worker on duty said the mother appeared to be stoned on crack. 'If you don't take her, I'm afraid I'll hurt her,' Lydia had told the worker.

A subsequent investigation revealed Lydia Jefferson's deterioration. Once a college student, she had lost everything because of a series of addictions. The form read:

The child alleges the mother's boyfriend abuses her and the mother does nothing to protect her. She also alleges that her mother had sold her on several occasions in exchange for crack. Physical examination showed that the child had been sexually active. She was also undernourished and had body lice. Her head was shaved. She was placed in foster care.

A series of forms showed that over the course of the next year things improved. Charmaine regained her health; she went to school. She still missed her mother. Toward the end of that year, Charmaine's foster family wanted to adopt her. Charmaine told the social worker that 'would be great.' She said she would like to have her new family's last name. The legally required search was made for relatives who might protest this adoption. None surfaced.

On the eve of the adoption, however, Charmaine's mother reappeared. Lydia had been newly released from prison, where she had given birth to a second child, Charmaine's half brother. She wanted her older child back. Lydia Jefferson regained custody.

The documents picked up again ten months later. Charmaine and her infant brother were found living alone in Washington, DC. The girl had been supporting the infant by prostituting herself. The children were separated, then placed in foster care. Charmaine was now a serious 'discipline problem.' She stole from her foster family and played hooky from school. She entered counseling. For a time she seemed to be improving. Then her mother reappeared and again won custody. Two months later Lydia died of a crack-induced heart attack. Charmaine was placed in a third foster home. She asked to attend her mother's funeral and had not been seen since. Not even Charmaine's birth certificate named a father.

O'Shaugnessy's beeper went off. He excused himself and headed for the pay phone. I sat and thought about the sequence of events that had turned Charmaine Jefferson into a fifteen-year-old prostitute named Porsche. When he came back, he said, 'A lot of phones are ringing off the hook. The DA, the department, *and* Hizzoner are being pressured to respond to your call for a special prosecutor. You'd better brace for their response.'

'Thanks. I think I'll pass.'

'You threw the rocks,' he said, 'now you wanna duck the ripples?'

20

It was almost midnight when I finally forced myself to go back to my apartment. I wished I had somewhere else to go. Millie wasn't back from Long Island yet. I remembered her warning that I was too often alone. That night the short walk from the center seemed terribly long. I could almost pinpoint the moment when my solitude shifted into a profound and threatening loneliness.

As I climbed to the first-floor landing glass crunched under my feet. Above, the light bulbs had all been shattered. It seemed that a black-ribboned wreath hung on my door. But when I reached the top of the stairs, I saw that the door's center panel was gone. I had been looking at the darkness within. Strangely the door itself was still locked.

With trembling fingers, I inserted my key quietly into the locks. One by one they slid back. As I pushed the door open the chain caught. Whoever had removed the panel to reach in and unlock the door had locked and chained it once inside. I turned and ran to the corner phone booth.

The phone took my quarter but gave no dial tone. I ran toward Manhattan Plaza. The complex had twenty-four-hour guards. Bill Crispo was on duty that night. If he wondered why I hadn't gone to the center, he didn't say so.

He listened to my story, then dialed 911. A call from Manhattan Plaza would be answered faster than any other call in the neighborhood.

Five minutes later a squad car pulled up in front of the building. I thanked Bill and ran back out. I recognized one of the two uniforms in the car.

'There's someone in my apartment.'

'You sure about that?' The older uniform, Klemperer, frowned.

'I'm sure.'

The backdoor unlocked electronically, and I slid into the squad car. Two minutes later we were looking up at my apartment. The window was open. The curtain fluttered.

'You stay here. We'll check it out,' Klemperer said.

As soon as the two cops went inside, I followed them. From the bottom of the stairs, I watched as they kicked my door open. Guns drawn, they went in. I waited. A minute later they came out.

'Lady, there's nobody in there.' The other cop, whose name tag said 'R. Reed,' sounded annoyed.

I climbed the steps. From the threshold of the door I could hear Beelzebub crying. I tried to step past the officers. Their bodies made a wall.

'I gotta get my cat.'

'There's no lights, ma'am.'

I pushed against their blue-coated bodies. Broken light bulbs, broken dishes, broken glasses crunched underfoot. Everything I owned was strewn on the floor.

'You the Eltern that runs Eden House?' Reed asked.

'Yes.'

'Playing with a fast crowd there, ma'am.'

I knelt to pull Beelzebub from under the couch. Small razor claws slapped my hand. I took her into my arms.

'What was taken?' Reed had his notebook out.

The television and stereo were still in their places.

'I don't know,' I said. 'I'll have to clean up before I can say.'

'Got any enemies?'

I thought of Blue Fly's warnings to get out of the neighborhood. I shrugged. 'The pimps, I guess.'

'Okay, Anna. We'll file a report.' Klemperer handed me a slip of paper. 'Here's your case number. As soon as you know what's missing, call it in. Wanna get community affairs over here? O'Shaugnessy can help you get this door fixed.'

'That won't be necessary. I'll call a carpenter.'

They ignored me and called O'Shaugnessy on the police radio. He came bounding up the stairs ten minutes later. I was sitting in the chaos that was left of my life, still holding Beelzebub. O'Shaugnessy's big shadow fell in the doorway. I got up and lighted a candle. The two bluecoats disappeared into the hallway.

'What the hell?'

In his big beefy hand, O'Shaugnessy carried a four-pack of light bulbs, which he proceeded to screw in around the apartment. Once the lights were on, the menace that had passed through the apartment was more clearly evident.

'What's missing?' O'Shaugnessy asked.

'Nothing, as far as I can tell. The TV and VCR are really all I had.'

'How about jewelry?'

'Don't own any.'

'How about downstairs in the office?'

O'Shaugnessy went first. I followed. Even in the darkness I could see that everything was in its place. The computer, the printer, the fax machine. Then something thumped quietly, steadily, on the staircase outside the door. O'Shaugnessy put a finger over his lips.

I stood very still. O'Shaugnessy drew his gun. He unlocked the locks gently and ripped open the door. I heard a high-pitched scream. Then O'Shaugnessy began apologizing. I stepped into the hallway. Millie stood halfway up the steps. One hand was over her heart, the other dragged a suitcase. Her face was ashen.

'Welcome home,' I said.

O'Shaugnessy, still apologizing, took the suitcase and carried it upstairs. I followed.

When she got to the landing, Millie peered past the shattered door. 'Annie, what in God's name?'

Millie went up to her apartment; I went into my bathroom. On the broken mirror someone had pasted one of Domingo's fliers, ripped in half. My reflection was split – half Porsche, half me. I screamed and sank to my knees. My fingers began to search the contents of the cabinet that littered the floor. O'Shaugnessy pulled me up and out of the bathroom. 'Don't touch anything,' he said.

In the kitchen I stopped whimpering. He asked, 'What were you looking for?'

'One of those snake rings where the snake swallows its own tail. Porsche gave it to me and it's gone.'

'You sure it was in there?'

'No, but she gave it to me so I'd never forget her, and now it's gone.'

'Anna, why would anyone steal a ring you can buy in every novelty store on the Strip?' O'Shaugnessy asked.

I nodded sadly, hoping Porsche's memento would turn up. O'Shaugnessy leaned out into the hallway. 'Get Crime Scene over here,' he yelled out to the two uniforms outside.

'Crime Scene on a burglary!' Klemperer came back into the apartment, scowling. Reed followed him sourly.

'You heard me!' O'Shaugnessy barked.

'They're not gonna wanna waste time on a burglary where nothing's missing.'

'Well, somebody took the *time* to do damage here, asshole. Now, call 'em.'

Reed got on his radio.

'Look.' O'Shaugnessy turned back to me. 'I brought some plywood from the precinct. It'll have to do for tonight. But I'm not gonna do anything until after Crime Scene dusts this place. It looks like the pimps really wanna scare you off.'

After a long half hour the forensics team arrived with their black doctor bags. They spread a white powder on everything. Most of the fingerprints were too smudged to be any good. Watching them work, I realized they would find Colin's and Porsche's prints. Still, I kept quiet.

'We're gonna hafta print the lady so we can rule out wild latents,' one of the forensics cops said to O'Shaugnessy as they were wrapping up.

'I'll take care of her myself,' he said, looking at me.

They thanked him and left. He went down to get the plywood for the door. Millie and I began the cleanup – books back on the shelves, clothes back in the drawers, dishes into Hefty bags. They were all broken or chipped.

'What about her? Can she be fixed?' Millie held the statue of Joan of Arc. Her head was cracked. The crack ran through her calm smile.

'Throw her out,' I said. 'She was a martyr.'

'No, she wasn't. She was a visionary.'

'It's the same thing.'

'What about this?' Millie asked a moment later. 'Not that you ever turn it on.'

'My beeper. Drop it in my purse.'

By the time O'Shaugnessy and I got to the precinct house, it was two in the morning. I was so tired, I felt that I was sleepwalking. He led me to the print area. He took my thumb between two of his fingers and rolled it on an ink pad. I felt the heat of his large body behind mine. He rolled my thumb onto a box on a card divided into ten boxes. In the alloted spaces on top he had written my name. I watched the topography of my thumbprint appear. Then he grabbed my index finger.

'Do you have to be so rough?'

'Usually when the department sets up a decoy, we like to know about it.'

'I thought the flier was a good idea.'

'Did you?' He rolled my finger on the ink pad.

'Domingo and I hung the fliers the night before we found Porsche's picture in the runaway-squad files. He made them himself. How could I turn him down?'

'I think the word is "no."'

'Besides, I figured if anybody knew who Porsche was, it would be one of the kids. And that they'd be more likely to talk to me than to the cops. I was just trying to help.'

'Is there anybody's job you're not trying to do?'

He rolled the finger in a box in the card. Another print appeared.

'These kids trust me.'

'Yeah, but can you trust yourself?'

Again I thought I should tell him about throwing Porsche and Colin out. But I had waited too long. We bickered until all my fingers had been inked and printed.

'The computer in Albany is down again this week. But when it's up, it will compare the prints from your apartment with all the prints in the system. Maybe we'll come up with something.'

'Who do you think it was?'

'The pimps telling you to back off.'

'Or maybe I'm right,' I said, 'and Colin isn't the killer.'

'Lady,' O'Shaugnessy said, 'this is one time you'd better hope you're wrong.'

21

'I've been reading the New York papers,' Beardsley said. 'Aren't you worried you're coming on a little too strong?'

'You mean calling for a special prosecutor?'

'Is that really appropriate?' He nibbled on his goat cheese.

'Even if I were wrong about Colin, what about the other three killings? The cops don't seem to be doing anything. They just don't give a damn about these kids.'

'The hearings will focus the media and get the public's attention. Then you'll get some policy changes. It seems to me that's infinitely preferable to a personal battle between you and the powers-that-be. The committee will galvanize the moral will to do something about the menace in Hell's Kitchen.'

I didn't mention that the menace had come off the streets into my apartment. I just put my golden fork into my mouth. After several days of lonely hibernation, I had taken Beardsley's offer to come to Washington and get to know him better.

'You remind me of myself,' Beardsley went on.

'How so?'

'Your work is your life.'

The chandelier above cast tiny rainbows in our water glasses. We were nibbling at our third appetizer.

'Maybe so,' I admitted, 'but there is a difference. You're a policymaker, and I work with people. I probably get more day-to-day satisfaction than you do. At least I used to, before all this fund-raising.'

He smiled. 'Who wants to work with *people!* They're so unpredictable.'

I laughed. 'The problem is institutions like the New York Diocese, which paid an ad agency millions of dollars to create an antiabortion campaign.'

'You'd rather they just gave the money to you.'

I laughed again because he was right. 'To my *kids*.'

'Is that why you left the Church?'

'The Church cares more about the unborn than the living. In Guatemala I worked with babies who were having babies, and I wanted to teach them about birth control.'

'The blind leading the blind.'

'What's *that* supposed to mean?'

'I expect you don't know a whole lot about sex.' He said it as if he would be more than willing to teach me.

'I know enough.' I sounded defensive and a little silly.

'Are you sure you didn't leave for a slightly more personal reason? Like David?' He said David's name as if he had known him.

'David was dead by the time I left the Church.'

'Did he ever try . . .'

'Why is it every conversation with you is an excavation into *my* past?'

'Remember when I asked you if you ever feel trapped?'

I remembered. At the Jefferson Memorial. Just before we kissed.

'I guess I was speaking for myself.' He smiled sadly. 'I want a new past.'

'Do we get to do that? Change the past?'

'If we change the present, someday we'll have a new past.'

I toasted that, but I was just pretending to drink my wine. I wasn't taking any chances.

'You'll like my house.' He added, 'I've prepared a room for you.'

'I booked a hotel.'

'Don't be silly. You're my guest.'

We crossed the P Street Bridge into Georgetown and the colonial past. It began to rain again. James's driver dropped us off at the top of a block where hitching posts prevented the entry of cars. James opened his umbrella; I slipped under it. A soft glow emanated from the old gaslights, which were now electric. A whisper of mist rose from the puddles on the cobblestones. A sudden wind flipped up his umbrella. In seconds we were drenched. He chuckled. 'I must be your rainmaker, Anna. Every time we go out, it rains.'

Laughing, we ran through the downpour toward a mysteriously secluded town house. Hemmed in by yew hedges, it nestled in the deep leaves of an old oak. He reached into his pocket for his key.

When he shut the door behind us, we stood in a glass-enclosed vestibule. I tried shaking the water from my sweater, but the cashmere had absorbed the rain, and even my underwear was damp. We took our shoes off.

'Wait here. I'll get us some towels.'

The eighteenth-century wallpaper was Chinese silk. A maze of vines among a riot of pink and yellow blossoms hid silent tropical birds. In a mahogany grandfather clock, the pendulum had stopped. A chill raced over my skin. A moment later James came back with two towels. I wrapped mine around my head.

'I'm going to change,' he said.

'Sounds like a great idea.'

I followed him up narrow stairs down a hall to the last door. Inside, I dropped my overnight bag on the bed. 'This was my mother's room,' he said. 'Every stitch of needlepoint is her own. It hasn't been used in years. Like it?'

'Very much.'

As he closed the door he said, 'See you downstairs.'

I sat down on the antique pencil-post bed. The room echoed an austere femininity. Above my head hung a starched canopy where crewel embroidery thistles glistened on cream-colored linen. From my bag I took jeans, a sweatshirt, and my new underwear. I decided to shower before changing. I even washed my hair quickly, as if I had to beat him back downstairs. To my surprise, I did.

The house was like a museum and just as immaculate. One sitting room led to another. I chose to sit on a Chippendale couch in a drawing room with rose-colored silk curtains. In front of me, on the Queen Anne table, sat a silver tea set. I picked up the pot. It was empty. Beneath me the couch's ball-and-claw feet gripped the polished floor.

The room was dark except for the recessed lighting fixtures in the rear extension. It was a while before I noticed the Flemish painting they illuminated. I got up to look.

Abraham, heeding God's command, is ready to sacrifice his son, Isaac. The knife gleams in Abraham's hand. Isaac, his face covered by his father's free hand, lies tied and naked. The boy can't see, he can't speak, he can't even breathe. Just before the knife plunges, the Angel of Mercy swoops from heaven to say that God was only kidding.

'One of God's nastier tricks,' James said. I hadn't heard him come in. He had showered and changed into a pale blue sweat suit.

He ruffled my wet hair. 'You look twelve years old, Anna. Let's go to the kitchen. I'll light a fire, make us some tea.'

As he led me through the dining room, where corner cupboards displayed salt-glazed stonewear, he explained that his father had been a senator from Massachusetts and this was his family's Washington home. How he had come to be its sole occupant he did not say. We passed through a smoking room. Glass cases lined the vertically striped walls. The cases displayed old weapons: knives, rifles with bayonets, handguns, even a diminutive cannon.

'Who's the collector?' I asked politely.

'My father,' James said proudly, 'and now me.'

He took my hand and led me through the kitchen to a sun room. Miniature lemon and orange trees bloomed in a forest of ferns. A potted orchid stood in a bed of smooth stones. Outside, the rain pattered down.

James knelt before the old brick fireplace. The flame

reflected on the glass wall between his indoor garden and the approaching winter outside, where the ivy climbed a very intricate trellis. How did it always know just where the next rung was? Raindrops slid down the sunroof's dome. The yard outside ended in a brick wall, where a plaster cherub nestled in the ivy. Miraculously balanced by the wings that spread behind it, the small chubby body clung to the top of the wall. The angel's hands covered its sex. Rain washed down its face.

I remembered the days and nights David and I had spent together searching for God in the jungle, finding only hungry children and each other. For the first time in a long time I remembered the night when David had touched me. The night before he was killed.

We had been hiding from the military, and we clung to each other, hoping for sleep. We were fully dressed. I felt his fingers crawling on my skin. I didn't move. It was getting harder to breathe. Trapped between revulsion and desire, I felt his hand between my legs. My body trembled. His fingers entered me as if I were water.

'Touch me, too,' he whispered.

But I was much too afraid.

'This room is my addition,' James was saying.

On the glass my fingers traced the falling rain as it quivered, clung, and let go.

'What are you thinking about?' James asked more softly, as if he had just noticed that I wasn't really listening to him.

'I was thinking about David.'

'What about David?'

'What it would have been like if . . . with . . .'

'Anna, I have to tell you something.'

I turned and looked into those changeable eyes. James Beardsley said, 'David was my half brother.'

I said nothing. I wondered how I hadn't known it sooner.

'I didn't know how to tell you. I tried that night at the memorial, but you misunderstood me, and I was afraid of losing any chance I had with you.'

'You should have told me the day we met.'

A harsh silence fell until he began to explain.

'David was the child of my mother's first husband. He died in a car accident, and a year later my mother married my father. She never loved him as much as her first husband. I don't know if that was the reason, but my mother never loved me like she loved David. David was the favorite son. Groomed to fulfill his father's ambitions. David turned his back on all that; he became a priest. And then he got killed.'

'What happened to your mother?'

'She died shortly after David did. Heart attack, broken heart. My father retired to England. I don't see him much. He's remarried. I'm glad for him. He finally escaped the shadow of David's father.'

'That's why you said you wanted a new past.'

He reached behind my neck and slid his warm hand against my backbone. My skin listened to his fingers move.

'Anna, are you going to come upstairs with me?'

'I don't see how I can now.'

'Because of David?'

'Because you're David's brother, and because you didn't tell me.'

'I'm not surprised.' He shook his head, then withdrew his fingers. 'I'll never escape that bastard.'

I felt claustrophobic. I looked around me. The house was so true to period that there were no telephones. 'What do you do when you want to make a call?'

He opened a cupboard, revealing a cordless phone. Across the room from me on a marble-top bureau stood a garden of photographs in ornate antique frames.

'Your family?'

'I found those antique-hunting. I don't know who the people are.'

'Why didn't you put your own family pictures in them?'

'I didn't like them much. Besides, how would it look – modern pictures in antique frames?'

'And you never married?'

'I was in love once, back in college. My mother successfully convinced me to let her go.'

I pondered that as the rain whispered.

'How well did you know your brother?'

'Enough to know David wasn't the saint you make him out to be. He always did exactly what he wanted. As if God had given him special dispensation.'

'Are you going to hold tonight against me?' I asked.

'It ain't over till it's over,' he said expressionlessly.

Later, in his mother's room, I undressed in the dark. I heard something just outside the bedroom door. Or were the footsteps in my imagination? I locked the door and went to bed. Above me the crewel embroidery gleamed like distant stars.

22

Monday evening when I got back from Washington, DC, Newark Airport seemed ominously empty. Tired travelers slouched in the waiting area's plastic seats. Sleeping children spread out on their parents' luggage. I headed for the bus back to the city, the emptiness of the terminal echoing around me.

We pulled out into the gray industrial wasteland of northern New Jersey. Chemical smells filled the air. I was anxious to get home, to kick off my shoes to sleep. The trip to Washington had filled me with a new sense of hope – not just for the program, but for myself, as well. In James Beardsley I had found a kindred spirit. He, too, was struggling. I had forgiven him for keeping his secret about David. After all, I had my secrets, too.

The bus entered the Lincoln Tunnel, and the harsh realities of the world I had chosen to make mine approached. In a car that passed I caught a glimpse of a young girl's head in the lap of a driver. At the end of the tunnel, he would toss her a five-dollar bill as she spat and staggered away. If she made enough money to get high and maybe buy a new miniskirt, she would feel proud.

The rushing insanity of Times Square was unchanged. As

I approached the storefront I saw a crowd outside my building. It took a moment before I made out the camera crews, reporters, and photographers. Had they heard about the break-in? Was it about Porsche's murder and Colin? Had there been a new development? As I stood on the curb deciding what to do, O'Shaugnessy's car pulled up. He leaned over and opened the passenger door.

'Get in.'

'What's going on?'

'They want to talk to you.'

'About the special prosecutor?'

'I'm afraid not.'

He took a folded *New York Post* from his dashboard and shoved it toward me. I flipped the paper open:

POST EXCLUSIVE
FALL FROM GRACE

Under the screaming letters two pictures were lined up like mug shots: an old photo of me next to a head shot of Lucky. I scanned the article. The exclusive carried Mike Taylor's byline.

His name is Lucky but he's not. In one week the grandmother who was raising him had a stroke, and one of his best friends murdered another in a crack rage. Sitting at Wendy's next to Playland, eating his first meal in several days, Lucky tells how he met his friends in the home of Anna Eltern, the director of Eden House.

'She would let you stay at her house, but if she liked

you, you'd have to have sex with her. My grandma was sick, so I stayed at Anna's place a lot. But then I got thrown out. Later she threw Colin and Porsche out because she was jealous of Colin. Everybody knew Porsche was her favorite.'

Lucky's father is in jail for dealing drugs. He doesn't know where his mother is. He lived with his grandmother in the apartment where a young girl's life was snuffed in the most brutal way imaginable, allegedly by preppy vagabond Colin Winklesworth III. Lucky lights a cigarette with trembling fingers and reminisces: 'After Anna threw Porsche and Colin out on Friday, they asked if they could stay with me. My grandma was in the hospital, but I had the keys to the apartment. That Saturday, Porsche was watching TV, and me and Colin went out to the park on Forty-seventh Street. Colin copped some crack. I smoked with him, and he started to get real weird. I stayed in the park and Colin went back to the apartment. I figure he killed Porsche cuz he was jealous that she would rather be with Anna than with him. I stayed out that night, and when I got back to the apartment, the cops were there. Everybody started telling me what happened inside, so I got scared and I split.'

Little is known of the private life of Eden House's mysterious founder, thirty-four-year-old Anna Eltern. The author of One Woman's Choice *is an ex-nun who worked with Covenant House in Guatemala. After leaving the Catholic Church in 1985, she returned to New York City, where she founded Eden House. Her work with the teenage runaways who haunt*

Times Square has received national acclaim. Repeated attempts to speak to Ms Eltern have been unsuccessful.

Whatever self-esteem I had drained from me as swiftly as air from a balloon. A dense cloud of shame descended. I thought about Toomey, the board, the kids. I tried not to think about the others – the anonymous readers for whom the *Post* was gospel. My hands started a frantic ripping until the paper lay on my lap like chunks of confetti. Outside the car window the West Side Highway sped by. 'I made a big mistake.'

'Why weren't you up front about those kids staying with you? Do you realize their prints must be on their way back from Albany? How the hell is that gonna look?'

'You believe it, don't you? You believe that crazy story!' I screamed.

'Why don't you tell me what did happen, Anna?'

When he said that, a twisted rage welled up in me. I started to cry. 'Don't,' he said. 'Please don't . . .'

But once I started, I couldn't stop. He pulled over and put his arms around me. 'All right, then,' he said softly as the traffic rushed by, 'let it out.'

He held me until my sobs died. 'How could Lucky turn on me like that?' I whispered, feeling that all my choices had been mistakes.

'Anna,' O'Shaugnessy repeated, 'what really happened?'

I explained about the board suspending Open Intake, how Colin and Porsche had come to be staying with me, and how I had lost my temper and thrown them out.

'What about Lucky? Did you throw him out, too?'

'No. Lucky was never *in* my apartment. Toomey threw him out of the storefront while I was in Connecticut when my grandfather died.'

'It makes no sense.' He rubbed his stubble. 'Why would Lucky be out to get you?'

The blood that rushed to my head was hot, and tears welled in my eyes. My voice came out in a hoarse whisper. 'I never . . .'

'I know that,' he said. 'I know you better than that. Protecting these kids has been your whole identity.'

'You believe me?'

'Of course I do.'

'Even after I tried to seduce you?'

'You and I are adults, Anna,' O'Shaugnessy said. 'It's different.' And he pulled back out into traffic.

O'Shaugnessy unlocked his door. I heard the dog dancing on the other side. The police lock slid back, and the shivering dog jumped up on her master, wagging her tail. O'Shaugnessy patted the dog's head. 'Just once, Anna. If you greeted me this way just once . . .'

The narrow hall with its velvet bulls and veronicas ended in the kitchen. When the dog stopped fawning, she turned to me, growling low in her throat.

'Don't mind her,' O'Shaugnessy said, 'she's the jealous type.'

Books, newspapers, and art journals were strewn across most surfaces. Unlike the night when I had come here drunk, I realized now that the mess was superficial. I sat down on the plastic-covered living-room couch. In front of me hung the kind of surrealistic painting that feels more real than a photograph. In a nest eggs were hatching. One was already cracked. A snake small as a thread was weaving its way out.

'I can't believe this is happening.'

'Now I know why you so desperately want Colin to be innocent,' O'Shaugnessy said.

'Colin didn't kill Porsche.'

'C'mon, now. Before his parents got that fancy lawyer, that kid confessed. You think he did that just because he needed attention?'

'Your buddies interrogated that poor kid for eight hours. I'd turn in my own grandmother after eight hours under the lights.'

'We have hard evidence. He was crazy about the girl – he told everybody so. The super saw him go into that building. Plus we got him going berserk in the video parlor screaming her name and about how he's sorry.'

I said, 'That's all circumstantial. You've got no witnesses.'

'Damn, Anna!' He stood. 'Even now you know everything better. Most murders don't have witnesses.'

'You've got connections – get the confession tape. See for yourself if it's fishy. The camera doesn't lie.'

'You want me to cheat and steal for your idea of justice?' He was yelling now.

'I'd better call Toomey to set up a board meeting. Then I'm gonna call a press conference.'

'And do what? Attack the department! That should be helpful. What you need is a lawyer with a rep to sue that rag so they know you mean business,' O'Shaugnessy said.

There was a long silence. The dog brought her leash to O'Shaugnessy and sat at his feet begging. O'Shaugnessy patted her head and rubbed behind her ears. 'All right, girl. You and me are going for a run.' He slipped the leash on the dog. 'Look, we both need to chill. Use the phone. Do what you have to. You can crash here. Use the loft.'

The dog ran forward until her leash snapped taut. As soon as O'Shaugnessy left, I called Millie. I knew she would be worried about me.

'Where are you?' she demanded. 'There's reporters everywhere.'

'I'm at O'Shaugnessy's.'

'Good. I always knew that was one man you could count on ... What are you gonna do, Annie? You have to fight back somehow.'

'I threw those two kids out onto the street, and I never told anybody, Millie.'

'That doesn't mean you deserve this kind of slander. I'm so mad I could spit. Toomey must be thrilled.'

'I'm going to call him now to set up a board meeting. After I've talked to them, I'm calling a press conference.'

Millie moaned. 'Anna, haven't you had enough press? That's how you got into this mess. Once they know you're there, they can turn on you whenever they want to.'

'I have to, Millie. I have to put my side on record. There's no choice now. Have you got any idea where Lucky might be?'

'No, but I'll find out. And, sweetheart, you *can* pull through this. You have to. You're just gonna have to believe in yourself more than you ever have.'

I pondered that contradiction. Believe in myself when I had nothing to pin that belief to? 'I love you, Millie.'

'I love you, too, Annie. And so do your kids.'

I called Toomey. His voice was cold and tight. At the end of our conversation, he asked if I was planning to offer a resignation. I told him I'd discuss my plans at the board meeting.

Then I climbed up to the loft bed in the alcove where O'Shaugnessy kept his easels and velvet canvases. I didn't even take my clothes off. And I didn't hear O'Shaugnessy come back in.

In my dream I sat naked under a Times Square movie marquee. Porsche, Colin, Lucky, Eclipse, and some of the other kids were sitting with me, wearing capes and bomber jackets. It was terribly cold. I tried to remember what had happened to my clothes. I was trying to hide behind the kids, hoping nobody would notice I was naked. Then I saw Toomey crossing the street toward me. I woke up fully clothed and drenched in sweat.

Outside, the city was coming to life. I heard toilets flushing, doors slamming, yelling, footsteps on the stairs, traffic. Soon I would have to face Toomey and the board. I climbed down from the loft. O'Shaugnessy was sleeping bare-chested. I knelt to whisper my good-byes; he opened his eyes.

'Thanks for last night. I'm going now,' I said.

He reached up and gently brought my head to lie on his chest. His St Jude medal was a small cold circle on my cheek. He ran his fingers through my hair. In a hoarse, sleepy voice he said, 'Take off the blindfold and stop flailing at the piñata,' which made about as much sense as any of his other aphorisms.

23

I climbed the steps to the center. I took a deep breath and opened the door. Rich Cannon looked up from his desk. Neither of us spoke. In his eyes I saw that he, too, was embarrassed. Then he smiled.

'I changed papers.' He gestured at the newspaper he was reading. 'I'm boycotting that lying rag.'

'Thanks,' I said, and took another breath. 'How do the kids feel?'

'See for yourself,' he said, and buzzed me in.

The autumn sun spilled over the dayroom; the smells of breakfast were still in the air. Kids stood around, getting ready to go to their classes. Dina spotted me first. 'Annie ... Annie ...'

All eyes turned to me. I felt transparent and fought for some kind of exterior that would make me seem less vulnerable. Then the kids began to surround me. A girl named Mellow threw her arms around me. She had come into the program with a three-week-old baby. She had run away from an abusive family. 'Anna, who you think paid Lucky to say those lies about you?'

'What makes you think somebody paid him?' I asked.

'What else?'

Juan said, 'Lucky didn't think up that craziness for nothing. Even he's not that far gone.'

Suddenly the chatter around us quieted. Toomey had come out of his office. He glared at the kids. 'What's going on here?' Without meeting my eyes, he said, 'We're ready for you. I suggest you send these young people to class where they belong.'

The kids stood around me, defiantly waiting for my response. In their eyes I saw the power I had lost.

'Go ahead, guys. I'll see you all at lunch.'

Toomey and the board sat in a semicircle; opposite them the empty seat was for me. But I took the chair protected by Toomey's desk. Their eyes fastened on me as if I were a calamity that mesmerized even as it revolted. 'The board members have all asked that we make this quick,' Toomey said.

This was the same group that attended all the meetings: Schneiderman, partner in a law firm and chairman of the board; Renée Delattre, the society hostess, in her designer suit; Buzz Greenberg, the real-estate tycoon; Arthur Baldwin, the limousine-service owner who had lost his son to drugs; and family-court justice Marianne Foster. Only the judge met my eyes.

'Thank you all for coming on such short notice.'

Schneiderman cleared his throat. Toomey inserted a finger under his collar. The judge's face became just a little colder.

'The statements in the *New York Post* article about me are false. The facts have been grossly distorted. The accusation of sexual misconduct is as far from the truth as anything could be.' I paused.

'Why don't you tell the board what did happen,' Schneiderman said in a tone that managed to be simultaneously compassionate and demeaning.

I explained exactly what had happened. When I finished, Baldwin softly said, 'You did this even after the board cautioned you not to?'

'Yes.'

Toomey added, 'Even after I personally went over there and threw the kids out?'

'Yes.' My voice trembled. I cleared my throat.

'Not too wise but understandable.' Judge Foster gave me an encouraging smile.

'The sin of pride.' Father Toomey shook his head sadly. 'You always know better.'

'From everything I've heard of these kids,' Baldwin exclaimed, his face red, 'they're unpredictable, they cheat, they lie.'

'These kids are what my life is about.'

'You still feel that way?' Renée Delattre sounded incredulous.

'I still feel suspending Open Intake was a mistake.'

In the silence that fell, I studied the scribble on Toomey's blotter. Schneiderman took a deep breath, stood, and leaned on the back of his chair as if he were about to begin a prosecution.

'The damage done to this program and the reputations of those of us who have agreed to be associated with it is inestimable, Miss Eltern. With the exception of one member, this board believes that perhaps you should step down.'

'I can't do that, Mr Schneiderman. That would be

tantamount to saying I'm guilty of the accusations in yesterday's paper.'

'Well, what do *you* suggest?' He sounded faintly sarcastic.

'Officer O'Shaugnessy, the precinct's community-affairs officer, has agreed to help me find Lucky Kelly. Once we locate Lucky, I feel certain I can get him to tell the truth.'

'What do you think this boy's motivation was in telling this story?'

'I don't know. When we find him, we'll ask. In the meantime I'm filing a lawsuit against the *Post*. In a few hours I'll hold a press conference. I won't hide from these charges. I'm going to confront them.'

'What about the proposals we have pending? How will they be affected?' Schneiderman asked.

The group leaned forward in their chairs, becoming a tight little circle from which I was excluded.

'That's precisely why we were wondering if it wouldn't be better for her to step down.' Greenberg spoke as if I were not in the room.

'A leave of absence maybe, until all this is cleared up,' Baldwin added hopefully.

'In the public mind, Anna Eltern *is* this program,' Judge Foster said crisply. 'If she steps down now, she will look guilty and you may lose *all* – not just some – of the funding we've applied for.'

'Perhaps Father Toomey should be the program's contact person with funders,' Schneiderman suggested. 'Just until you've cleared your name, Anna.'

I agreed to that and stood up. 'Will any of you be joining me at the press conference?' I asked.

Renée Delattre looked away. The other board members each explained that they were busy. Father Toomey said, 'You should definitely have your lawyer at your side, Anna.'

'I don't think so. I'm not a criminal. I can speak for myself.'

Back in my office I wrote a press advisory:

FOR IMMEDIATE RELEASE:

TIME: 1:00 P.M.
PLACE: ON THE STEPS OF EDEN HOUSE RESIDENTIAL CENTER *1933 Tenth Avenue*

Anna Eltern founder and director of Eden House will announce a slander suit against the New York Post *and will address the charges made against her in Mike Taylor's* Post *column at a press conference on the steps of the Eden House residential facility at one o'clock today.*

I faxed the advisory to Associated Press, United Press International, and the major dailies. Then I called Washington. I didn't know if James had seen the *Post*, but I wanted to tell him what was going on. As the phone rang I broke out in a cold sweat. His secretary, Dottie, picked up. He was not in his office, she said. I left a message that I needed urgently to speak to him. She didn't know when he would be able to get back to me. I went to the cafeteria. A group of kids waved for me to join them at their table.

As I pushed my food around my plate Juan asked, 'What are you gonna do, Anna?'

'I'm having a press conference here at one o'clock to answer Lucky's charges.'

'I think you should just kill the bastid,' Juan declared.

'Why you, Anna? You never hurt nobody!'

'She don't even like sex. Do you, Annie?'

'I never seen her with nobody.'

'C'mon, guys. You should know better than that. Whatever I do or don't like, sex is for adults, for people mature enough to handle it.'

'Why didn't you pick me? I love you,' one of the newer kids said.

'Don't joke like that.' Juan's face turned purple. 'Can't you see she's hurting? We all know you're on the up-and-up, Annie. Everybody who knows you knows that.'

'Can we come with you?'

I wanted to say yes. No statement I could make could equal the simple purity of whatever the kids would say. But when Toomey entered the room, his glare told me this would be impossible. The board would terminate me for sure.

'It's sweet of you to offer. But I don't think so.'

'We could tell them about the ID cards. Why else did we get them if we weren't going to tell anybody?'

'The board wouldn't like it, Juan. This press conference is about the charges against me. It's up to me to answer them.'

24

The glare of the klieg lights was blinding. As my eyes adjusted I saw that the sidewalk in front of the center was crowded with camera crews and reporters from every paper and every television station in town. I felt a momentary jolt of power. Then I saw Mike Taylor. His presence choked me with hatred.

'Ladies and gentlemen, thank you for coming on such short notice.'

Someone coughed. Or were they laughing? Across the street curious neighborhood residents were stopping, staring. I launched into my defense. When I had finished, I heard myself say, 'I challenge the *New York Post* to produce Lucky Kelly. I want to face my accuser.'

Then the questions came fast and hard. The same questions again and again. Over and over I affirmed my innocence.

'Are you saying that you violated your own board's policy?'

'Yes, I am.'

'When you threw them out, did you know that Colin Winklesworth had homicidal tendencies?'

'No, I did not. And neither do you. I'd like to remind you that Colin Winklesworth is innocent until proven guilty.'

The reporters started shouting.

'If Colin Winklesworth didn't kill Charmaine Jefferson, who did?'

'What about Winklesworth's confession?'

'I've said this before. Colin confessed after an eight-hour interrogation without the assistance of counsel. I doubt that his confession will hold up in court.'

'Are you saying that the DA indicted the wrong man?'

'Colin is not a man, he's a boy. And yes, I'm saying I believe that's a definite possibility.'

'Are you still calling for a special prosecutor for these murders?'

'Yes, I am. And I want to know why the police have made no arrests on the killings in July and August.'

'Why do you think Lucky Kelly said what he did?'

'I don't know the answer to that. I do question the *Post*'s printing his accusation without bringing him to face me and without speaking to me.'

'We tried to get your reaction before going to press,' Taylor called out.

'No, you didn't. I wasn't even in town.'

The reporters and cameras all turned toward Mike Taylor.

'We tried,' he repeated indignantly.

'No, you didn't, and those facts will be brought out in my suit against the *Post*.'

Goose bumps rose on my flesh, and I glanced across the street at a face that was watching me with a chilling intensity. As soon as I looked up, he turned to walk away. I didn't recognize his gait. But the shape of his balding head – I knew that. He lumbered heavily away, and the noon sun gleamed off the wad of keys attached to his belt. He crossed the street. I heard a small voice behind me. It was Dina.

'Annie Eltern is the best thing that ever happened to us. We know she never did any of the stuff Lucky said. And she's doing a great job helping us.'

Her voice became stronger as the cameras and reporters turned to her. She held up the fake ID she had purchased the night of Colin's arrest. The other kids all held up their fake IDs, too.

The elation of being so spontaneously defended by the kids mingled with a quick fear of how the board would react. I tried to coax them back inside.

'All of us bought fake IDs on the Strip with *no* problem,' Juan called out. 'That proves somebody's not doing their job, and it's not Anna Eltern. Annie's good people. We can count on her. The charges against her are bull—'

Dina interrupted him. 'The charges are all lies!'

'C'mon, guys, let's go in,' I said as the clamor grew louder.

Impulsively I turned back to the lights. 'Lucky, if you're watching, all is forgiven. Just come back and tell the truth.'

'Masterfully manipulated!' Taylor shouted as I ushered the kids inside.

The kids' faces were flushed. My heart pounded in my ears. I hadn't won anything yet, and things were a long way from normal. The dayroom was empty; classes had begun.

'Thanks, guys, but you didn't have to do that.'

'We wanted to, Annie. And we're gonna tell Toomey it was our own idea.'

'You'd better get to class before Toomey really gets upset.'

'Did you see all them cameras? We gonna be on the news tonight for sure.'

I was trembling. I went to my desk and pulled out the folders of the proposals I had submitted to various agencies and foundations. I made a list of contact people and wrote a status report. I hid my terror in a ruthless efficiency. Finally I could no longer avoid confronting Father Toomey. Without meaning to, I lingered in his doorway for a moment.

'Come in. Sit down.'

'These are the files on the proposals you'll be taking over for now.' I put them on his desk.

He patted the folders into a neat square. 'I'll do what I can.' He flipped through them, reading the labels.

I said, 'I never did like fund-raising.'

'What about the federal proposal?' he asked.

'I want to continue handling that one. The contact person on the committee is a personal friend. I need to talk with him before turning the proposal over to you for follow-up.'

He was staring at me sorrowfully. 'I think the diocese may pull me out of here,' he said.

'Is that what you want?'

The slight shift of his facial muscles said I should know better. 'I'm a misfit like you, Anna. I'm much more comfortable out here on the crumbling edge of a social order I don't respect anyway, than squarely in it. I'm just not as crazy as you are.'

'You know I'm innocent, don't you?'

He took off his glasses and cleaned them. 'I hate to say I told you so, but I told you so. Even here on the margin where everybody makes up the rules as they go along, your methods are too unconventional, Anna. You left yourself completely unprotected.'

'The kids came outside at the end of the press conference. Spontaneously.'

He put his glasses on before sighing deeply. There was no more resistance in him. As I got up to go he said, 'I'll tell the board that, Anna.'

My emotions were flickering, one moment hopeful, the next despondent. I walked around the corner to the apartment because I couldn't risk falling apart in front of the kids. As I unlocked my door the telephone was ringing. I ran to get it.

'What the fuck is going on in the rotten apple, Annie? I saw you on a news bulletin,' my sister Angie said.

'It's bad,' I answered, 'but it's not true.'

'Wanna come home?'

I considered in silence the option I hadn't considered in twenty years. 'I don't think so. I have stuff to do here. I've got to find that kid.'

'The one who calls himself Lucky?'

'If I find him, I can get him to tell the truth.'

'We had a big storm here last night. It snowed a month too early. The power went out.'

In my mind a curtain parted. I felt again the magical days of childhood when the power went out and the world stood still. If only that could happen now.

'Does Mom know what happened?'

'She reads the *Post* right after she reads the Bible.'

'Did she say anything?'
'Nope.'
We were both silent. Then Angie said, 'Keep in touch, okay? I worry about you.'

I tried Washington again. Still no James. I left another message. I was crying at the kitchen table when I heard the rapping on the door. I let O'Shaugnessy in.

'Hey, kid. You okay?'

I blew my nose. 'I'm whipped. Finished. *Basta.* Blotto.'

'Maybe this'll perk you up,' he said, walking toward my living room. 'Got a minute?'

'What is it?' I asked, already grumpy at the slickness with which he had butched his way into the apartment.

'It's the tape you asked for, Annie. Not the whole eight hours, but a pretty interesting excerpt. I got it from a friend at the DA's office.'

He extricated a videotape from the envelope he was carrying and inserted the tape into the VCR. 'This is about seven hours into the interrogation,' O'Shaugnessy said.

We sat down on opposite ends of the couch.

Colin was shaking. A hand from offscreen lit his cigarette. Bruises and swellings distorted his face. His lips were swollen.

'I don't think you're crazy, son, but I do think you need help.'

'Because I don't remember hurting her . . .'

'Because the polygraph says you did.'

'I thought I was taking that test to show I was innocent.'

'So did I, Colin, but I can't deny what I see here on the chart. Your heart jumps every time I ask you about hurting Porsche.'

'Couldn't that be because I love her?'

'I think you've got your doubts.'

'Because I remember running upstairs to Lucky's apartment, and then I don't remember much until I got arrested.'

'It's happened before, a kind of a blackout, a person snaps and does something they don't want to remember.'

'I *was* jealous.'

'And smoking crack.'

'I'm scared because I don't remember it.'

'And now there's doubt.'

'In my mind there's doubt. Maybe . . .'

'Well, let's go over it again from when you were in the park. Maybe we can spark your memory and that would help us all.'

'Me and Lucky were smoking. We didn't have a pipe, just a glass stem. We were laughing because the old guy was talking to his dog, fixing his Zorro hat. The dog looked like he was talking back. We laughed so hard the old man got mad. He tried to get the dog to attack us. That made us laugh even harder. The old man was buggin'. So we went around the corner to the mural.'

'Go on.'

'We smoked some more. I was feeling good till Lucky mentioned about Porsche being in his apartment with the john and I started to get jealous. I remember Lucky tugging on my sleeve because he didn't want me to go. But I punched him in the arm and left.'

'You see, son – you do get violent sometimes.'

'I guess I do.'

'Go on. What's next?'

'The next thing I remember is I'm in front of Lucky's building trying not to go up because I know she'll be mad. Anyway, I couldn't get in cuz the buzzers were busted, and I couldn't ring up. But then somebody came out and I went in.'

Colin rubbed his fingers over his forehead as if trying to dislodge something.

'You do have a good memory, Colin. I've had lots of people right here in this room whose memories weren't able to focus like yours can. What then, Colin?'

'My heart was making a lot of noise. I remember running up the stairs. I remember the apartment wasn't even locked.' Fighting back tears, Colin pulled on his cigarette.

'Then what?'

'I went in. At first I thought she was in there. I thought I saw her on the bed. Then I saw that it was just bloodstains. The place was empty. The bed was a pool of blood. A pool . . .'

'That must be the moment.' The voice is gentle.

Colin cocked his head, puzzled.

'The moment you snapped . . . the crack . . . the jealousy. She probably was there and then she wasn't because you killed her and threw her out the window.'

'Are my fingerprints there?'

'That's gonna take time to ascertain.'

'I feel sick . . .'

'What you're feeling now is shame, son. You don't remember because you're too ashamed to admit it even to yourself. But once you get it out and we get you some help, it'll be over with. Everything will be better once you get it out.'

'I want to tell you I did it . . . I'm just not sure.'

Static filled the screen. The tape ended. O'Shaugnessy turned to me. 'He's hooked. Twenty minutes later they reel him in and he signs the confession.'

I listened to the tape's annoying crackle. I couldn't speak.

'You were right, I was wrong,' O'Shaugnessy was saying. 'That kid was railroaded.'

'But why?'

'A thousand reasons. He was an easy target, the captain wants the case, the mayor needs good press, the suit from Washington is bringing hearings to the city. Just people, going along to get along.'

25

I didn't want to wake up, but Millie kept knocking. The knot in my chest had tightened during the night. I padded angrily toward the door. She stood there, arms full. I let her in, leaving the door ajar for air.

'I brought the papers, Annie, and breakfast.'

'I'm not hungry, and I don't want to read those rags.'

'Oh,' she said softly, 'I see all our best characteristics coming to the fore.'

She dropped the papers on the table, the *Post* on top. The headline said ELTERN DENIES ALL CHARGES, ATTACKS DA.

'When did I attack the DA!' I yelled.

'When you said they arrested the wrong man, I guess.'

I grabbed the paper. Aside from a few quotes in which I proclaimed my innocence, most of the text was devoted to my call for a special prosecutor.

'Boy, they really know how to twist—'

'I think the *Post* paid Lucky,' Millie said.

'Naw.' I shook my head. 'Even the *Post* isn't that crazy. They wouldn't have printed it if they didn't believe it was true.'

I picked up the *Times*. They, at least, had printed my

279

explanation in detail. They talked about the effect of the budget cuts just as more kids were fleeing the streets because of a rash of murders. They even mentioned my opposition to suspending Open Intake.

'You don't want this?' Millie started eating my bagel. When I get nervous, I can't eat. When she gets nervous, she can't stop eating. When I had finished reading all the papers, I began again with the *Post*. She took it from me and tossed it into the garbage.

I called Washington. Still no James Beardsley. And yes, Dottie had given him my messages.

Millie chewed her last piece of bagel and said, 'Lucky's grandmother is in St Clare's.'

I shot up. 'Why didn't you say so?'

Maureen Kelly lay on the bed, yellow as parchment and almost as transparent. The smell of illness and death was laced with ammonia. A tube dripped water into her arm. Maureen Kelly was eighty years old. Her heartbeat was a blip on the monitor. Millie stood over her, chubby and alive. She ran her fingers gently across the old woman's forehead. On the night table an unopened heart of chocolate truffles matched red roses in a vase. A banner read I LOVE YOU GRANDMA.

She opened her eyes. 'Millie.'

'Good to see you, Maureen.' Millie took her hand. 'What happened?'

'I heard a rushing in my head, and the next thing I know, I see St Peter's beard. The doctors say I had a little stroke.'

'Where's Lucky?' Millie asked.

'He was just here.' The old woman raised a finger toward

the roses. I stepped up to the bed. I kissed her damp forehead.

'Annie.'

'How you doing, Maureen?'

'Much better.' Half her face smiled. The other half didn't move. Her eyes told me that she knew nothing of the murder in her apartment.

'The boy,' she whispered. 'You'll take care of him, Annie?'

Millie shot me a look for which I had no words. 'We don't know where Lucky is right now.'

'He'll be right back . . .' A teardrop grew in the corner of Maureen Kelly's eye and slid down a bony cheek.

'I pray for Lucky,' she wept, 'and for his mother, but I don't have my rosary. The one I brought from Ireland. Lucky went to get it for me.'

I heard a rustle in the doorway. Lucky stood there holding the pink glass rosary beads. His eyes reflected that special horror of facing someone you've wronged.

'Don't run,' I said. 'Your grandma needs you.'

'Look who's here,' Millie said, grabbing Lucky's arm. We led him to the bedside. The old woman wept with one side of her face.

'I'm sorry, Grandma. I didn't mean to make you sick.'

Maureen took the rosary with her good hand. 'You're gonna be all right now, Lucky. You stay with Annie Eltern.'

She looked up at me as if I were the answer to a prayer, and then she fell softly away.

'Is she dead?' Lucky whispered.

'No,' Millie said. 'She's resting.'

Millie and I took Lucky into the hallway.

Millie said, 'Maybe you don't understand what you did, Lucky. If you don't tell the truth, Eden House will be shut down. All the kids will be back in the street.'

'*I'm* in the street,' Lucky said, 'and I don't want to be dead like Porsche.'

'The roses you gave your grandma are beautiful,' I told him. 'That was a nice thing to do.'

Pride and panic mingled on his face.

I said, 'They must have been very expensive.'

He kicked me in the shin, pulled away from Millie so hard she fell, and dashed out the emergency exit. I ran after him. When I got down to the street, I saw him ride off on a new bicycle. I ran after him, screaming his name. When he turned the corner toward Broadway, I stopped. Of course, there were no cops around. I stood there, my heart pounding in my throat, feeling so much anger that it made me sick. I headed back to the hospital awning, where Millie was hobbling toward me. We stood staring across the street.

Millie hooked her arm into mine, and together we walked home. It was midmorning, and the neighborhood shops and restaurants were coming to life. A well-dressed woman carrying a briefcase rushed along next to a bag lady whose shoes didn't match. Drivers were unloading their wares to *bodegas* and greengrocers. I heard Spanish, Russian, Korean. It would be hours before the addicts and their dealers came out of the basements, abandoned buildings, and rooftops where they slept.

'That little bastard,' Millie muttered. 'How could he do this to the one person who really tried to help him?'

'He'll come back, Millie. He's got nowhere else to go.'

Millie went to the center, and I went home to call O'Shaugnessy.

'I saw Lucky,' I said when he picked up.

'Where the hell have you been? I've been worried sick. I thought we agreed you were going to keep that goddamn beeper on.'

'It's on.'

'The hell it is.'

I reached into my purse. The beeper I pulled out wasn't mine. It was a fancy job with a clock and a ten-number memory. 'That's strange. I've got an extra beeper.'

Then I saw the little *P* scratched into the corner. 'I've got Porsche's beeper.'

'Great. But it's not doing me much good when I'm trying to reach *you*.'

I pressed a few buttons on the beeper. 'There's a number in the memory – 917-546-2222. The call was entered at one-twelve p.m. on Saturday, October ninth. Isn't nine-one-seven the car-phone area code?'

'Yes, it is.' He sighed, then added, 'Porsche was killed that night. I'm gonna put you on hold while I try the number, Anna.'

A few minutes later he came back on the line. 'It rings, but it doesn't pick up. Car phones aren't in the Reverse Directory, so I can't look it up.'

'What's that?'

'Just what it sounds like, you look up a number and get the name attached to it, also the address. The squad has one, so does the public library. Anyway, I have a source at the phone company. I'll check the number with her. In the meantime hang on to the beeper. It's evidence ... Where do you think Lucky went?'

'I have no idea. He was riding a brand-new bike, though. He seems to have come into some money. He brought his grandmother some very expensive gifts.'

'Weird timing,' O'Shaugnessy mused. 'Look, I gotta run, but please keep your beeper on, okay.'

After I hung up, I sat there wondering how Lucky had come by his good fortune. It seemed for a moment that the puzzle wasn't far from coming together. But the missing pieces were those crucial ones that made placing the others possible. The phone rang. It was Mike Taylor. And everything turned upside down again.

'A woman named Dixie Lee Brown has told the *Post* of another incident like the Lucky Kelly one.'

'I don't even know anybody by that name.'

'She alleges that you coerced her daughter, a girl named Eclipse. That you made Eclipse stay at the storefront even though she has a home. That you molested her there.'

'It's a lie.'

'Well, Ms Eltern, what would you say motivates all these people to lie about you?' he asked softly.

'Have you talked to Eclipse?'

'We can't find her.'

'Don't you think you should?'

'We're going with the mother's story. I'm calling to give you a chance to respond.'

'I think you should wait until you find the girl. She'll tell you it's not true.'

'I'm offering you a chance to respond now.'

I slammed the phone down. I had to find Lucky or Eclipse before morning.

26

'Are the hot plates in the food truck working?

I unpacked groceries onto Millie's kitchen counter. I had brought rice and the makings of chili, hot chocolate, and coffee.

Millie looked up. 'It's all working. But what about Toomey and the board?'

'What about them? They can't take the truck away from me. I own it.'

We hadn't used the food truck since the last series of budget cuts. Whenever we took the truck out, kids asked to spend the night at the storefront. Sometimes this led to an actual enrollment in the program. Often it was just a night off, a respite from the street. I had stopped the food runs rather than face turning kids away.

'I've got to find those kids tonight, Millie. You know the rule – if you don't disprove a media lie within twenty-four hours, the lie becomes the truth. But I hate taking the food truck out with ulterior motives.'

'We all have ulterior motives,' Millie said. 'This time you just know what yours are.'

I peeled an onion. Its pungent odor made my eyes tear. 'I've always had ulterior motives?'

'You need to be needed. That's what makes you feel good. Me, I prefer to volunteer with kids rather than at the senior-citizen center. I like to feel young.'

'Are you saying nobody ever does anything out of the goodness of their heart? That no motive is pure?'

She salted the water. 'I'm just saying in life it's never just one way.'

Millie turned the gas up under the pot of rice. The flame was a spectacular blue. The water began to boil. She adjusted the flame down. It went orange at the edges.

For the next few hours Millie and I cooked. We made rice, chili, corn bread, and coffee. Then I walked over to Forty-fourth Street and Eleventh Avenue to get the truck from the open-air lot with no gates where all the parked cars had seen better days. Tufts of weed grew from the pavement. A half-moon hung over the river beyond the lot. I knocked on the truck door. The parking-lot attendant opened up, sleepy-eyed. He napped in the truck, and in exchange I parked free. The hair net that cupped his beard and head told me I had caught him with his turban off.

'Hi, sorry to wake you. I need to use the truck.'

'Okeydokey, no problem, I am just finishing my dream.'

The truck smelled of sweat and feet. I opened the windows. The ignition struggled before catching. I drove to the storefront, where Millie waited on the curb. She sat at the wheel while I made several trips upstairs. In midtown even a vehicle of mercy would be towed if left unprotected for five minutes. We loaded the food tureens, several gallons of apple juice, coffee, paper plates, and cups. We headed for Forty-second Street.

Under a black sky the Strip rose ahead of us like Las Vegas from the desert – vibrant, electric, hollow. Kids darted in and out of doorways as if following the clues of a treasure hunt.

Millie sighed. 'It all looks so much worse when you've been away.'

I said nothing, wondering if the kids were getting younger or if I was just getting older.

Four teens pooled their money under a marquee that read WET PUSSY AND THE WICKED DICK OF DEATH. The kid who was doing the counting shook his head in frustration. The others dug deep into their pockets and came up with another quarter, dime, nickel. Triumphantly one kid found a penny gleaming in the gutter. I pulled up alongside them.

'You guys hungry?'

They looked at me, then back at each other. Food wasn't what they had been thinking about.

'Whatcha got?'

'Chili, apple juice.'

'Any coffee?'

'Yep.'

As I hopped down from the cab Millie pushed her bulky little body between the seats to the back of the truck and opened up. The smell of food wafted out. A couple of kids came over. Ahead of us, four movie marquees were dark, the letters removed, the theaters going under. We served coffee. The kids played with their change. This was a crowd of newcomers to the street, not yet hardened, still caught up in the adventure of living on the edge, out of reach of adult authority.

'Wanna make a donation?' One of them smiled broadly. He was about fifteen with golden curls. His teeth were rotting.

Millie reached into her coat. 'This is it, though,' she said, handing over some coins.

'Beats a blank,' the boy said, proud of his street lingo.

I filled a plate for a girl named Sweets. She had earned her nickname because she still had the Iowa cornfields written in her freckles. 'Hey, Lucky dissed you bad.'

'You heard?'

'Yeah. It's whack.'

I watched her eat greedily, then said, 'I'm looking for Lucky or Eclipse. You seen them?'

'What for?' A young boy I'd never seen before eyed me suspiciously.

'Whattaya think? What he said about her is some serious shit,' Sweets told him.

I said, 'I just want to talk to them.'

'Eclipse is back on the street. Her moms got arrested. And Lucky done disappeared from his grandmother's crib.'

'Where is he?' I handed a tall, emaciated redhead a plate. Her skin thin as tissue paper, she came and went like an apparition.

'I ain't seen him in a while,' Sweets went on. 'It's getting cold out here. I be sleeping in the Port Authority.'

Millie and I looked at each other. This was the point where we should have been able to offer the kids shelter, even if only for the night. Instead we said our farewells and climbed back into the truck.

The kids wandered up the avenue. Millie and I headed east. Past Broadway, Fifth Avenue was dark, empty. On Times Square itself the night moved fast. Desperadoes and tourists brushed elbows in the garish light of stores offering radios, CD players, tape recorders, ivory, and Oriental rugs. The after-theater crowd rushed toward elegant late-night suppers and decaf cappuccino. In front of the Army Recruiting Center, a stand-up comedian competed with two thirteen-year-old hip-hop dancers. The recruiting center was closed. Tomorrow it would open again seeking to attract some kids still well enough to send to war. We parked in front of Playland.

From the arcade rolled an electronic pitch, high and penetrating. Car, plane, and helicopter crashes mingled with the blows of hand-to-hand combat and the electric screams of women and men going down for the last time. Young men and boys played with a life-and-death intensity. The more they maimed and killed, the longer the machine let them play. Most were alone, playing against the most efficient killer, the machine. Among them pederasts offered quarters and waited patiently to strike. In the novelty section a dust-covered Frankenstein mask was surrounded by condoms, dildos, rubber vomit, glass eyeballs, and fake IDs from Harvard.

Some kids came out to the truck and asked for coffee and food. I knew several. After we had served the food, Millie and I sat with them on the milk crates we carried in the truck. This was a tougher crowd. Many had been in the street for years. Most had been so misused by adults, their anger made them unpredictable. Any scam was justified.

'Why haven't they fixed those machines?' I asked.

'I guess they waitin' on the Mafia to bring some new ones,' a kid named Double J answered. Double J was a lanky seventeen-year-old from Harlem whose nights in the street had already burned him out. His teeth rotting, his clothes dirty, he had become the rough trade only a down-and-out pederast might buy. He practically lived in Playland.

I asked, 'Are those the machines Colin broke?'

Double J eyed me. 'What's it to you?'

'She's just talking to talk.' Millie sipped her coffee.

'It's like they packed it up, packed it in, disappeared. All three of 'em,' another kid mused.

'That white nigger could pull some crazy skins.' Double J shook his head.

'Shi-it, all the pussy Lucky pulled had crabs goin' round in the naps.'

'I can't get with that.'

'Anyways, it ain't true. Chicks pay him to use his crib, that's all. He do get dumb dollars.'

Listening to the kids' coldhearted chatter, I wondered what had made me think I could ever make a difference. Sitting in front of Playland was like sitting in a foxhole. The noise began to nauseate me.

I asked, 'Does anybody have any idea why Lucky said what he did about me?'

A silence fell. In the strobe that illuminated a novelty-store window on the corner, a red-faced devil jumped back and forth.

'That thing gives me the creeps,' Double J muttered.

A kid named Radio tossed his coffee into the gutter. 'This is some vile shit.'

'It is bad,' I agreed.

In the flash of the strobe, the devil rocked toward the glass that separated us. 'That sucker's sweatin' me,' Double J said. 'I ain't 'shamed to say it.'

Radio's laugh was bitter, old. 'You scared of the wrong thing, my man. It's these fools out here you need to be worrying 'bout.'

'Can I get an answer?' I glared at Double J.

'I don't know why Lucky dissed you. The last time I seen Lucky, he had new clothes and crazy loot. He didn't even see me.'

He got up to help me put the milk crates away. When we were between the truck's doors, I slipped him a five-dollar bill. He whispered where I could find Eclipse in my ear. 'But you didn't get it from me,' he said softly.

Back in the truck's cabin Millie and I shared another cup of coffee. 'This really is bad,' I said.

'I don't think they're out there.'

'A little bird whispered in my ear that Eclipse is working at the Pussycat Lounge.'

'How'd she get a job in that hellhole? She's underage.'

'What else is new? Anyway, it's early for the Pussycat Lounge. Let's try the crack house where Lucky hangs out. The one on Forty-seventh.'

It was a four-story prewar building two doors down from the pocket park on Forty-seventh Street. On the upper floors senior citizens and single-parent mothers lived with their children behind iron-gated windows. Last year a college student had tried to organize the tenants against the crack dealers on the lower floors. A dealer had shot her in the back. She died; he set up shop in another building. These days tenants barely spoke to each other. Window-box gardens hinted that the struggle continued in lonely silence. In the alley there was a side entrance to the basement. It was open to all who dared enter.

I followed rancid garbage cans to the boiler room, then waited for my eyes to adjust to the darkness. I knocked. Above me a toilet flushed. The roach-covered walls shimmered and shifted. Mildew grew on old clothes spilling from ripped plastic bags. Rusty pipes creaked. I knew the teenager who came to the door. His name was Dutch. He didn't remember me. Dutch's once-solid build had become a narrow frame that held some sagging skin. He was seventeen, but he looked eighty. I said, 'I'm a friend of Lucky's.'

A water bug popped underfoot. 'So?'

I held up a twenty-dollar bill. 'Is he here?'

He snatched the bill with his withered hand. His bulging eyes rolled in the direction of the boilers. Permission to enter.

Trembling fingers had written names in the soot that covered the boiler. It cranked up, groaned, and then died. In a pile of ash, rats nibbled a decomposing carcass. I slipped sideways through the space between the boiler and the wall. The stench of vomit, urine, and feces devoured the air. Across the room a hand I couldn't see lit a Bic. A crack pipe gleamed in the darkness. In it the milky smoke of death uncoiled. Matches flickered like Connecticut fireflies in August. I stepped between the mattresses looking for Lucky. Groaning skeletons curled to the wall in fetal positions. Other bodies scurried and scrambled toward the ever-flickering crack pipes. I heard a whispered negotiation.

'Not my ass, man,' a young girl's voice pleaded.

'I don't want no pussy I can drive a truck through.'

'Gimme my hit first.'

A match flared. The rock cocaine crackled as it burned with a high, sweet smell. The little body turned on its knees.

With the pipe in his mouth as he rode her, the man was weirdly luminous, his thin limbs elongated. I could hear his lungs sucking the pipe. The crack dissolved into a glowing ember. He groaned. She whimpered. Around her, three emaciated bodies writhed like snakes in a nest.

'Hey, baby, a hit for a hit.'

In the skeleton that faced me, two eyes burned fiercely. I turned to leave. Bones grabbed my arm. 'Hey, what are ya, a cop?'

I didn't answer. 'If you ain't a cop, take a drag.'

I tried to pull away. The skels rose from their mattresses. I saw an Uzi, a handgun, and the glint of a blade. The pipe neared my lips.

'Just a puff, baby.'

I inhaled. A thin line of smoke slithered down my throat.

I felt, for a fleeting second, the lightness of my soul, the racing of my heart, a sweet freedom from memory and pain. The world that opened up was inside me. The ugliness around me disappeared. My skin melted in ecstasy. Someone laughed. Dutch spun me around.

'Don't be wasting my shit on her!' He shoved me toward

the exit. Blindly I clutched the boiler, the walls, the door. 'That'll cost you a bill,' he said.

I handed him the rest of my cash.

Outside, the night air seemed unbelievably sweet. I was bathed in sweat. My molecules vibrated so fast, I was afraid they were jumping from my body, that I was disappearing. I hobbled toward the food truck. Around me the buildings seemed to crumble. But the night was far from over. I dropped Millie off, went home, changed clothes, and called O'Shaugnessy.

27

I used the cornucopia knocker on O'Shaugnessy's door. Inside I heard him come grumbling to the door.

'Who is it?'

'Me. Anna.'

The door opened. The dog jumped up to sniff my crotch. I pushed her back.

'God Almighty, Eltern, Halloween isn't until Monday.'

I pulled Porsche's black wig from my head. 'I'll wait in the truck.'

Ten minutes later he came out in jeans and a Yankee jacket and cap. Because I was nervous, I asked him to drive.

It was midnight. On Tenth Avenue a lone butcher puffed on a cigarette under the slaughterhouse awning. The rust-colored blood-stains on his frayed white apron shifted in the play of passing headlights.

'What if some reporter spots you?'

'That's what the disguise is for.'

'And if you do get in? Will you be able to handle it?'

'I have to. Eclipse won't talk to you.'

I put the wig back on. He kept his eyes on the road. To break the silence I said, 'There's only one way the killer himself could be in a position to pull the strings on this smear campaign against me.'

'How's that?'

'It's Dr Love or Blue Fly himself. They can terrorize kids like Lucky into saying whatever they want.'

On the avenue ahead, all the lights were green. He pressed the pedal. I saw the muscle in his thigh contract. 'What about Eclipse's mom?'

'What about her? She's a hooker. They probably run her, too.'

We parked as close to Broadway as we could get and walked to the Pussycat Lounge. Smiling clowns with red, orange, and green balloons lit the narrow stairway. Music pounded on the floor above. On the wall, mirror chips shattered our faces. O'Shaugnessy shepherded me past the bouncers into the main room.

It was a huge room decorated to look like a circus tent. The walls were black, the carpet red. A bar snaked from one end of the room to the other. Tables lined the walls. From the bar, poles rose into the ceiling. The kind that firemen slide on. The girls were naked in a variety of ways. Some wore just G-strings, some push-up bras. One Oriental girl wore a negligee that reached just to the top of her legs.

I was the only woman patron. O'Shaugnessy and I sat down at an empty section of the bar. Suddenly I resented him intensely. He was one of them. The men. The girls kept peeking at me. Was it because I had my clothes on? Without wanting to, I mentally compared my body parts to theirs.

Through the legs of one of the girls, I saw a young man's face angled upward in awe. When he saw that I was watching him, he smiled sheepishly and moved one hand over the other to cover his wedding ring.

A large blonde danced above us. She wore only fishnet stockings. She squatted down to talk, her legs spread wide, her young eyes glassy.

'He your guy?' she asked me, pointing at O'Shaugnessy.

He kicked my foot. 'Yeah,' I said, 'I guess he is.'

'You jealous? Cuz I don't wanna disrespect you.'

'Nooo,' he answered for me. 'Coming here was *her* idea.'

'Got any matches?'

O'Shaugnessy handed the blonde a book of matches. She split two marches in half, giving them legs. With a little spit she fastened the matches to her nipples and lit them.

'Blow 'em out,' she told me.

I raised my head and blew the matches out. She smiled proudly.

'That's some trick,' O'Shaugnessy complimented her.

'Yeah, I'm the only one here that can do it.'

She patted her thigh where a garter displayed dollar bills. O'Shaugnessy slipped a dollar into the garter. I wondered how many kids she was feeding. She asked, 'That's from *both* of you?'

I had no singles. I put a five-dollar bill under the garter. In the holes of the fishnet I saw needle bruises. The barmaid came to take our orders.

'Could I have a drink with you?' The naked blonde smiled down at us.

'Maybe later,' O'Shaugnessy answered.

She moved on. He explained that a drink with the girls

cost twenty dollars. O'Shaugnessy ordered a beer. I asked for Coke. Across the room an archway opened into another room, a room that contained many little rooms. Rooms with doors. In front of each door a barely clad girl rubbed her body suggestively. One girl had placed a leg up on a chair to advertise her wares. A shapely black girl faced a mirror. She looked like Eclipse.

I got up. 'Be right back,' I said to O'Shaugnessy.

When I got to the next room, it was a mirror. In it Eclipse was walking toward me. The real room was behind me. I turned. Eclipse went to the women's room; I followed.

Eclipse entered one of two red lacquer stalls. I waited by the mirror. I heard her sniffing coke; then she flushed and stepped out.

'Hey, hey.' Even in her spiked heels she was just a naked little girl.

I pulled the wig from my head.

'Anna!'

'What are you doing here?' I asked her.

'I'm sorry about what my mom did to you, but don't let the boss see we talking.'

'Do you know why she did it?'

'She didn't have no choice.'

'We always have a choice.'

She laughed sourly. 'Who told you that?'

I said, 'You could choose to do right by me.'

She walked up to the mirror to deepen the color of her crimson lips. After she blotted the lipstick, she said, 'You look silly in that wig. Is that what you gotta do now, hide out?'

The disco beat in the main room thumped steadily on the

walls; the stink of stale urine consumed the little air we had in that windowless room. She studied herself in the mirror, hard woman one minute, lost child the next. She was weighing the odds, trying to figure out whom she could trust. I leaned back. A foot kicked the door behind me.

'Hey, you giving *birth* in there?'

Eclipse shuddered. I saw goose bumps on her midnight skin. 'Look, I don't want my mom to get hurt, but I wanna help you, Annie. Can you meet me at the Forty-seventh Street park? I get off in an hour.'

The banging on the door became angrier. As I moved aside, Eclipse went back into a stall. Over her shoulder she whispered, 'Bring a flashlight and don't let nobody follow you.'

I unlocked the door, and an angry dancer pushed past me. 'I damn near pissed on a customer.'

Back at the bar a buxom dancer stood over O'Shaugnessy.

'It wasn't Eclipse,' I told him. 'Let's get out of here.'

'Sit down. I gotta pay the tab.'

He signaled the waitress. The dancer squatted, reached down between her legs, and with two fingers spread her labia. Inside, it was pink with folds and layers. She wet a finger and flicked her clitoris. It popped up like a rosebud. I felt my heart beat in the hollow of my throat.

'Got a cigarette?' she asked.

O'Shaugnessy handed her a cigarette. She inserted it into her vagina. I saw her muscles contract. A tuft of smoke rose from the cigarette. O'Shaugnessy slipped a bill into her garter.

'That's from both y'all?' Her smile showed teeth that

needed braces. She took the cigarette from her vagina, placed it between her lips, and took a drag. 'You don't like my trick?'

I put five dollars in her garter. O'Shaugnessy paid the barmaid. I headed for the stairway to the street. When I got out there, Broadway was spinning.

'C'mon, it wasn't that bad,' he said.

I kicked him. 'You enjoyed that.'

He bent to rub his shin and seemed to speak to the shards of glass glittering in the cement. 'I told you before I'm not that hard up.'

I started running toward the truck. I was still trying to unlock it when he walked up, calmly. My knees were shaking. I heard car horns, a siren, the backbeat of hip-hop. We got into the truck. The Times Square billboard and all the lights on Broadway shifted.

'Just take me home,' I said savagely.

'Get off your high horse, Anna, and walk down here with the rest of us.'

'That Pussycat Lounge is pathetic.'

'Oh, so that's my fault, too.'

I said, 'I'll drive you home.'

'Forget it, just head for the lot. I'll walk you home and grab a cab.'

'That's okay.'

'I *said* I'd walk you home.'

We drove back to the lot in an angry silence. Finally he said, 'I can't win with you. It doesn't really matter what I do. You hate me. I might as well accept it. The next time you come knocking on my door at midnight, I'll remember not to answer.'

Walking back to the storefront, I kept hoping he'd say something. I wanted to make amends but couldn't find the words. I unlocked the door slowly, stalling for time. But O'Shaugnessy didn't even stop. He'd reached the corner before turning back to say, 'Porsche's killer's out here, Anna. So quit playing detective.'

It was still dark when I went back out to meet Eclipse. I grabbed my flashlight and took a detour to the Forty-seventh Street pocket park. The old man slept on a bench, his dog in the shopping cart next to him. When I walked toward them, the dog started to howl. Tangled bodies slept under the mural.

'Anna!' Eclipse sat on the broken swing seat. 'Let's go before somebody sees us.'

I followed her to the last boarded-up building on the block, her high heels clicking on the pavement, my sneakers squeaking.

'You sure you weren't followed?'

'Positive.'

We stepped into the alley between the buildings. I heard her feel for a loose board. She pulled it out, set it on the ground, and climbed into a hole in the darkness.

'Step where I step,' she whispered.

When we were inside, she put the board carefully back into place. It seemed to take a very long time. Only when the window was again covered did she say, 'Okay, now you can use your flashlight.'

We were in the bedroom of a first-floor apartment. I followed her to the living room. Here the floor was just a ledge to a large, jagged hole into the basement below. Eclipse stepped up to the edge. An old armchair on which two mice played tag hid the top of a ladder. She shoved the chair aside.

'Gimme the flashlight. I'll light you from below.'

She began her descent. I waited. A few minutes later a beam of light illuminated the rungs of the ladder. I climbed down toward what looked to be a mountain of ceiling mortar, floorboards, and rotting furniture. She took my hand and led me around the mountain to a basement grotto.

Everything stood on a fake Oriental rug: a couch that matched the chair upstairs, a chest that served as coffee table, a milk crate that propped up a painting of Palestinian women peering through the mesh fence of a detention camp. Colin, Lucky, and Domingo sat on the same side of a picnic table, the mosaic of their faces shifting in the flicker of a patio candle. An unopened bag of White Castle miniburgers and a bag of doughnut holes were on the table.

'Annie, it's our turn to feed you,' Domingo said proudly, opening the bags.

'You fixed this place up nice,' I told them.

'Nobody can find us here,' Domingo said. 'Not even the crackheads who use the empty apartments upstairs.'

'Who are you hiding from?'

'The grown-ups.' Colin passed the food.

'I'm sorry I let you guys down.'

'Anything to drink?' Eclipse asked.

'We got a forty.' Lucky got up to open a picnic cooler standing in the darkness at the edge of the rug. He came back with a quart of beer, opened it, took a swig, and passed it on.

Colin looked like a concentration-camp survivor who ages a decade in a year. His blond hair seemed streaked with silver, but it could have been the light. 'What are *you* doing here?' I asked him.

He shrugged. 'My parents bailed me out, but they don't really believe I didn't do it. I couldn't stay there.'

'If you jump bail, everybody's going to think you're guilty.'

'Not if we prove he didn't do it.' Domingo poked a finger into the paraffin circling the candle wick. He withdrew his finger and peeled off a perfect wax fingerprint. 'You could help us,' he said.

'Help is a two-way street, Domingo.'

'Promise you won't tell anybody about this place,' Eclipse said.

'I won't tell if you don't want me to, but if we're gonna prove Colin's innocent, we need Officer O'Shaugnessy's help.'

That frightened the kids, and they stared into the darkness around us. In the candle's flicker their faces kept changing shape.

I said, 'O'Shaugnessy's already on your side, Colin. He saw the tape of your confession, and he says you were railroaded.'

'Hey-Zeus is not like the others,' Eclipse said. 'He's never tried to get free sex from me. When he picks you up, all he ever does is send you to the program.'

'I did a stupid thing, Annie.' Lucky frowned. 'I wanna tell the truth, but we gotta get the killer first.'

'Was it your own idea?' I asked.

He shrugged. 'That jive reporter kept coming around.

Everybody knew it, and then Blue Fly gave me mad bucks to tell that story. After I saw the papers, I felt real bad.'

Eclipse added, 'Then you gave that press conference and Blue Fly was pissed. He went around looking for somebody else to lie about you. He tried with me, but I said he should just kill me.'

'So how did he get your mom?'

'He didn't, I don't think. Moms got picked up for loitering. When they let her go, she went straight for the phone.'

I said, 'I don't get it.'

'She was in the precinct-house pen. The killer musta got to her hisself.'

Domingo shoved an envelope toward me. 'Open it,' he ordered.

It was the photograph of Porsche, the copy Domingo had made for himself, just a bit bigger than the original. He pulled the candle closer and tilted the photograph to its flicker. The flame seemed to jump into the picture, right into the gleam on the third cop's hand. The cop who wasn't in the picture.

'See that?' He pointed.

He pulled out a strip of photograph paper that was still in the envelope. It was an enlargement of the hand. On the pinkie I saw a golden snake ring.

'There's lots of rings like that,' I said. My heart, though, was remembering Porsche's gift to me. How I had placed it in the medicine cabinet for safekeeping. How after the burglary, I had never seen it again.

'Porsche had a ring just like that,' Domingo said firmly. 'She told me a john gave it to her.'

'You think the cop and the john are the same person?' I asked.

Eclipse nodded. 'Porsche told me she hadda play along with this cop freak because he was a friend of Blue Fly's. He would tell Blue Fly when the busts were coming, and Blue Fly made sure he got all the free sex he wanted. That cop was her first client.'

'We're gonna need O'Shaugnessy's help,' I urged.

'We know he hangs out at Circus World, Porsche told me that,' Domingo said.

'We can't get him arrested without some proof,' I said.

'We don't need to arrest him. We could just kill him,' Lucky suggested. 'Everybody knows the law don't work.'

'If you do that, Colin will never be free. They'll convict him.'

'I don't care,' Colin said fiercely. 'Just bring him here and we'll ice his ass.'

'We do this my way,' I said, 'or we don't do it.'

When I left the kids, *New York Post* trucks were already rolling to newsstands across the boroughs.

28

The picture was blurred, a grainy moment of happiness gone by. I was dancing, lost in the rhythm, laughing with Juan, that day of the protest on the plaza of the Harlem State Office Building. The moment had been frozen, captioned, and changed into a cardinal sin. I had dared to have fun. The story read:

EDEN HOUSE SIN HOTBED

In a modest Hell's Kitchen apartment a young mother weeps bitter tears as she describes her daughter's ordeal at Eden House. Dixie Lee Brown the second person to come forward and accuse Eden House founder and director Anna Eltern of sexual misconduct with the program's clients said that she did not want her address revealed because 'that woman has goons all over the neighborhood. She thinks she can do better than us parents. Why don't she stick to runaways like she supposed to?'

Dixie Brown has had her share of troubles and heartaches. The daughter of a Georgia sharecropper who died when she was only twelve, Dixie married at sixteen. At eighteen she was pregnant. At nineteen her husband left her. Dixie does not deny that when she became homeless she resorted to shoplifting to feed her infant daughter and herself. Currently on welfare, she is attempting to climb out of poverty by returning to school. But once again her family has been ripped apart. She explains, 'Eclipse be acting strange, not eating, not going to school. She wouldn't talk to me. Some nights she wouldn't come home. Then one night I follow her and come to find out she's staying at that storefront. She talks about that Eltern woman as if she were some kinda saint. But I knew something was wrong. Last week, after I read about Lucky Kelly, I sat Eclipse down and made her talk. She said it happen to her, too. Eltern likes young meat. That's why she has that program. Why else would she be in this neighborhood when she don't have to be? Now Eclipse run away for real, and I could just kill that Eltern. I hope the law does its job for once and puts that woman away.'

A ribbon of bile rose from my stomach. I pressed my face against the table's cool surface. I was whipped. There was no fight left in me. Had I really done this to myself? I felt the city closing in on me. I got dressed and headed for the parking lot. I didn't know where I was going, just away to breathe, to think.

I was already on Forty-second Street when I realized I had a flat tire. After kicking the tire a few times and stubbing my toe on the rim, I opened the trunk and checked for a spare. Then I slipped the jack under the car and began cranking it up violently. My despair had shifted to a mute rage.

'Need a hand?' I didn't bother to turn around. O'Shaugnessy's Puerto Rican drawl was unmistakable.

'That's okay. This won't be the first tire I've changed.'

'I'm sorry about last night, Eltern.'

I nodded. The kinder he got, the more I wanted to cry. Obviously he had read the morning paper.

'Where you headed?' he asked when I didn't answer.

He brought a hand big enough to cover my face under my chin and forced me, gently, to face him.

'I don't know,' I said, avoiding his eyes, 'for a ride.'

We finished changing the tire together. 'Listen,' he said, 'I got a sick day comin' to me. Lemme go with you. I want to talk to you about the case, and other stuff, too.'

We wound up going in his car because it seemed safer, but he let me drive. I needed to drive. Driving gave me a focus other than my pain, my confusion. Without thinking, I headed up the Saw Mill toward what had once been home. After a while O'Shaugnessy said, 'Eclipse's mom called Mike Taylor from the precinct pay phone as soon as she walked. She was never booked, they didn't bother.'

'How do you know that?'

'They were gossiping about it in the precinct house.'

'What are you telling me?'

'I'm not sure. It just seems odd . . . as if the person who put her up to attacking you was right there in the precinct house.'

I concentrated on the road for a while. As we got out of Manhattan the roadside shimmered with autumn colors and the leaves that swirled on the pavement disappeared under us as we passed.

'It does make sense,' I said finally, 'if what the kids told me last night is true. I thought they were just paranoid about cops at first, but now ... I wonder.'

'Last night! I thought when I dropped you off at home last night you quit playing detective.'

'Before you go off, do me a favor, just listen for a minute.'

'I thought I told you not to play detective.'

I told him about the snake ring on the hand in the enlarged photograph. The ring just like the one Porsche had given me. The ring I had been looking for the night of the burglary. The ring *he* didn't think was important. The snake that swallowed its own tail. 'The kids said this cop gets free sex in exchange for warning Blue Fly when a bust is scheduled to go down.'

'Did you ever find that ring?'

I shook my head and asked, 'Any word on the phone number in Porsche's beeper?'

'It's definitely a car phone. It's listed to a limousine-rental firm. But I haven't been able to find out who was renting the limo it was in yet. I know Blue Fly sports one now and then.'

'The kids are fingering a cop. Did you hear me when I said that? They told me he hangs out at Circus World.'

'I heard you,' he said. 'This time I hear you. I'll stake out Circus World myself when we get back.'

We rode in silence until he said, 'There's only one good thing about all this mess.'

'What's that?' I took my eyes off the road to look at him, just for a second.

'You never would have let me get this close any other way.'

I was sweating slightly in the autumn sun refracting through the windshield. I wiped the dampness over my lips with a finger and thought how to answer. Any other time I would have denied it. But trapped in the car with him as I was, it didn't seem possible. So I just turned into a diner. 'Hungry?' I asked, parking the car.

'Yeah,' he said, 'hungry.'

We got out. The morning was brisk. Above us, dying leaves rattled like a shaman's bag of bones. I put an arm through his. 'All right,' I said, 'I admit it. You've been good to me.'

'Naw – naw.' He removed my arm and left it dangling at my side. 'Don't patronize me. You have feelings for me or you don't. Which is it?'

We reached the space between the outside and the inside doors of the diner. Beyond, the grill shimmered in its own heat; next to us stood the newspaper rack. My ruin was statewide, not just local.

'Look in your heart and answer me,' he demanded.

I grabbed the handle of the diner's heavy inside door. It resisted opening until O'Shaugnessy applied some muscle. We were at the counter watching the short-order cook pour batter into the waffle iron when I finally said, 'I guess there's a reason you're always getting under my skin.'

'Admit it, goddammit, you have feelings for me!'

He opened the menu to hide a twitch of the lips that threatened to become a smile. I turned to look at him then. His eyes were deep enough to swim in.

'Trying to start something?' I asked just to be sure.

On the counter he put his paw over my hand. 'Yes,' he said, 'I am.'

'All right, then. Let's see where it takes us.'

We ate listening to the banter of the waitresses and the working stiffs who ate there every day. After that we drove to Kent at the foot of the Appalachian Trail to walk and do our own talking. We walked until lunchtime and then followed the scenic route to Cornwall, Sharon, and Litchfield. Somewhere in the glorious gift of autumn colors that surrounded us, we decided to spend the night together. As the day was ending we drove along the Housatonic to find the right spot. I was at the wheel when I saw a sign that read HOUSATONIC MOBILE HOME PARK. My heart quickened. I stopped the car.

'What is it?'

'My dad lives down there. I haven't seen him in almost two decades.'

He leaned over and kissed my lips softly. 'I'll wait here.'

My father stood in the river between two hills, where red leaves flickered in the first moments of dusk. He reached into the water and studied the handful of mud he brought up. After a while he rinsed his hand, straightened his derby hat, and began to cast. In the dance of light and water, the fishing rod in his hand seemed to be holding him. I remembered how hard I had worked to forget him. And then I remembered how much I had loved him. He hooked a fish.

I listened to the click of the unwinding reel as he let a long line out. The fish fought for its freedom, but he anticipated its run. When he had reeled it in, he reached down into the water. In his hand the fish gleamed silver against the olive river. My father unhooked it and held it for a moment in the dying light. He returned the fish to the water, reached into his pocket, pulled out a flask, and took a swig. The current seemed to be holding him in its grip.

I walked down to him.

'Annie?' He squinted into the evening sun. 'Annie?'

Before thinking, I attacked, 'Did you hear that Grandpa died?'

'No habit?' he said, gesturing at my blue jeans and plaid shirt. 'Is it really you?'

'I came to tell you that Grandpa died.'

He struggled for an appropriate reaction. 'Jody died last year.'

Jody was his dog.

We stood in silence. I read the map of his face, its roads of laughter and pain.

'Still hunt?' I asked, searching for a kinder subject.

'Only in my dreams. In a green field with Jody. She lived a long time for a dog.'

I sat down on a rock that hung over the river. He pushed his derby back, and as he climbed out of his wader and put away his gear, he talked. I had forgotten what a storyteller he was.

'In this dream – it's a recurring dream – the wind in the tall grass sounds like waves coming to shore. Jody and I are walking. Ahead of us, the pheasant go up. I hear their wings beat the sky. I aim; I squeeze the trigger. A pheasant falls. Jody runs. She brings it back to me. I feel its pulse in my palm, fast the way a bird's pulse is. I open my hand, throw it up, and watch it fly back to heaven.'

'Like playing God, isn't it?'

'Just a dream,' he said noncommittally. 'I'm an angler, not a hunter or a fisherman.'

'How come you never tried to reach us?'

He turned to me, his bloodshot eyes pleading. 'Your mother always knew where I was.'

I mulled that over in silence. His hair and his beard were white. Above us, the geese cried.

'So you just forgot us?'

I took off my shoes and stepped into the water. It was cold, golden and silky soft. A school of tiny fish darted into the shadows of a rock. I curled my toes into the mud, which was warmer than the water. He sat on his hands to keep them from going for the flask, I assumed.

'I didn't forget. How could I forget? I'm the one that lost everything.'

He opened his tackle box. Inside were feathers, beads, hooks, and wires. He picked up a red-and-green-striped fly with wings of silver. 'In the river the fish really believe this sucker is alive,' he said proudly.

'What were Grandma and Grandpa like?'

He reached behind his ear as if dislodging something. 'They didn't like me much. They wanted your mom to marry an Italian, not a Polack like me.'

A breeze stirred the flame-colored trees across the river. They shivered in the water and the sky.

'Look,' he said, 'You may not believe this, but I love you. I just . . .'

I stepped out of the river, patted my feet dry on the grass, and put my shoes back on. 'It's okay, Dad, I just came by to tell you about Grandpa. To see how you are. To tell you I love you.'

He turned his glistening eyes to the other shore. 'I appreciate that, Annie. I'm fine, really I am.'

We said our good-byes, and I walked back up the hill to the car. It was empty. I turned to the crunch of footsteps on fallen leaves. Between the white beeches moist with dew, O'Shaugnessy walked toward me. He stopped to lean on a craggy old maple. I rested my body on his. In the oncoming cool of evening, he felt warm and safe. Solid as a tree with arms. Only the pounding of his heart said he was fragile, too.

'He's an old drunk,' I whispered as if it were a secret I had to keep even now.

'Doesn't mean he doesn't love you,' he said. 'Just means he didn't have the strength to live it.'

I cried a little bit, and then we walked for a while, holding hands.

'What were you searching for when you drove up here, Annie? Do you know?'

'I'm not sure. Everything that's been happening has made me want to look at the past again, at my choices, why I ran into the arms of the Church. I always thought it was devotion, and lately I've begun thinking about what lies behind the fierceness of my devotions – when I chose them.'

'Needs,' he said, 'needs of the heart. You weren't just running from, you were also running to.' He pounded at his chest with a fist.

I caught his hand just to stop him from thumping at himself. 'All right,' I said, 'I get the point.'

The bed-and-breakfast was in an old Colonial home. The logs in the living-room fireplace crackled in their flame cloak, and I smelled pine. Our room at the top of the stairs was wallpapered in pink and chartreuse stripes like gift wrap. An old four-poster bed was covered in a quilt my grandmother might have made. A cat slept on the rocking chair that seemed just this moment to have stopped moving. The lace curtains shimmied.

Our window opened onto a brightly lit Congregational church next door. We undressed in its reflected light, and O'Shaugnessy pulled the quilt back. I slipped under the covers. The sounds of choir practice joined us. As our bodies met, the children's voices rose high and pure and full of hope. Once in a while they faltered, giggled, then began again. And that was us, too. But all in all, we did all right.

Long after he had begun a slight snoring, I lay awake, content and still. The moonlight had turned the room to silver and sable and I felt that I was cracking through a shell. In that soft colorless light, I heard the bittersweet stirrings of a self I had denied, had run too fast to hear, had buried in the variety of my quests. I caressed O'Shaugnessy's sleeping back and listened to the hum of our naked bodies. We were so different, I thought. I had always had so little tolerance for him. In my annoyance with his style, I had overlooked his integrity. He turned to hold me, and in his arms I found a deep and trusting sleep.

Just before dawn we began the drive back to the city so that O'Shaugnessy would arrive in time for the first dayside shift. I let him drive so I could snooze. Also because I felt shy with him now and didn't know what to talk about.

'Call you later,' he said when he pecked me on the nose good-bye.

I walked home wrapped in last night's glow, feeling not a single premonition of what was to come.

29

The phone was ringing. It was Dottie, James Beardsley's secretary, calling from Washington. 'Mr Beardsley is on his way to New York. He should be landing in La Guardia in half an hour. He asked me to call you so that you'd be available at nine-thirty. He wants to talk to you before the day gets going.'

I thanked her. For a moment I was elated. I would finally get to explain to Beardsley and maybe save my funding. Afraid that he would get too busy to call, I asked, 'Could you give me a number where I can reach him, Dottie? Just in case I have to step out for a minute.'

'Certainly.' She read me the number. I wrote it down. I asked her to repeat it. She did. It was the phone number on Porsche's beeper. I folded my arms, cupping my elbows in my hands. The apartment was so quiet I thought the world outside had disappeared. Then the refrigerator began its obnoxious whir. The thinnest hand rounded the face of the battery-operated kitchen clock, second by soundless second. The phone rang again.

'Anna?' James sounded as if he were in a tunnel.

'James . . . I guess Dottie told you I've been trying to reach you for a week . . .'

'I've read the papers. To tell you the truth, Anna, I didn't know what to say.'

A surge of anger rushed through me. 'If you had returned my calls, I could have told you what's really going on. I guess you just didn't want to talk to me.'

'Do me a favor. Don't read my mind. You're not very good at it.'

I took a deep breath. 'I found Charmaine Jefferson's beeper in my apartment. Its memory shows that you called her from your car the morning of the day she was killed.'

The line went dead. I put the receiver down. The phone rang. I picked up.

'Sorry about that. We hit a dead zone. Happens all the time on this route. Anyway, Anna, I'd rather discuss this face-to-face. Meet me in an hour at the Plaza, room four-oh-five. We'll talk.'

I walked through the Plaza's lush mezzanine. In the Palm Court, elegant tourists enjoyed a variety of breakfasts under trees that belonged in the tropics. The shops on the way to the elevator offered lavish displays of gold, silver, pearls, silk, and buttery leather. In the elevator I was joined by a couple carrying Bergdorf Goodman and Versace shopping bags. They got off on the third floor.

The fourth-floor hallway was quiet. A deep crimson rug absorbed my footsteps. I knocked. He opened immediately.

'Come in,' he said, and closed the door quickly. A pale

peach floral rug seemed to float under the antique furniture. A heavy curtain blocked not only the noise from the street but the daylight. Inside the room there was no telling day from night. I had expected him to be angry, but instead he looked like a runaway who'd just realized the pimp is inescapable.

I said, 'Let's take a walk.'

An equestrian General Sherman guarded the entrance to Central Park. Just in front of him, on foot, Victory carried her palm. The statue, no longer covered in its original gold leaf, had been newly cleaned. I stopped to look up at it. 'Nobody remembers the misery Sherman left in the path of his march,' I said nervously.

'Even saints devastate somebody along the way,' Beardsley snapped. 'That's just nature's way. Heroes aren't perfect. What counts are the results they achieve.'

He headed toward a dozen tired old horses hitched to carriages alongside the park. Flies swarmed at their swishing tails. Blinders prevented them from seeing the cars that drove inches from their flanks. Big, soft eyes seemed to plead for release. Some of the carriages were open-air. The more old-fashioned ones had canopies with backdrops. Once inside, you couldn't be seen.

'I don't feel like walking,' Beardsley said, climbing into one of the older carriages.

I looked around.

'Hop in, ma'am.' A young man in a top hat and a black overcoat smiled down at me. His yellow teeth were coated in something that resembled cream cheese. I climbed in. I smelled the horse's sweat and my own.

The driver sat above us. I watched his back as he picked

up a thin whip. He made an odd clucking noise with his tongue. The horse tossed its head. The driver cracked the whip in the air. We began moving into the park.

Traffic became a hum in the background. The horse's hooves fell as slowly as if it were pulling a hearse. Our breath made little clouds in the air. I wanted to explain to Beardsley about the articles. But he launched right into his own defense. 'My mistake,' he said, 'was not reporting my wallet stolen the night you gave me the tour.'

'The wallet?'

He took his glasses off and cleaned them with the lining of his yellow silk tie. 'The girl called me. I didn't know who she was. She said she had my wallet. She said if I wanted it back, to call the next time I was in the city. So I did.'

'Why didn't you tell me?'

'There was nothing to tell. I beeped her when I returned to New York, but she never called me back.'

'Why didn't you say something when I came to Washington looking for her picture?'

'I didn't know it was the same girl. How could I have known that? I never saw her.'

My face and hands were cold.

'Where's the beeper now?' Beardsley asked.

I looked into his ever-changing eyes. The lie came to my lips with amazing speed. 'I gave it to Officer O'Shaugnessy. He's going to issue you a subpoena.'

In the Sheep Meadow a soccer game was in progress. Beardsley's skin was flushed with rage. His lips were smiling. He said, 'The officer doesn't have to subpoena me.

I'll gladly tell him what I know.' He looked down at his Rolex. 'I'll just call Dottie and have her push all my meetings back an hour. Then we can go see this cop.'

Back at the hotel I offered to wait in the lobby. As soon as Beardsley went up to his room, I moved to the pay phone. O'Shaugnessy wasn't at the precinct. I beeped him. Two minutes later the phone rang. 'Listen, I don't have time to explain. I'm on the way to the precinct with James Beardsley. The phone number on Porsche's beeper is his. He decided to come and talk to you voluntarily.'

'Where are you?'

'At the Plaza.'

'I'm all the way downtown.'

I slammed the phone down and ran up to the lobby, beating Beardsley by seconds.

'My car's out front,' he said when he came back.

In his car, he asked me about the *Post* articles. As often as I had rehearsed what I would say to him, I was tongue-tied. I just said, 'None of it is true.'

He looked at me for a long time. Finally he said, 'I believe you that it's not true, Anna. But how do you expect me to get your funding now?'

'I expect to find those kids and clear myself before the week is out.'

It was moving day at Manhattan South. The precinct was returning to its newly renovated headquarters on Fifty-fourth Street. Vans lined the block. Boxes and furniture littered the sidewalk. O'Shaugnessy was just locking his car when we pulled up. Over his shoulder hung a red robe. A rubber mask was squished under his arm. In his other hand he carried his canvas briefcase.

'Officer O'Shaugnessy,' Beardsley called.

O'Shaugnessy turned. 'Anna.' He smiled.

'You remember James Beardsley? We happened to run into each other and I mentioned the subpoena. He hasn't got it yet.'

O'Shaugnessy glared at me, then caught on. 'That's because we haven't issued it yet.'

'Can we talk inside?' Beardsley asked.

O'Shaugnessy grinned. 'Sure thing.'

We started up the precinct-house steps. A huge box came bouncing down the steps on a hand truck. The box bumped into O'Shaugnessy. The mask fell from his arm.

'Watch it Dowd,' O'Shaugnessy growled, rubbing his leg.

Beardsley picked up the mask. 'What on earth?' he asked, pushing two fingers through the eyeholes.

O'Shaugnessy grabbed the scarlet mask back. 'That's my Halloween costume. We're having a brand-new undercover detail at the parade, volunteers, boroughwide. There's been a little too much gay bashing this year. I'm thinking of getting them for all my volunteers.'

'An undercover detail of devils?' Beardsley smiled nervously. O'Shaugnessy chuckled. The hand truck continued on down the steps.

'Please' – O'Shaugnessy pointed once we were inside his office – 'have a seat.'

His desk stood in the center of a stack of boxes. There were only two chairs in the room. Beardsley sat down. I walked to the newly washed window. O'Shaugnessy opened a folder and studied its contents.

'You rented a car, driver, and phone from the New

Amsterdam Limousine Service on Saturday, October ninth?' O'Shaugnessy slammed the folder shut.

'Let's skip the preliminaries, Officer. My wallet was stolen during a tour of Times Square with Ms Eltern. A few days later I got a call from a young woman saying that I could get it back in exchange for three hundred dollars. She gave me a beeper number and said to call the next time I was in the city. And that's exactly what I did.'

'Three hundred dollars! Had you reported the wallet stolen?'

'It's one of a kind,' I interjected. 'Given to him by the president himself.'

'The president of what?'

'*The* president,' I said.

O'Shaugnessy's eyebrows fluttered.

'Unfortunately I did not report the incident. At the time it seemed a futile gesture that might unnecessarily embarrass Ms Eltern. She already seemed to feel responsible for the theft. I did call all my credit-card companies, of course.'

O'Shaugnessy pulled out a pocket calendar. 'Let's see if we can nail down these dates. What night was this wallet stolen?'

I said, 'It was a Monday.'

O'Shaugnessy shot me a silencing look and asked Beardsley. 'When did Charmaine Jefferson call you?'

'A couple of days later. I don't remember exactly.'

'I see. So when you came back to New York, you called the girl's beeper.'

'Yes. But she never called back.'

I said, 'But you came to New York that Saturday. The Saturday after the closing ceremonies we attended in Washington?'

'As a matter of fact, I did.'

'She was murdered the day you beeped her ... that night,' I said softly.

O'Shaugnessy's eyes shot daggers at me.

Beardsley sighed. 'Check the credit-card companies,' he told O'Shaugnessy. 'They'll tell you I reported the wallet stolen.' He looked at his watch. 'I'm afraid I have to be going. Is that it, then?'

O'Shaugnessy got up. 'The officers on the case will want to talk to you at greater length, Mr Beardsley. Will you be in town?'

'In and out.' Beardsley nodded and offered O'Shaugnessy his business card.

O'Shaugnessy took the card and asked, 'Will we be seeing you at the Eden House floating fund-raiser on Halloween?'

'Of course,' Beardsley said, looking at me as if I had set him up. But I was as surprised as he was.

'Anna,' O'Shaugnessy said, 'I need to talk to you about a couple of open files. Kids I can't locate. Can you hang around for a minute?'

I nodded, relieved that Beardsley would have to leave without me. As he headed toward the door the phone rang and O'Shaugnessy answered it. From the window I watched Beardsley leave the building, his back so stiff he seemed one-dimensional.

When O'Shaugnessy hung up, I asked, 'Why'd you push him into going to the fund-raiser? What was that about?'

'Let him show some heart. It'll be good for you, people will see he hasn't backed off your program.'

'I wasn't planning on going. Anyway, how did you know about it?'

'I'm the community-affairs officer, remember? They invited me; I'm taking you.'

'I don't want to go. I forgot all about that damn Halloween fund-raiser, so much has happened.'

'You have to go, Anna. You can't hide out.'

I stared at him, trying to recover the tenderness of only a few hours ago, but he was wearing his cop facade, and it wasn't easy. He said, 'Beardsley's some piece of work. I don't believe his story. Do you?'

'What else could explain his number on the beeper?' I asked.

'He could be the john Colin talks about on the tape. He could be the killer.'

'You're reaching.'

If the phone hadn't rung, we would have begun to argue again. It was O'Shaugnessy's telephone-company contact calling to tell us what we already knew. After he hung up, I stared out the window. He stared into his own palm as if reading it. Then he got up and came to stand behind me. He ran a finger over the top of my hand. 'It's gonna get rough. If we're not careful, we'll lose each other before we've even begun.'

'Maybe this isn't the time to be falling in love,' I said.

'You're not falling, Eltern, you're choosing. In fact, last night I'd say you chose. Don't chicken out on me just because you're back in the soup.'

On the street below, Beardsley's car was sandwiched

between a moving van and a UPS truck. I said, 'Last night seems so far away now.'

He kissed me lightly. 'Do me a favor,' he said. 'Don't go back to your apartment now. Take in a museum, a movie, dinner. I've got a long day ahead of me. Tonight I'm gonna stake out Circus World. In the meantime buy a costume for the fund-raiser.'

'I told you I wasn't planning on going.'

'Well, change your plans, Eltern.'

I have forgotten what I saw at the museum and what I ate for dinner. Buying the costume I remember vividly. I found it in a Times Square novelty shop. I remember trying it on – the white shirt, the blue pants. I remember knotting the tie that felt like a noose around my neck. I remember wrapping the garrison belt around my waist. It was so heavy it hung down onto my hips. But it was when I stepped into the shoes, the men's shoes, that I felt the transformation. I rocked on my heels, absorbing the power of the uniform. For a moment, I actually believed I was the law.

I even bought a .38. Only its weightlessness in my hand revealed that it was fake. I stuck it into my holster and hoped O'Shaugnessy would get a good laugh when he saw me. I didn't think that my real reason for choosing this particular costume was probably a little closer to home – that for the fund-raiser, I needed the toughest exterior money could buy. By the time I carried the bagged costume up the stairs to my apartment, night had come to Hell's Kitchen.

The apartment was dark. I went to the living room to make sure the front gates were still locked. Beardsley sat by the window, holding his head in his hands. I tried to back away quietly. His hand shot out and grabbed my wrist. A headlight from below opened the darkness just long enough for me to see that his eyes had lost their color.

'Millie let me in,' he rasped.

'What do you want?'

He pulled me down next to him. His hands were cold.

'Don't look at me like that,' he whispered. 'I'm not going to hurt you.'

'Let go.'

He uncurled his fingers. I stroked the ache they left behind. He reached for the lamp on the side table. A circle of light opened the darkness.

'I came to tell you the truth,' he said.

I moved to a chair opposite the couch, where I could see him better than he could see me. Beardsley twisted his fingers. Some indelible horror had chiseled itself into his features. Something old that had risen from within.

He said, 'She was going to blackmail me.'

His head dropped into his hands, and a strangled sound came from deep within him. When the sound died, he looked up at me, his face wet and contorted as a newborn's. I knew what he was going to say. They had been lovers and he had killed her.

'She told me on the phone . . .' He choked up again. 'She told me she was my daughter. She wanted to blackmail me. She had a picture, a picture of me with her mother. Lydia was pregnant when I let my mother talk me into abandoning her.'

'Have you got the picture?'

He shook his head. 'I never saw it.'

'So you can't really be sure.'

He looked up at me carefully, an odd confusion in his eyes. I knew what mattered was that his guilt had borne bitter fruit.

'When I got there, the place was empty, the door unlocked, blood everywhere, the window open. I saw her down in the air shaft. I ran . . . I ran from her when she was born, and I ran from her when she died. She was my child, Anna, and she died despising me.'

In the way his hands gripped each other, I saw the lifetime he had spent building his own prison. And I felt the pain that now ripped him open. In that, he reminded me of myself.

'Did you see anybody,' I asked, 'when you went there?'

'On my way out I saw Colin standing outside. That's why I believed he had killed her.'

'Nobody else?'

'There was one other guy. I passed him on the stairs on my way in. A heavy guy with a big wad of keys on his belt. I assumed he was the super. He smelled terrible, I remember that.'

'Do you remember anything else about him?'

'He was bald, heavy, lumbering. I didn't want him to look at my face, so I didn't look too carefully at his. But I remember the extraordinary number of keys hanging from his belt, and that terrible odor he had. Oh, Anna what kind of human being am I?'

'The fallible kind . . . like me . . . like the rest of us. We both knew more than we told. We both made our mistakes.' My voice cracked. 'I threw Porsche out into the street.'

He looked up from his hands and reached to stroke the

hair away from my face. 'When those articles came out, I was prepared to think the worst about you, Anna. Can you forgive me?'

I said, 'Forgiving myself is harder.'

He smiled sadly and said nothing.

He got up. 'I'll do whatever I can to help clear you,' he said. 'Just tell me what you want me to do. Maybe I'll have to go public.'

'Don't be in a rush,' I said. 'The media is not a good confessional.'

I searched his eyes for the past – not just his, but mine with David. 'I thought I was falling in love with you,' I whispered. 'Before you told me about David.'

'Just as well,' he said. 'We could never have overcome the past, you and I. Besides, I think we're probably too much alike to ever have made each other happy.'

I felt the terrible loneliness of his guilt and heard myself say, 'You know I have to tell Officer O'Shaugnessy.'

'You'll do what you have to do, Anna.'

Then, as I opened the door, Beardsley practically stepped into O'Shaugnessy's beefy fist about to knock. The two men studied each other as if waiting for an introduction. O'Shaugnessy's face twitched and rearranged itself.

Finally I said, 'You remember James Beardsley?'

'How could I forget?' O'Shaugnessy snapped, pressing past Beardsley and into the apartment. 'Remember something more you wanna tell me?'

'No need to be rude, Hey-Zeus,' I interjected nervously.

O'Shaugnessy loosened his tie and planted himself at the kitchen table. A blind man would have seen it as a territorial gesture. Beardsley seemed unable to react. He just headed down the stairs and without turning he said, 'Good night, Anna. You know where to find me.'

'Take care of yourself,' I called after him. I wanted to say more, but I was afraid O'Shaugnessy would erupt again. After I shut the door, I yelled, 'How old are you? That was ridiculously adolescent.'

'I'm the jealous type,' he said unstrapping his shoulder holster. 'It's in my blood.'

'That's not gonna fly with me,' I snapped. 'Apparently I'm not the only one in this relationship who has a few things to learn.'

'Maybe.' He put the gun and holster on the kitchen table.

'What happened on the stakeout?' I asked, suddenly realizing why he looked so tired.

'*Nada*, just *nada*.' He took a soda from the refrigerator. 'What did *he* want?'

It was quiet in the apartment. I heard the snap of the tab that opened the can. I heard his swallows, one by one. I was pacing, wringing my hands.

'Sit down. You're making me nervous,' O'Shaugnessy said.

I explained about Beardsley. O'Shaugnessy scratched his beard. It wasn't a real beard, just the shadow that appeared on his face between shaves.

'Poor bastard,' O'Shaugnessy said when I had finished. 'I shouldna jumped down his throat. Colin's defense will want him to testify, especially about that guy he saw on the stairwell.'

He got up and walked to the window in the front of the apartment. I followed. In front of Samsara Video the street was hopping. He studied the action for a while before saying, 'It's coming to a head, Anna, believe me when I say that. I'm gonna put this sick cop in a vise, and when he tries to break out, I'll be there waiting.'

'You figured out who it is, didn't you?'

He looked at his watch. 'I'm going to Circus World. Promise you'll stay put?'

'You're not going to answer me?'

'No, Annie, I'm not. Just promise me that no matter what, you stay put tonight?'

'Where am I going?' I grumbled. 'I'm tired.'

It seemed O'Shaugnessy had barely had time to walk to the corner when sirens began their electronic wail somewhere very nearby. Then I heard popping noises and screams on the street below. I told myself it was nothing, just a truck tire exploding or some girls fighting over a john. Still, I ran to the front of the apartment. I got to the window just in time to see a squad car pull up. A fraction of a second later Samsara's display window splashed to the sidewalk like a glass waterfall. Oddly the cops had arrived before the crime. The cops ran inside the video store and I ran downstairs.

Pedro the *bodegero* and a few neighboring residents clustered in front of Samsara. The girls who usually hung out on the corner had all disappeared, and there were no cars with Jersey plates lined up on the block either.

'What happened?' I asked Pedro.

'Somebody break theee window,' he said.

Just then backup arrived. That meant the team inside had found more than they could handle. A few minutes later a cadre of young girls in hooker regalia were followed by a bluecoat carrying evidence bags. But it was the backup team who emerged with the big prize – Blue Fly. His hands were cuffed behind his back and he was crazy mad.

I leaned on a car, calm, casual, and unbearably excited. 'Leaving the neighborhood by any chance?' I asked as they walked him by me.

A few dusty pearls of cocaine glistened on his nostrils, and I could tell he was flying. He fought with the humiliation of being in handcuffs. 'Don't worry,' he said, 'I'll be back.'

'What happened to your friend at the precinct? No time to warn you.'

'What's that supposed to mean?' His pupils widened and I could see the well of evil within.

'Nothing, just that I'm sorry your friend let you down.'

'You drop a dime on me?' Blue Fly studied me with a twisted mix of admiration and venom.

A bluecoat turned to me. 'Was it you that made the 911 call, Miss Eltern?'

'You bitch,' Blue Fly said as if he had just added two plus two. 'Your ass is grass.'

'Shut up, asshole!' The cop pushed Blue Fly into the squad car.

I headed back across the street wondering who had called 911. From the squad car rear window Blue Fly grimaced at me menacingly. I remembered my promise to O'Shaugnessy, went home, and locked the door.

30

Caught in the grip of an undertow, I fell from one bad dream to another. Death was chasing me, and death was a crooked cop. My mind struggled toward consciousness, but my limbs refused to move. If I couldn't rouse myself, he would catch me and I would die in my sleep. Then I was looking up into their faces: Eclipse, Lucky, Domingo, and Colin. Porsche wasn't there. They tapped on the window. For a time I studied their prints, miniature maps, ghosts on the pane. Then I sat up and opened the window.

'What are you guys doing?'

They climbed in quickly, their bodies so agile they seemed like much younger children. I followed them to the kitchen.

'He was out there, Annie. Last night he was watching you from across the street. We seen him.'

'What are you talking about?'

The fog around me was so deep, I was having a hard time deciding that I was awake. 'What are you talking about?' I heard myself repeat.

'The cop, the bald guy, we seen him. He circled your block all night long. One time he went into the *bodega* for beer. We couldn't see his face, but we saw that huge wad of keys he carries and we got his license plate. He's onto you, Annie. We gotta do something.'

'We? I thought I told you guys to stay put.'

'Annie.' Domingo pulled at my arm. 'You're not listening. He's after you now. That's what we're trying to tell you. Let's go tell O'Shaugnessy.'

'I thought you guys didn't trust cops.'

'We trust you,' Eclipse said, 'and you trust him. So let's go. You said O'Shaugnessy would help.'

'I can't risk exposing you guys like that.'

'Annie, something happens to you, we'll be in *real* trouble. Nobody will believe us about this cop.'

'What if this cop sees us at the precinct house? He knows us and we don't know him.'

'What if he does? He'll be more careful if he knows we're talking to somebody.'

'More careful or more crazy.' I sighed.

Domingo put his hands on his little hips. 'We're goin', you comin'?'

Since I had waited a long time for these kids to trust a cop, I said I'd go.

By the time I had showered and dressed, the fog had lifted a little. An oyster dawn had spread over the city, and we were inside the shell. We headed for the new precinct house, which was actually the old precinct house after a two-year renovation. We left Colin at the apartment.

Inside, everything smelled clean and new. We asked for Officer O'Shaugnessy at the desk. His office, we were told, was on the first floor in the back. In the newness of the space, I felt that I would never find him. I felt that I had walked into a maze. Telephone cords that hadn't found their hiding places yet snaked across the floors. Stacks of boxes formed walls of varying heights. On the landing above, O'Shaugnessy was pushing a folder into an envelope while bending a stick of gum in half with his teeth. When he saw me, a rage of emotions distorted his features. He looked angry, guilty, compassionate, sad, and helpless.

'He was stalking her. We got his license number,' Eclipse yelled up the stairs.

O'Shaugnessy placed a finger over his lips. The same kids who less than an hour ago had acted like adults were now just some children running scared. I felt a chill as if someone had walked on the spot where my grave would someday be.

'I'm kinda busy now,' O'Shaugnessy snapped.

'He's gonna kill her! She's next if you don't protect her,' Domingo insisted angrily.

The kids went berserk, all four of them screaming and yelling at him, saying that I had promised he would help.

'Anna,' he said as casually as he could manage, 'take these guys into my office.'

The office was immaculate. Obviously O'Shaugnessy hadn't occupied it long. The kids were agitated.

'What's wrong with him?' Eclipse demanded.

'I thought he wanted to help us.' Domingo planted his hands on his hips.

Lucky just listened.

'Give him a chance. Maybe he just didn't want you guys screaming everything you know in the stairwell.'

A moment later O'Shaugnessy came in. 'Anna,' he said through his teeth, 'take these kids back to where they're safe. And stay out of this case. How many times do I have to tell you that?'

'The case seems to be chasing me.'

'Look.' He pulled me to the corner of the room. 'He was at Circus World last night. His name is Dowd. He's a drunk, but he's the captain's brother-in-law. He's a cop, only he shouldn't be, and most of all he's dangerous. Stay out of it now. I'm handling it. Back off just for today.'

He turned to the kids. 'You kids have been a great help, and we're gonna get this guy, but we gotta get him legal. The only thing you guys can do now is fuck it up.'

'What about Anna?'

'Let me worry about Anna.'

'We got his license plate.' Domingo handed O'Shaugnessy a scrap of paper.

'Great. But coming to the precinct house wasn't the smartest thing you guys ever did. C'mon, I'll walk you out.'

We stepped out into the hallway. As the kids headed back down the stairs O'Shaugnessy said, 'Pick me up tomorrow at eight on the steps of the Market Courthouse. We'll go to the fund-raiser from there.'

31

I elbowed my way through skinheads, members of the Moral Majority, latter-day Nazis in work boots, God-fearing Catlicks, and bored teenagers looking for a head to bash. They were bonded by their desire to see gays return to the closet. To make their point, they were going to disrupt the Halloween Parade, which, given its West Village roots, had always been heavily gay. As they moved down into the Village it became impossible to distinguish protesters from revelers. I looked at my watch. I was early. Despite the din that surrounded me, I had the odd sensation that I could hear the second hand ticking.

Near Sheridan Square, the streets were clogged with tourists, vendors, wandering teenagers, and local residents. Jack-o'-lanterns gleamed in store windows. Partying crowds spilled from the White Horse Tavern and the other neighborhood joints. Along the parade route the crowd was eight deep, jostling cheerfully behind police barricades, climbing street lamps and traffic lights to see the marchers and the floats. There was a red devil on almost every corner.

I ducked under a barricade. A cop pulled me back. 'Hey, lady, you think I can't tell that's a costume?'

I headed for the next corner and tried again. But the cop had followed me. 'Hey, you deaf?' he yelled as I was about to try again.

'Officer, please, I have to meet somebody.'

When he turned away, I joined a troop of dancing dominoes and made it across the street.

He was up there on the steps to the Market Courthouse looking down at the crowd, holding a walkie-talkie. The devil mask covered his head completely, and the red robe flowed from his neck to his ankles. As I climbed the steps he came down to meet me halfway. He wrapped me in his arms and began to dance to the music rising from a band in the parade. We pirouetted behind a column. The world of the street below disappeared. He brought his rubber lips in close. His breath tickled my ear.

'Honey,' he said, 'when you dance with the devil, the devil dances with you.'

Even before I saw the ring on his pinkie, I knew. I kept dancing, hoping O'Shaugnessy would show up, hoping I could just slide out of Dowd's grip and lose myself in the crowd. I tried leading him down the steps. He pulled me the other way. I grabbed for the walkie-talkie. It fell. He kicked it away. 'You should have left well enough alone,' he said.

Below us on the passing floats, the gossamer wings of giant butterflies sailed over a lone drag queen on roller skates. I kicked David in the groin. As he doubled over I ran down the steps and into a family of papier-mâché reptiles. For a moment the crowd closed around me. I saw another red devil caught between bodies, pushing toward me from the other side of the street. O'Shaugnessy pushed his mask back and I reached for him. Laughing cadavers on stilts separated us. Then Dowd pulled me back, away from the parade. He had me by the hair. We waltzed that way, the crowd pointing and screeching. I bit him. I screamed. I kicked. The crowd applauded wildly. Dowd pulled me into a doorway.

I ripped at his mask. He took it off, laughing. Pictures squirmed in the sludge of memory – his face in the box at Circus World, him standing across the street during my press conference, Beardsley's description of the man on the stairs. For a moment we just stood there, wrapped in the cocoon of our hatred. From under his robe he pulled out a box cutter.

'You gotta go with the others,' he said. 'You turned Blue Fly against me and you talk too much.'

'How many went before me?' I asked softly. 'Besides Porsche?'

'Them other three,' he said. 'That's all. I didn't mean to kill nobody, but you know how it is when you're having fun.'

An apartment door opened. A man holding a garbage bag appeared in the doorway.

'Call 911!' I yelled. 'Please call 911!'

The door slammed shut. Dowd turned. He was between me and the door. I ran up the stairs. I heard him huffing and my own breath wheezing. The window on the first-floor landing was open. It led to a fire escape. I climbed out.

One of the revelers spotted me. He began waving and cheering. The crowd joined in noisily. Dizzy and out of breath, I began my descent. Dowd came to the window. His big body loomed over me. I felt him as he got closer.

His fingers closed around my arm. 'You,' he said, 'shoulda left well enough alone.'

He tried to push me off the fire escape. I clung to the railing. I bit his hand. He pulled me toward him, twisting my arm behind me. When I refused to fall, he tried pulling me back up the fire escape. But I kept descending. He ripped at my arm. Pain shot up into my shoulder. I slapped his face. I kicked his shins.

'Go to, honey,' somebody shouted from below.

I pulled free of him. My arms and legs flew at him in an uncontrolled frenzy. He slipped and fell to the sidewalk, which by now wasn't very far below. I jumped to where he had fallen. The crowd parted, laughing and pointing. I grabbed the gun from my holster. I heard sirens, but they may have belonged to the parade.

'Don't shoot,' he pleaded, and got to his knees.

I put the gun in his big gut. I pulled the trigger. I pulled and pulled and pulled. And as I did I kicked him with a vicious fury that left me limping. I don't think I would have stopped if I hadn't felt the hands on my shoulders and heard Hey-Zeus O'Shaugnessy say, 'All right, Anna, that's enough.'

He took the prop gun from my hand. As I caught my breath the world went from slow motion to real time. When I looked around me again, the crowd had parted, and I was surrounded by red devils. Some bluecoats were cuffing Dowd. O'Shaugnessy was giving him Miranda.

In the craziness of the pagan wilderness in which we stood, I looked at O'Shaugnessy with renewed respect. 'You set me up, didn't you?'

'You left me no choice. I knew he'd come after you. I

wanted it to be when I was around. I was going to be here before you. The protest almost screwed everything up.'

'You made that phony 911 call.'

'You *are* a good detective,' he said. 'Maybe you should take the test.'

'You broke Samsara's window.'

'I used a B-B gun. The broken window was my excuse to call 911 and get the cops inside. I knew they'd find plenty. I wanted Blue Fly to turn on Dowd. You made yourself the target when you didn't keep your promise to stay home.'

Some bluecoats pushed Dowd into a squad car. The crowd applauded as they pulled out, sirens, lights, and all.

'What do you really know about him?' I asked.

'We called him the broom. Every precinct has one. He's a guy who's been shot down so many times he has no business on the force. Instead of taking his badge and gun, the department hid him away. He cleaned the cells, kept the precinct house stocked. He was a lot like the kids he killed, a guy society swept under the rug, who just blew up.'

Twenty thousand celebrants fluttered through the night like migrating birds on a noisy shore. A Dixieland band came up the street. The crowd went wilder yet. Deafeningly they sang, 'Oh when the saints, oh when the saints go marching in. Oh Lord, I wanna be in that number, when the saints go marching in.'

'Any chance of that?' I asked O'Shaugnessy.

The devil's mask was crumpled on his head like a cap. 'Not much, Anna,' he said wistfully. 'It's hard enough just being human.'

Epilogue

The noisy hearing room fell silent as we walked up the center aisle to the witness table: Colin, Lucky, Eclipse, Domingo, and I. Reporters and spectators alike, they knew of Dowd's arrest. He'd been charged with all four Times Square killings. In the press, Lucky and Eclipse had cleared me.

Sitting in the audience were O'Shaugnessy and almost a hundred graduates of Eden House: college students, secretaries, a 911 clerk, a bus driver, a social worker, a transit cop in uniform, and several mothers and their babies. They had come to show their support. Through the glare of the lights, I saw James Beardsley in his usual spot at the chairman's ear. He gave me a warm and welcoming smile. I knew he was in my corner.

Thunderous applause filled the room. When it quieted down, I began: 'We're here today in memory of a young girl who lost her life because the grown-ups who run her country have lost their way.'

A selection of bestsellers from Headline

HARD EVIDENCE	John T Lescroart	£5.99 ☐
TWICE BURNED	Kit Craig	£5.99 ☐
CAULDRON	Larry Bond	£5.99 ☐
BLACK WOLF	Philip Caveney	£5.99 ☐
ILL WIND	Gary Gottesfield	£5.99 ☐
THE BOMB SHIP	Peter Tonkin	£5.99 ☐
SKINNER'S RULES	Quintin Jardine	£4.99 ☐
COLD CALL	Dianne Pugh	£4.99 ☐
TELL ME NO SECRETS	Joy Fielding	£4.99 ☐
GRIEVOUS SIN	Faye Kellerman	£4.99 ☐
TORSO	John Peyton Cooke	£4.99 ☐
THE WINTER OF THE WOLF	R A MacAvoy	£4.50 ☐

All Headline books are available at your local bookshop or newsagent, or can be ordered direct from the publisher. Just tick the titles you want and fill in the form below. Prices and availability subject to change without notice.

Headline Book Publishing, Cash Sales Department, Bookpoint, 39 Milton Park, Abingdon, OXON, OX14 4TD, UK. If you have a credit card you may order by telephone – 0235 400400.

Please enclose a cheque or postal order made payable to Bookpoint Ltd to the value of the cover price and allow the following for postage and packing:
UK & BFPO: £1.00 for the first book, 50p for the second book and 30p for each additional book ordered up to a maximum charge of £3.00.
OVERSEAS & EIRE: £2.00 for the first book, £1.00 for the second book and 50p for each additional book.

Name ....

Address ....

....

....

If you would prefer to pay by credit card, please complete:
Please debit my Visa/Access/Diner's Card/American Express (delete as applicable) card no:

Signature .... Expiry Date ....